Redneck days . . .

"Are you seeing this Hollywood producer again? You know money, Jamie Lee, doesn't make the man."

"I'm just showing him around town, Mama."

"Why don't you set your sights on some local boy instead of Mr. Hollywood?"

"I'm not setting my sights on anyone."

"Jamie Lee, you are a catch for any man, Hollywood or not. But you can't get reeled in if you don't jump in the water."

Hollywood nights.

DARK ROOTS AND COWBOY BOOTS

LuAnn McLane

A SIGNET ECLIPSE BOOK

SIGNET ECLIPSE
Published by New American Library, a division of
Penguin Group (USA) Inc., 375 Hudson Street,
New York, New York 10014, USA
Penguin Group (Canada), 90 Eglinton Avenue East, Suite 700, Toronto,
Ontario M4P 2Y3, Canada (a division of Pearson Penguin Canada Inc.)
Penguin Books Ltd., 80 Strand, London WC2R 0RL, England
Penguin Ireland, 25 St. Stephen's Green, Dublin 2,
Ireland (a division of Penguin Books Ltd.)
Penguin Group (Australia), 250 Camberwell Road, Camberwell, Victoria 3124,
Australia (a division of Pearson Australia Group Pty. Ltd.)
Penguin Books India Pvt. Ltd., 11 Community Centre, Panchsheel Park,
New Delhi - 110 017, India
Penguin Group (NZ), cnr Airborne and Rosedale Roads, Albany,
Auckland 1310, New Zealand (a division of Pearson New Zealand Ltd.)
Penguin Books (South Africa) (Pty.) Ltd., 24 Sturdee Avenue,
Rosebank, Johannesburg 2196, South Africa

Penguin Books Ltd., Registered Offices:
80 Strand, London WC2R 0RL, England

First published by Signet Eclipse, an imprint of New American Library,
a division of Penguin Group (USA) Inc.

First Printing, August 2006
10 9 8 7 6 5 4 3 2 1

Copyright © LuAnn McLane, 2006
All rights reserved

SIGNET ECLIPSE and logo are trademarks of Penguin Group (USA) Inc.

Printed in the United States of America

To small-town girls everywhere,
this book is for you.

ACKNOWLEDGMENTS

I would like to extend a very special thanks to my fellow authors Dianne Castell, Rosemary Laurey, Toni Blake, Shiloh Walker, Karen Kelley, Lucy Monroe and Janice Maynard, who make up *vampsscampsandspicyromance@yahoogroups.com*. Not a day goes by that I don't value your friendship, support and inspiration. I also want to thank the dedicated readers on this loop. Your posts keep a smile on my face and my fingers on the keyboard.

Thanks so much to my editor, Anne Bohner, for her knowledge, enthusiasm and unending support. You are a pleasure to work with.

As always, a big thank-you to Jenny Bent. Your guiding hand has pushed me forward and kept me on track. I couldn't ask for a better agent.

1

Hollywood Comes to Hootertown

Lifting the edge of the cotton strip and the plastic cap, I check on the status of Irma Baker's perm. "Just a little while longer, Miss Irma," I assure her after unwrapping a limp gray curl from the curling rod.

"Not too curly, now, Jamie Lee," Irma warns me in her gruff smoker's voice. "I don't want to go outta here lookin' like some danged poodle."

Patting her hand, I tuck the curling rod back underneath the cap. "Now, Miss Irma, you know I won't let that happen."

Irma waves her blue-veined hand in my direction. "I know, I know. You're every bit as good as your mama. I'm just flappin' my jaws."

I smile at the compliment, knowing Irma isn't one to throw praise around lightly. It just isn't her way. Now that Mama has retired, I try hard to keep her old clients at Cut & Curl happy while drawing in some of the local college coeds. Handing Irma a copy of *Ladies' Home Journal*, I walk over to the front of the shop and open the door, letting the cool morning breeze chase away the pungent perm fumes. Since the bright sunshine is already cutting through the chill, I decide to prop the door open. The day promises to be another hot one even though it's only June.

"Mornin' Jamie Lee," Rose Jenkins says with a smile on her weathered face as she wheels a sale rack of clothing through the front door of Second Hand Rose, her vintage clothing shop.

I return her greeting with a smile and a wave. Main Street in Hootertown is coming alive. The small Kentucky town teetering on the Tennessee border is a throwback to yesteryear, kept thriving by nearby Lake Logan Resort where summer vacationers come to rent houseboats, fish, and swim. Hootertown handles the spillover from the Logan Lodge at the Mid-town Inn, and offers an array of antique shops, boutiques, and restaurants, including Flanagan's Tavern, which as far as I'm concerned serves the best food on the planet. Not that I'm an expert or anything. Stuff like sushi and escargot will never pass these lips.

I wave to Macy McCoy, who is pulling her beat-up red Blazer into the gravel parking lot across the street where most of the Main Street employees park, leaving the street open for customers. Macy has been my best friend since we were knee-high to a grasshopper and we always dreamed of running a beauty parlor together. Mama used to let me and Macy come into her shop on Saturday mornings and play pretend hairdressers until one day we got the bright idea to really cut each other's hair. Lordy, it took six months for our hair to grow back in, and Mama banned us from the hair stations until we had our cosmetology degrees.

So here we are some twenty years later, cutting and curling side by side, just like we always wanted. A minute later, Macy crosses the street while sippin' on a diet Mountain Dew. She's not fit for human contact until she has at least three Dews under her belt, so I always make sure we're stocked up.

"Hey," she says and musters up a grin. "What's shakin'?"

"I'm giving Irma a perm. She's just about done. Your ten o'clock called to say she would be running late, so you can take a walk-in this morning."

"'Kay," she says, hiding a discreet little burp behind her hand.

"Your hair's looking good today," I tell her. "The curl has relaxed a bit."

Macy reaches up and fluffs her chin-length auburn hair highlighted with chunky blond streaks. Just like when we were kids, we are forever playing with each other's hair, sometimes with good results, but more often than not with disastrous ones. With our customers we're conservative, giving them the styles they want while extending our expert, but subtle, opinions. But with each other, we go all out. My own hair at this given moment happens to be shoulder-length honey-blond, but next week, who knows?

"I'm actually starting to like it," Macy says after a long swallow of Dew. "In a couple of weeks it will be perfect."

I have to grin. In a couple of weeks we'll play around with another color or cut, never giving the perm a chance. It's a wonder we're not both bald. We're about to go into the shop when a sleek silver sports car glides slowly down the street, drawing our attention.

"I do believe that's a Jaguar," Macy says, shading her eyes against the glare of the sun.

A moment later the car pulls into a vacant spot directly across the street. Macy and I watch, rather slack-jawed, as the silver door opens wide, and then as long jeans-clad legs unfold followed by wide shoulders and a shaggy blond head that's sexily messy, but I know the look is from a precision haircut from a fancy salon.

"Mercy," I say with a low whistle.

Bending over, the blond god reaches into the car. We both angle our heads to get a better view of his very fine butt. He straightens up, holding a small camera, shuts the door, and begins taking random pictures.

"Nice ass," Macy comments.

"Well, shut my mouth and slap my grandma," I agree. "The man is sex on a stick."

"Girl, you got that right. I wonder who he is, and why he's taking pictures of, like, everything?" Macy's hand closes over my arm. "Jamie Lee, he's comin' our way." Her voice is an unnatural squeak.

"I've got to go in and check on Irma."

"Don't you even think about leavin' me to find my voice. You know how I get all tongue-tied around good-lookin' men. What if he needs directions or somethin'? You know how I am with directions. Oh God, he's crossing the street. He's looking right at us."

"Macy, get a grip. He's just a guy." I don't want to let on that my own pulse is pounding harder with each long-legged stride that the blond god takes toward us.

"Good morning, ladies." His voice is deep and rich, oozing over me like thick maple syrup. He flashes us a smile revealing very white, perfect teeth. In the Hootertown land of dip and chewing tobacco, white teeth are a glorious feature to behold.

"Mornin'," I manage, feeling like I should curtsey. Macy remains mute and I want to give her an elbow, but I'm afraid she'll fall over.

"So this is Hootertown," he says, flashing those awesome teeth.

I nod, waiting for the jokes to begin. Having been a Hootertown Hornets cheerleader, I've heard every hooter joke known to mankind and although this guy is really hot, I don't feel the need to hear another.

"Home of Oliver and Lisa Douglas," he says with the grin remaining. "You know, *Green Acres*."

Okay, at least it wasn't a hooter joke. "No, that was *Hooterville*. This is *Hootertown*," I explain.

"Oh." The thousand-watt smile fades a bit, but then he shrugs.

"We get that a lot," I feel compelled to explain. "You know, because of the *'Green Acres'* reruns on Nick at Nite. So if you think you're taking pictures of Hooterville, well, you're not." I could have explained that there wasn't a real Hooterville, only on television, and the fictional town was supposed to be somewhere in Missouri, not Kentucky. But at this point I really have to get back to Irma before she gets all poodly.

He shrugs again. "Well, it doesn't matter." He looks around with an appreciative smile. "This town is the perfect setting."

"For what?" I glance at Macy but her eyes are fixated

on him like a bird dog's on a pheasant. For a moment I think she might even point.

"A movie," he says with a grand wave of his hand. "I want to film a movie here."

"Really?" I have sudden visions of Brad Pitt or Orlando Bloom rolling into town. "What movie?"

"Vanquished," he announces, with feeling.

"Vanquished?" I parrot, without too much feeling. *Vanquished* doesn't sound very romantic.

He nods vigorously, making his perfectly cut hair lift and move, and then fall back into beautiful disarray. "Yeah, it's a horror flick about a small town that gets terrorized by vampires."

"Vampires?" Ew.

"Yeah, I've been searching all over the country for the perfect town to film *Vanquished*." He looks down the street and then slaps his thigh. "I think I've finally found it."

"Cool," I say, but I'm not really sure if this is a cool thing or not.

"Hey," he says turning back to me. "Would you mind showing me around town?"

My stomach does a weird little flipping thing at the thought. "Uh, I'm in the middle of doing a perm."

Macy finally finds her voice. "I'll finish Irma up," she offers and gives me a discreet elbow to the ribs.

I shake my head and ignore Macy's you've-got-to-be-crazy-he-is-*so*-hot look. "I've got a highlight at ten."

"Jamie Lee, I'll reschedule her."

The blond god interrupts us, saying, "How about lunch?" He gives me this bone-melting smile. I notice a dimple in his cheek and have to repress a sigh. Macy elbows me again.

"Uh, okay." I am such a dork.

"Any suggestions on where to eat?" he asks.

"Flanagan's Tavern, two blocks down the street, serves a very nice luncheon buffet," I say in a prim and proper voice that would make my mama proud. I am giving him a very ladylike smile but my nose starts to twitch when I detect the strong, very close, rotten-egg odor of perm solution. I turn and see Miss Irma standing in the doorway. I can see that she is about to give me a lecture about turning her into a poodle when she spots the blond god and her wrinkled cheeks turn all pinkish.

"Well, howdy do," Irma says in her gruff voice and it is apparent that she, too, is smitten. Her hands go all fluttery and she gives him a coy smile, obviously forgetting that she has a plastic bag wrapped around her head and smells none too pretty.

I want to shoo her back inside, but of course, I don't.

"Parker Carrington," the blond god says, and taking a step closer extends his hand to Miss Irma.

"Irma Baker," she roughly croons, letting her frail hand be engulfed in his grasp. "Are you of the Fayette County Carringtons? I have a cousin, Clay Carrington, twice removed on my mother's side. Very respected family except for that no-count Leroy who ended up in the pen, but I suppose every family has a bad seed, don't you agree?"

Parker blinks at her for a moment and I'm guessing he is trying to process what she just said. "Uh, I'm from L.A., so I don't think Clay or Leroy are relatives."

Irma squints her eyes at him. "You sure? You kinda look like Leroy around the mouth—"

"Miss Irma," I interrupt with a gentle smile, hoping Parker will think she is senile or something, "Let's get you inside and rinse, okay?"

Irma's eyes go wide and she puts a hand up to her head, realizing how she must look. Glaring at me like it's my entire fault, she says, "Lordy, I'm going to look just like a danged toy poodle. You might as well put a bow in my hair and get me a can of Mighty Dog." Throwing her hands in the air, she turns on her soft-soled heel and heads back into the shop.

At this point I truly believe that Parker Carrington of the L.A. Carringtons is going to sprint across the street, hop in his silver car, and hightail it out of Hootertown. But he is smiling and says, "I love this place."

I'm not quite sure what to make of that comment so I let it go.

"I'll see you around noon at Flanagan's Tavern, Jamie Lee," he says and then smiles at Macy. "And you are?"

"Macy McCoy, senior stylist," she says and extends her hand, fingernails up, showing off her French manicure.

He grins and asks, "Of the famous Hatfield and Mc-Coys?"

Now, I realize he's making a joke and I have to hide a smile behind my hand because I know what's coming.

Macy's chin comes up and she no longer seems befuddled by Parker's awesomeness. "Yes, I most certainly *am* a descendant of the *real* McCoys of Pikeville, Kentucky."

Macy has this look like she is going to tell him the whole feud thing, about which she happens to be quite the expert, so I grab her arm and say, "Macy, we have to get to work."

"You mean they really exist? There really was a feud?"

"Most certainly."

"Wow," he says, and a slow smile spreads across his face. "I *love* this place."

After bidding Parker a polite "Good morning," I watch him head off down the street, snapping pictures like a kid. Now, I realize that I'd be doing the same thing if I were in L.A., but somehow it doesn't seem quite the same. This is Hootertown. Still pondering this, I head back inside where I'm relieved to see that Macy is already rinsing Miss Irma.

"That was one fine specimen of a man," Miss Irma says in a gruff but dreamy voice while Macy squeezes the excess water from her curling rods. "Why, if I was thirty years younger, I'd want a piece of that."

"A piece of that?" I have to laugh. "Miss Irma, where'd you learn such talk?"

"HBO. Hey, I know who Mr. Big is."

I start to unclip her curling rods, relieved to see that the curls aren't too kinky. "You have cable out on Pikeville Road?"

"Satellite dish," she announces proudly. "Griffin Sheldon hooked it up for me. Quite the handyman, that one, and a fine specimen, too, I might add. Not all flashy like that Parker fellow, but he's an eyeful without his shirt."

"Now, Miss Irma," I ask, "just how did you manage

to get Griff to shed his shirt?" Griff is my brother Luke's best friend, and a good friend of mine. I can't imagine him showing off his muscles for Irma. He's a pretty conservative guy.

"Griffin is building a deck off of my kitchen and since it had been hotter than blue blazes, I let him know that I would not be offended in the least if he happened to shed his shirt. Whooo, baby, that boy is built like a romance-cover model."

"Miss Irma, you're somethin' else," I tell her with a chuckle as I begin to trim her hair.

"I will take that as a compliment," Irma says with a grin.

She and Macy get into an in-depth discussion of their latest romance reads. I listen with half an ear while I think about my upcoming lunch date with sexy Parker Carrington. It's been a long while since a man has made me feel all fluttery and I rather like the feeling. After having had my heart broken by Travis Tucker, my high-school sweetheart, I dated a steady stream of frat boys from Payton College. But at twenty-six, I'm getting too old for college boys. Mama has started grumbling about grandkids, and truthfully, I'm beginning to long for that direction myself.

Irma and Macy's conversation goes from romance novels to soap operas while I wonder what I'll order at Flanagan's. I don't want to get something too messy or that could get stuck in my teeth. I'm just thinking that I'll stick to the soup and salad bar when I look up to see my brother enter the shop.

"Hey there, Luke," I call over to him with a smile. "What brings you in here?"

He reaches up to run his fingers through wavy brown hair that he keeps clean-cut short. "I need a trim," he says with a nod to Macy and Irma. "Morning ladies."

"I'm busy here with Miss Irma, but Macy can take you."

"Jamie Lee, I have a cut and color at ten." She gives me this don't-make-me-do-this look, but I ignore her. She's always had this huge crush on Luke and while I know cutting his hair will make her nervous as all get-out, she needs to get over it. I'm sure that if Macy would give Luke any indication at all that she is interested, he would ask her out, but she's too damned stubborn about this stupid notion that she's not good enough for my brother.

"Macy, you have plenty of time," I tell her firmly. "He only needs a trim." I wave my hand toward Macy's station and say, "Luke, have a seat." I give Macy a look that screams, *I'm having lunch with Mr. L.A. Parker Carrington, so you just quit being such a wuss and cut his hair.*

Macy purses her lips and narrows her green eyes at me.

"Uh, I can come back later," Luke offers.

"Sit your butt down," I tell him.

"Jamie Lee," Macy begins, but I cut her off with a bug-eyed stare that tells her to shut up.

Luke gives her a grin and says, "I showered this morning, Macy. I brushed my teeth and gargled so I smell just fine, if you're worried about getting too close."

Macy's cheeks turn all pink. "I didn't mean any offense, Luke. I just don't like to be rushed, is all." I notice that her fingers are trembling ever so slightly while she fastens a blue smock around Luke's neck, and I feel a little sorry that I pushed her.

Luke has just returned home to coach football at Payton College. He was a big star at Hootertown High and went on to quarterback at the University of Kentucky. He was always our hometown hero, and it looked like he had a shot at the pros, but a shoulder injury cut his career short. All through college he dated Shelly Montgomery, a Lexington debutante, but when his football career came to an abrupt end, so did their relationship, and while I personally believe he is better off without her and her uppity attitude, Luke was devastated. After basking in the limelight for so long, Luke was completely undone by his string of bad luck. He floundered around, going from job to job, drinking too much, and not giving a rip about anything. Griff finally hauled his sorry butt back to Hootertown and thank God the coaching job at Payton College opened up.

I look over at Macy as she sprays down Luke's hair. She might not be a beauty queen, but there's not a mean bone in her body and she has, in my opinion, more class in her pinky finger than Shelly Montgomery has in her entire Barbie-doll body. It must be said, however, that I tend to be very opinionated where my friends and family are concerned. I decide I had better make some conversation before Macy goes into a meltdown, so after instructing Miss Irma to bend her head forward so I can trim her neck, I ask, "What are you fixin' to do today, Luke?"

"I promised Dad I'd go fishing with him."

I chuckle. "So, did Mama call you up and beg you to get Daddy out of her hair?"

"Yep. She claims that he follows her everywhere, even out to her flower garden, giving her advice she doesn't need or want." He turns to look at me with a grin and I know that if it were anyone else, Macy would have told him to hold still, but she patiently waits until Luke turns his head forward so she can begin cutting his hair.

"How's your Daddy doin'?" Miss Irma asks. "No more heart trouble, I hope?"

I check her neckline to make sure I've trimmed it straight across. "Oh, healthwise, he's just fine. Mama makes sure he stays on his heart-healthy diet. He's keeping his weight down and they walk in the evenings."

"Is he still working the farm?"

"No, they still live in the house, but he leases out the land." I turn to Luke and ask, "Have they talked about traveling?"

Luke turns towards me again and Macy nearly snips his earlobe. "They can't agree on where to go. Mama wants to go to the beach and Dad insists he wants to go out West."

Miss Irma shakes her head, making her curls bounce. "Lordy, lordy. Tell them to flip a damned coin."

"Not a bad idea," Luke answers. "Hey, by the way, who owns that silver Jag sitting across the street?"

"Some Hollywood producer," I tell him. "He wants to film a movie here in Hootertown. Can you believe it?" I leave out the fact that I'm having lunch with him and I meet Macy's eyes in the mirror, warning her with a look not to tell Luke, who tends to be an overprotective brother, but I can tell by the look she gives me that she's going to pay me back for making her cut Luke's hair.

"Jamie Lee is having lunch with him," Macy says with a smug smile in my direction.

"That so, Jamie Lee?" Luke asks. "Just what do you know about this guy?"

I inhale and blow out a big sigh. "Luke, he seems real nice and I'm having lunch with him at Flanagan's in broad daylight."

"Hmmm," Luke says rubbing his chin. "I haven't had lunch at Flanagan's in a while . . ."

"Luke! Don't you even think about showing up there!" I glare at Macy.

"Don't worry, little sis. I promised Mama I'd have lunch with her and Dad before we go fishing. She'll have my hide if I don't show up. I'm just playing with ya." He grins at me in the mirror, but then says, "I want you to watch yourself, though."

I have to roll my eyes. "Luke, I'm a big girl. I can take care of myself."

"Okay," he says slowly, "I guess some habits die hard. Say, listen. I've got to interview some chick over at Payton later on for the cheerleading coach's job." He shakes his head and complains, "I don't know why I have to be the one to interview her. I know football, not cheerleading. But anyway, will you come over there with me and give me your two cents?"

I could, but I suddenly have a better idea. "I've got to work until eight tonight." I look over at Macy, whose green eyes go wide. "But I bet Macy could go with you."

"I'm here 'til six, Jamie Lee," she says tightly. "Besides, I don't know that I'm qualified to give my opinion."

"Don't be silly," I counter. "You were head cheerleader both junior and senior year. And I happen to know that the Hootertown High cheerleading coach has asked you to help choreograph their dance number this year."

"Would you mind, Macy?" Luke asks.

"I have to work."

"I'll have Mama come in to cover for you," I insist. "She'll be glad to."

"How about it, Macy?" Luke meets her eyes in the mirror and, of course, she caves.

"Okay."

Luke smiles at her and she looks ready to melt. "Great, I'll swing by and pick you up here around five. I'll pay you back with pizza and a pitcher of beer."

"Y-you don't have to do that," she says while busily brushing the loose hair off his neck. "Short enough?"

Luke nods. "Perfect. And I insist on taking you for a bite to eat." His eyebrows rise in question while Macy tugs at the Velcro on the smock. "Unless you have plans. I don't want to mess up your evening."

Macy hesitates and I give her a don't-you-dare look. "No," she finally says, "I don't have any plans." She leans forward and removes the smock, shaking Luke's brown hair onto the floor. "All done," she tells him with a shy smile and walks over to the register. After Luke pays and bids us all goodbye, Macy turns to me with her hands on her hips. "Jamie Lee Carter, you need to mind your own business. You know danged well that Luke isn't interested in me."

"I don't know any such thing. Give him half a reason and I'd bet the farm that he'd make a play for you."

Macy stomps her foot. "Oh, come on. Just look at me! I'm five foot three and twenty pounds overweight. I'm not in Luke's league."

I have to throw my hands up in the air in protest. "Oh, yeah, like tall and skinny Shelly Montgomery was a good choice. It's about time that Luke dated someone other than the Barbie dolls he's been dating all of his life. That boy needs a real woman!"

"Damned straight!" Irma chimes in and we both look over at her. She slaps her knee and then points to her wrinkled face (framed with very nice curls, I might add). "See this old mug? Someday you'll be sittin' in my orthopedic shoes, your youth done gone. I'm tellin' ya ta go for it. One day you'll wake up an ol' cuss like me and you don't want to have a long list of things you wish you did." She points at Macy. "You, young lady, are a beautiful woman and don't let no magazine ad tell you any different. So you got a little meat on your bones? So danged what? Maybe Luke likes a little *junk in the trunk*. Shake it like a salt shaker, sister!"

I burst out laughing and Macy joins in. "Miss Irma, you are a piece of work." I turn to Macy and plead, "Don't be mad at me."

She blows out a sigh. "I'm not. You know, I think Miss Irma has it right. We're not getting any younger, Jamie Lee. We need to get off of our cans and go after what we want. I've been moonin' over your brother for too danged long. I'm going to give it a shot or move on." She points a finger at me. "But don't you dare let on, you hear me."

I nod. "I swore back in fourth grade not to tell Luke that you were sweet on him. If something happens between you two, then it was meant to be." I refrain from letting her know that this doesn't mean I can't arrange ways for them to *just happen* to be together.

Macy nods, making her tight auburn curls bounce. "You know somethin'? We both need to quit pussy-footin' around, and just go for it. If we don't get it, at least we tried. Let's make a pact right here, right now, to make this summer one to remember." She holds out her hand and we do our secret handshake like we did when we were kids. Pump twice, high five, and then a knuckle bump.

Miss Irma slaps her knee and says gruffly, "Now there's the spirit."

I go over and show her the secret handshake. It takes her three tries and then she gets it. "You rock, Miss Irma."

"I know, I know." She looks at her watch and says, "Finish me up, Jamie Lee. Griffin will be over to work on my deck soon. I don't want to miss a minute of that." She points to my cutoff jeans and advises, "Change into something suitable before you have lunch with your Hollywood hottie."

"Oh my gosh, you're right." As I style her hair, I mentally go through my wardrobe, wishing I had something new.

As if reading my mind, Macy suggests, "Wear your black capri pants and your white sleeveless shell. Oh, and those strappy little sandals you picked up at Payless last week." Macy nods and says, "Yep, that outfit is classy, Jamie Lee. Parker Carrington won't know what hit him."

2

A Long Time Coming

Flanagan's Tavern is one of the oldest buildings in Hootertown, built before the Civil War. The brick has weathered to a muted orange and the steps leading to the entrance are dipped in the middle from wear. I sometimes fantasize about what it would have been like to live in the era of hoopskirts and horse-drawn buggies and I think it would be really cool to take a trip back in time. Well, for a day or two. The lack of essentials like deodorant, dental floss, hair spray, and, most importantly, tampons, would make me want to come back to the future real quick.

I open the heavy front door and step into the cool interior, inhaling the delicious aroma of Southern fried chicken, and the thought of mere soup and salad isn't too appealing. A rather narrow hallway with an uneven hardwood floor leads to the back of the building and the main dining room. I can hear the clinking of silverware against plates and the buzz of conversation as I draw closer to the room. I pause before entering, putting a hand to the sudden butterflies in my stomach.

Now, I'm not really nervous because Parker is a good-looking guy or he's from L.A. or he drives a fancy car. My daddy has farm equipment worth a lot more than that silver Jaguar. The butterflies are stemming from the pact I made with Macy. Ever since we were kids, if we made a promise to each other, we kept it. Today, we promised to get off our cans and go after what we wanted. *This* has me nervous. Excited. What I want may or may not be Parker Carrington, but somehow, walking into that dining room has me feeling like it is a big step in determining my future. Silly, I know. But that's how I feel and it's a long time comin'.

I take a deep, cleansing breath and tuck a lock of hair behind my ear before entering the room. I spot Parker right away at a table for two over by the window that I know overlooks a rose garden. He sees me, gives me a dazzling smile, and waves, but it takes me a while to make it over to the table. I recognize most of the people in the room, and of course I must do the polite thing and stop at several tables to greet folks. I realize that all eyes are on me when I sit down with Parker and I do have to say that I feel a little special. I also know that my mama will know of my luncheon with the handsome stranger before I take my first sip of water. Small towns mean big gossip, and the invention of cell phones has brought the Hootertown grapevine to a whole new level.

"You look nice, Jamie Lee," Parker comments. "I feel a little underdressed in my jeans. When you said *tavern*, I was thinking burgers and pub fries." He waves a hand in the air. "This place is really beautiful. The rose garden is magnificent."

I nod and can't help but feel a sense of pride. "Flanagan's Tavern was the original name, dating back to the mid-eighteen-hundreds. I'm sure it was a steak-and-ale type of place." I give him a reassuring smile. "Don't worry about the jeans. There's no official dress code, just the wrath of my mama. If I would have come in here in my cutoffs, she would have been mortified. You should be honored, though. I don't get even this dressed up except for Sunday services. I'm a jeans-and-T-shirt kinda girl. I'd go barefoot all day long if I could get away with it."

"Very bohemian. I like that."

I chuckle softly. "Most people would call it *redneck,* but call it what you like." I put my palms up and tell him, "I am what I am."

"And I like it," he says, giving me this slow, sultry smile that heats my blood. It's not one of those leering, giving-you-the-once-over kind of smiles, but one of male appreciation that has me feeling sexy as all get-out. I don't know quite what to say, so I reach for my water and take a sip.

"So, what on the menu would you recommend?"

"I would go for the buffet so you can sample a little bit of everything."

He nods. "Variety is the spice of life. Is that what you're going to do?"

I nibble on the inside of my lip. "I shouldn't. I always overeat at the buffet."

"Oh, come on, go for it." He looks past me at the piles of food. "I need you to help me choose."

"There's nothing free-range or made of tofu up there," I warn.

"No problem. I enjoy down-home cooking."

"Really? You look like a tofu-and-sprouts kinda guy."

He grins. "Well, let's just say it smells heavenly."

I groan and say, "You're tempting me." Boy, was he ever. Just then our waitress comes over and asks if we want a menu or if we are having the buffet.

"Jamie Lee?"

"Oh, I'll have the buffet."

"Make that two," he tells the waitress.

"Anything to drink?"

"Sweet tea," I tell her with a smile but her eyes are already on Parker.

He hesitates and then says, "I'll have the same."

"Enjoy," she says with a flirty smile at Parker. She's young, probably a Payton College student, but as we approach the salad bar I see other women eyeballing him as well. He doesn't seem to notice, and I'm flattered that his attention doesn't stray from me.

"Sweet tea means iced tea, right?"

I nod. "It's the drink of choice in the South. But you could have had a beer or whatever. We're wet here in Hootertown."

His eyebrows shoot up. "Wet?"

"Well, actually the correct term is moist."

"Moist?"

I grin. "We're a wet city in a dry county. Meaning we are allowed to sell alcohol."

"Oh." He nods his head as if he understands. "You mean some counties can't?"

"Oh, sure. I think around sixty. But there are all kinds of rules and exceptions. For example, the golf course out by Lake Logan can serve alcohol, but the lodge at the lake can't." I shrug my shoulders. "Go figure. We supply the world with bourbon and half of Kentucky can't sell it."

He shakes his head. "Sort of an oxymoron."

"You could say that. No wonder people have stills."

His eyebrows shoot up. "You mean moonshine?"

He seems so fascinated that I have to laugh. "Yeah. It's becoming a lost art, but they still exist."

"Let's get our salads and you can tell me more."

I choose the Caesar salad but Parker samples a bit of everything. He is delighted with things like pickled beets, spoon bread, and country ham. I find myself relaxing with him, flirting a bit and basically just having fun.

When we return to our table, he puts a thin slice of country ham on a cracker and takes a bite.

"Well?" I ask. "It's a little too salty for my taste."

"I like it," he says. "Different."

I swallow a bite of salad and then nod. "You're brave. I generally stick to things that I know I like."

Parker forks a slice of pickled beet, looks at it, and then pops it in his mouth. Chewing thoughtfully, he swallows and then wrinkles his nose. "Now, that I don't like." But then he looks at me and says, "But I never would have known if I hadn't tried."

"So my mama likes to tell me. I confess that I've always been a picky eater."

"Your mama is a smart lady. And I bet she's beautiful, like you."

"You are a smooth one, Parker Carrington. I do believe you could sell snow to an Eskimo." I laugh, but of course I'm eating it up. I glance at my watch and see that the time is passing all too quickly. I've got a client at one, so I say, "We had better get our main course. I've got to get back in about thirty minutes."

We head up to the buffet and of course I pile my plate with way more food than one person could possibly consume. I would feel like a pig, but Parker's plate is worse than mine. We sit down and I say, "My God, I can feel my hips gettin' wider just looking at all of this food."

"Let's just throw caution to the wind and enjoy," he says.

"Sounds like a plan." I take a bite of creamy mashed potatoes and almost groan. Macy, who is always into the latest diet craze, is convinced that carbs are evil, so she has me avoiding anything white.

"This," Parker says pointing to the blob of corn pudding on his plate, "is amazing. What is it again?"

"Corn puddin'."

"Puddin'?"

"Pudding," I slowly repeat.

He grins. "I'm going to have to learn the lingo if I'm going to be here for a while."

"I'll be glad to help you learn Hootertownese." I feel a rush of excitement knowing that he is planning on staying in town.

He polishes off his corn pudding and pats his flat stomach. "That was too good. I'm going to have to go for a run tonight."

"Actually it's more of a custard than a pudding.

Made with milk and eggs, a dash of salt, and corn. You bake it in a pan of water in the oven."

"You cook, Jamie Lee?" He looks at me like it's an amazing thing to do. I'm guessing that most women he knows don't know how to boil water and probably eat very little anyway.

"Not as much as I would like to. I'm busy at the shop, but I do love to cook. I learned from my mama and she's awesome. She still fixes pot roast with all the trimmings every Sunday." It's on the tip of my tongue to invite him, but I don't want to appear too forward.

"That's nice," he comments.

Uh-oh. *Nice.* That means boring. It dawns on me that he is used to sophisticated women who talk about worldly things like trips to Paris. Lordy he must think I'm a real fuddy-dud. Or maybe just a dud. I take another bite of mashed potatoes and it sort of sticks in my throat. I have to take a big drink of tea to wash it down.

"Can you recommend somewhere in town to stay?"

"There are a few bed-and-breakfast inns. But your best bet is the Mid-town Inn on Main just a block from where your car is parked. The rooms are nice. How long are you staying?"

He swallows a bite of chicken and says, "Well, I'm going to check out the town and surrounding area, take more pictures, and make sure that Hootertown is the right place. I will also have to get permission from your city to film the movie here. Do think anyone will object?"

I have to consider this. "I'm not sure. We have quite a bit of summer tourism that overflows from Lake Logan and I know they won't want to scare people off.

And the whole horror-flick thing might not go over too well."

"We wouldn't do any actual filming until the fall. And as far as the horror aspect, well, it's more of a spoof than scary. Probably a rating of PG-13. I've got a portfolio to present to your town council. You wouldn't happen to know when the next meeting is, would you?"

"Next Tuesday." I refrain from telling him that my uncle is the mayor of Hootertown. I glance at my watch. "I've really got to get going, Parker. I hope things go well for you."

"Did you just give me the brush-off?"

"Well, no . . . that is I—"

"Good. Then you'll consider showing me around town later this evening?"

"I have to work until eight o'clock. Maybe another time."

"You *are* giving me the brush-off."

"I am not!" I say this a little too loudly and draw some stares. "I most certainly am *not*," I say a little more softly.

"Jamie Lee, the night is just beginning at eight."

"Not in Hootertown," I tell him, and he really seems disappointed, which gives me a little boost of confidence. Just maybe he finds me as refreshingly different as I find him. "Listen, if you stop over around eight-thirty or so, we can go for a short drive and I'll show you around. If you want to check out the lake this afternoon, take a left at the end of Main and follow the signs. Payton College is in the other direction."

His face lights up and he says, "Great. Thanks for having lunch with me, Jamie Lee."

"The pleasure was all mine," I tell him and mean it. Parker might be polished and sophisticated but there's an endearing, almost shy, quality about him that I really enjoy. Not only does he appreciate me as a woman, but he seems to value me as a person as well. He stands up when I get up to leave and reaches for my hand. I think he is going to shake my hand, but he kisses it instead, and ohmigod, I think I might just melt into a puddle right there on the floor of the dining room. It's just too danged romantic for words. Repressing a sigh, I give him a smile that I think might be a little shaky around the corners, but I can't help it.

I walk out the door and for the first time I totally get the expression "walking on air." I feel as if I'm floating back to Cut & Curl. Maybe I'm just on carb overload, but I feel energetic, excited. I can't wait for the evening when I'll see Parker Carrington again.

Of course Macy pounces on me like I'm a Hershey's Kiss on a PMS day as soon as I enter the shop, not that I can blame her. Since the shop is momentarily empty, I tell her every last detail, more than happy to relive my lunch with Parker. I have to tell her the kiss-on-the-hand part twice.

"That's just so romantic," Macy croons. "Why can't there be romantic men like that in Hootertown? Huh? Is a kiss on the hand asking too friggin' much?"

This thought seems to put Macy in one of her pissed-off-for-no-apparent-reason moods, and because of my carb high or whatever, I develop an attitude of my own. Not a bad mood, really. Just an attitude. For example, when the UPS guy blows into the shop and gets all snippy with me when I have hair gel on my hands and can't sign his clipboard like, right this danged minute, I sashay right over there, grab his old pen in my gelled hand and scribble my initials. My reward is seeing his mouth drop open like he's a frog trying to catch flies.

"You got goop all over my pen."

"Sorry, I didn't realize," I tell him in a voice dripping in sugar, and I give him a look that just dares him to cross me. He doesn't. Now, this leads me to our next secret-handshake promise after I declare, "We are *not* going to take crap from jackasses any longer." Of course that was after he had left the store in his dorky brown shorts. It must be said that we don't really a get a lot of crap anyway, but it sure felt good getting all fired up. Unfortunately, this exuberance leads to cutting way too much hair off of Trudy Wilson's head and I glance over at Macy in horror. Luckily, Trudy thinks that the mere two inches of red hair sticking up on her head looks *sassy* and she loves it. *Whew*.

I realize that although Macy and I have done a good job with Cut & Curl and have some future plans for expansion like tanning beds and such, we've been on cruise control. This whole going-after-what-you-want thing is something that really has been a long time coming.

"Macy, look at the time," I tell her while sweeping up tumbleweeds of red hair. "Luke is going to be here soon. You wanna go home and change or anything?"

"No! I don't want to look like I primped for him."

"Macy, I thought you wanted to give him the impression that you're interested?"

She nods as she tidies up her station. "I know, but I need to take it slow. Give me some space, Jamie Lee."

I put my hands up. "Okay, okay." I would say more,

but Mama breezes into the shop and gives Macy a hug and me a glare.

"What?" I ask, all innocent-like.

"You didn't return any of my phone calls, Jamie Lee Carter. Not a one."

"Mama, we were swamped." I look to Macy for help. "Weren't we, Macy?"

"Yes, Mrs. Carter. We surely were. All day."

Mama purses her perfectly lined lips and fluffs her very big, very red, Naomi Judd hair. "Well then, why don't you just tell me if there is any truth to the rumor that you dined at Flanagan's Tavern this very afternoon with that handsome stranger who has been tooling around town in a flashy silver car? I've heard that he might hail from *California*! Explain yourself, Jamie Lee."

Of course Mama already knows this to be a fact and I think about denying it just for fun, but Macy, who knows Mama can get rather dramatic, gives me a discreet shake of her head and a very slight widening of her eyes, meaning: *don't do it*. I'm convinced that Macy and I could probably carry on an entire conversation without verbalizing a single word. The problem is that Mama knows this, and is watching us all squinty-eyed. She can't really figure out what we're conveying, just that we're somehow talking behind her back . . . sort of.

"Well?" Mama demands, hands on her hips. She is petite and has delicate features, but she is a ball of fire, a steel magnolia, through and through. "Did this event occur?"

"Yes," I tell her.

"And just who is this man?"

"His name is Parker Carrington. He is a movie producer and wants to film a movie right here in Hootertown."

A worried frown puckers her brow. "And how do we know he is trustworthy? This sounds rather far-fetched if you ask me."

I roll my eyes. "I'm not askin' you."

"Don't you get all sassy with me. Jamie Lee, I do think you should keep your distance until we know more about this man."

Macy knows that I'm seeing Parker tonight and, like the loyal friend she is, remains silent.

Mama turns to Macy and asks, "Don't you agree, Macy?"

Macy swallows, clearly not wanting to cross my mother, whom she loves dearly.

"We could Google him," Macy suggests.

"Do what?" Mama asks. The Internet remains a mystery to her. She won't even go near a computer. "Now, how might one go about *Googling* him?"

"Well, first we have to take off his clothes," I say with a grin.

"Jamie Lee!" Mama exclaims.

"Oh, Mama, it just means we can look him up on the Internet. That's a good idea," I tell Macy. I have to admit that I'm a bit curious myself as to the magnitude of Parker's success. I follow her over to the computer at the front desk. She brings up the Internet and types in PARKER CARRINGTON.

"Wow," Macy says when we find pages and pages of sites featuring him. She clicks one and there is an article about his production company and his movies, and a picture, leaving no question that he is on the up-and-up.

"Looks like he's the real McCoy," I say and get an elbow from Macy. "See, Mama," I say with a little lift of my chin, "he *is* on the up-and-up."

She lifts the reading glasses dangling around her neck from a beaded chain and puts them on. She peers at the monitor for a minute and then looks at me. "Are you seeing this Hollywood producer again? You know money, Jamie Lee, doesn't make the man."

"I'm just showing him around town, Mama. No biggie."

Mama blows out a long sigh. "Why don't you set your sights on some local boy instead of Mr. Hollywood?"

"I'm not settin' my sights on anyone."

"Well, maybe you should."

"Mama—"

"Jamie Lee, you are a catch for any man, Hollywood or not. But you can't get reeled in if you don't jump in the water."

I want to tell her that I'm not a small-mouthed bass, but I don't. I know that she means well, and that there's more than a little truth to what she's saying. I'm saved from further comment when Luke arrives. He's wearing tan khakis and a dark blue Payton Panthers logo golf shirt that brings out his blue eyes. I see Macy look down at her jeans with a small frown. I give her an I-told-you-to-change look, and she shrugs her shoulders.

"Lucas!" Mama says, rushing over to him for a hug. "What brings you here? You certainly don't need a haircut." She reaches up and smoothes his brown hair. "Looks nice."

"Macy gave me a trim this morning," he says and looks over at her with a grin. "Macy, you ready?"

"What's this?" Mama asks. "A date?" She looks pleased as punch. Mama has always adored Macy.

"No!" Macy says quickly, her cheeks going all pink. "I'm just doing Luke a small favor, is all."

"Macy has been kind enough to assist me in hiring a new cheerleading coach. I don't have any idea why I'm in charge of this task, but somehow I got roped into it."

Mama nods. "Well you're certainly qualified, Macy." She glances down at her slim gold watch and then over at Luke. "Now, you're going to get her somethin' to eat, aren't you? She's been working all day and I understand they've been swamped."

Macy and I exchange a guilty look.

"Of course, Mama."

She reaches up and pats his cheek. "That's my boy."

Luke leans in and kisses Mama on the cheek. "You raised me well."

"That I did." She plucks a tiny speck of lint off of his shirt. "That blue suits you, and as always, you are neat and tidy."

Of course I have to interject something to end this drivel. "And what was I, raised by wolves?"

Mama arches a delicately plucked eyebrow. Ha, she thinks she will be able to comment on my attire, but I'm still in my black capri pants and white shell instead of my usual jeans and T-shirt. Unfortunately, I'm in my bare feet, ruining the total effect, although my toes are a nice shiny shade of red. But hey, those strappy sandals were uncomfortable. Mama, of course, focuses on my feet.

"My shoes hurt," I tell her a bit defensively.

"You look very nice *today,* Jamie Lee," Mama comments, which is sort of a backhanded compliment. "Very professional." Her look says that I should dress like this all the time.

"Mama, if I had wanted to dress up every day, I would work in one of those fancy day spas. I prefer to be comfortable when I work and I do believe it puts the customer at ease, as well."

She flips her hand in the air, making the bling on her wrist jangle, and says, "Whatever." Mama gets dressed up just to go to the grocery store.

"Macy, are you ready?" Luke asks.

"Sure," she says and then glances at Mama. "Thank you for covering for me, Mrs. Carter."

"No problem, sugar. Truth is, I'm tickled to get out of the house. Tom was gettin' on my last nerve. I do love that man, but I needed a break." She does a shooing motion with her hands. "You two just go have fun."

Macy opens her mouth and I'm sure she's going to protest again that this isn't a date, but I squelch her with a look. This isn't officially a date, but it *is* one in a manner of speaking, and she should treat it as such. *Flirt*, I mouth at her while Luke starts walking towards the door.

Macy gives me a panicky little shake of her head and I would draw her aside to whisper my two cents, but a customer walks in and she escapes. Mama takes the walk-in since I have a client due and we are surprisingly busy for a Wednesday evening. By eight o'clock I'm beat, but then I remember that Parker is coming over and I want to hurry up to shower before he arrives.

"So, tell me about Mr. Fancy Pants," Mama says as we clean up.

"He's nice, Mama. Very polite and respectful."

She doesn't look convinced. Putting a hand on my shoulder, she says, "Just be careful."

I kiss her on the cheek. "I will. And thanks for coming in tonight."

"Oh, I enjoyed it. You're doing a fine job here, Jamie Lee." She gives me a smile and puts her hands to her cheeks. "Oh, do you think Macy and Luke might start seeing one another? Wouldn't that be wonderful?"

"Nothing would please me more."

"Well, I'm off. Call me tomorrow, okay?"

"I will." I show her to the door, lock up, and then head upstairs to my apartment. My heart starts to pound harder when I think about Parker and I stop by the fridge and snag a longneck, more to calm my nerves than to quench my thirst. Twisting off the cap, I take a long swallow, feeling the cold liquid all the way down my throat to my belly. This reminds me that I have skipped dinner, but I head to the shower thinking that I don't have time to fix something to eat.

I groan when the hot water pelts my tired body. The beer has relaxed me a bit and although I long to linger in the steamy stall fragrant with peach-scented shampoo, I finish up quickly so I can dress and primp a little. I don't want to go all out and give Parker the wrong impression, but I do want to look nice. Not wanting to waste makeup-applying time, I choose a fairly new pair of Levis and a scoop-necked red blouse.

I add some product to give my hair body and blow it dry. Luckily I'd just done my roots, so I'm quite pleased with my hair. Now, I know I'm a hairdresser, but my favorite way to wear my own hair is in a simple ponytail; however, tonight I let it hang loose. This is my favorite length as well, long enough to do stuff with, but short enough to swing about my shoulders. My bangs are fringy, thanks to the trick of trimming with the tip of my scissors pointed up. Okay, I know I'm goin' on about my hair, but it is my bread and butter, after all, so deal with it.

I'm finishing up my makeup when I hear my doorbell chime. With a quick inspection in the mirror, I add a dab more pink lip gloss and hurry down my short hallway to the door. I put my hand on the doorknob, take a big cleansing breath, and swing it open with a welcoming, lip-glossy smile.

"Griff?" I ask in surprise. "What are you doin' here?"

3

Friends in Low Places

"Well, hello to you, too, Jamie Lee," Griff says with a grin, but his brown eyes have a little hurt look to them.

"I'm sorry, I didn't mean to be rude," I tell him. Griff is my brother's best friend and dear to me as well, so of course I must invite him in. Besides, he looks tired and thirsty. While I really don't want him here when Parker arrives, I figure I have a few minutes to spare. "Come on in and have a beer," I offer and I'm rewarded with a warm smile.

"Thanks. I could use a cold one."

He looks down at his dusty work boots and is about to take them off, but I wave it off and say, "Don't worry about your shoes. A little dust won't hurt anything."

He grins. "You just don't want to smell my sweaty feet."

"Guilty," I tell him and he laughs.

"Here, this is for you," he says and thrusts a jar of strawberry preserves at me. "It's from Irma Baker. I'm puttin' a deck off of her kitchen and she asked me to bring this to you on my way home."

"Griff, I'm not exactly on your way home," I say as I reach in the fridge for a beer.

"No big deal," he says, shrugging his shoulders and then wincing.

"What's wrong?" I twist off the cap and hand him the cold bottle.

"Sunburn. It's been so hot out that Miss Irma said I should take off my shirt and I guess I didn't realize how much sun I was gettin'."

I try not to grin, but fail.

"What's so funny?" he asks, wiggling his shoulders, and winces again. He takes a long pull off his bottle and then says, "It hurts."

I can't tell him that I'm picturing Miss Irma ogling him, so I say, "Nothing. Do you have any aloe at home?"

After taking another swig of beer, he chuckles. "Do I look like the kind of guy that would have aloe in his cabinet?"

"Point taken." In his scruffy brown boots, work-worn Wranglers torn at the knees, and a faded blue T-shirt stretched across wide shoulders, he certainly looks all man. The thought skitters across my brain that Parker *would* have aloe in his cabinet and I'm not sure what that means, so I shake it off. "Well I do. Follow me, and I'll get you fixed up."

I hear Griff's heavy boots clunking on the hardwood floor as I head down the short hallway to my bathroom. Opening the medicine cabinet over the sink, I locate a bottle of aloe. "Take off your shirt," I tell him while I unscrew the lid. "This will cool the burn and help heal your skin."

With a nod, he polishes off the remainder of his beer and then peels off his shirt. "Work your magic," he says.

"Sit down on the commode so I can put this on you." I make tisk-tisk noises with my tongue when I see his red shoulders and back. "Griffin Sheldon, you should know better." Squirting some of the green gel onto my palms, I gently begin to smooth the sticky stuff over his shoulders.

"Wow, that's cold," he says with a hiss.

"Feels better, though, huh?" I squirt some more aloe from the bottle. "Lean forward so I can get your back." Griff is a big guy, six foot three or so, but not quite as bulky as my brother. His strength is from hard labor, giving him more of a whipcord-lean, muscled physique than machine-generated muscles. After applying a generous amount of the sticky stuff to his back, I ask him to turn around. "Let me see your chest."

"Yes ma'am." He scoots around on the toilet lid and looks up at me. "Well?"

"Not as bad." I put a smaller dollop in my palms. "Lean back a little." I smooth the aloe over his upper chest, lightly furred with dark hair. He smells of the outdoors, a bit like sunshine and musky man and a hint of aftershave, and suddenly I get this unexpected pull of sexual attraction. A bit startled, I look at his face and his brown eyes lock with mine and for a weird moment, I think that he's feeling it too.

"You need a haircut," I tell him, trying to break the spell, but my voice sounds all husky and needy. I clear my throat and say, "Pretty soon you'll be needing a ponytail." I'm trying to joke, to chase away the urge to lean in and kiss him. I'm wondering what the hell has gotten into me. I've known Griff all my life. He is a nice guy, a great friend, and I remind myself that I'm looking for a little excitement, which is about to arrive on my doorstep in the handsome package of one Parker Carrington. That's gotta be it. I'm looking forward to some male attention and I'm so worked up about my date with Parker that I'm feeling things that I shouldn't. I mean, let's face it. Griff is a good-looking guy and I'm just so revved up that my body is reacting to a bare chest, *period*. Not *Griff's* chest, nice though it might be. I certainly don't feel that way about him. He's like a brother. Nothing more.

Okay, I know I'm protesting a little too much and not really being honest with myself. But I don't want to have feelings for Griffin Sheldon. *I don't have feelings for Griff!* Not like that. I've been down that road.

God, he's got a great mouth.

Oh stop! If he knew what I was thinking, he would laugh his ass off. I'm the pesky little sister that he and Luke always tried to shake. He would never be interested in me.

Griff reaches up and runs his fingers through his dark hair, causing a ripple of muscle that sorta has me fascinated.

"Maybe you can do me tomorrow? Think you could fit me into your schedule?"

"D-do you?" God, is it hot in here or is it me?

"I could even stop in after hours."

"After hours?"

"Jamie Lee, you okay?"

No, I am most definitely not okay. "I'm . . . fine. Now what were you sayin'?"

"I want you to cut my hair tomorrow if you can squeeze me in." He grins. "Where's your brain wanderin' off to?"

"I'm sorry, Griff. It's been a kinda crazy day. Sure, I can trim you up tomorrow. Just stop in after you get done at Irma's." I begin washing the dried aloe off my hands.

"Okay." He clears his throat. "Hey, you wanna go grab a pizza? I haven't gotten a chance to eat."

I open my mouth to say sure, when the doorbell chimes. *Parker!* Oh my! I do believe my brain has taken a holiday.

"You expectin' someone?"

"Uh, yeah."

"Macy? 'Cuz she can go with us."

"No, not Macy." I check my hair in the mirror. "Griff, I've got to get the door. Put your shirt on, okay?"

Frowning, he nods.

I rush to the door that is chiming again and swing it open with a smile. "Hi, Parker. Come on in."

He steps inside. "Your place is really nice." Looking around, he says, "Very eclectic."

I have to chuckle. "You mean very garage sale?"

"Country chic," he comments with one of those dazzling smiles. "I love the exposed brick walls and hardwood floors."

"It's a work in progress. Took a lot of elbow grease and help from friends to get this place livable." I would say more, but Griff walks into the room. Parker's eyebrows shoot up and there is this sort of something or other that passes between them. Like they are sizing each other up. Maybe I'm just imagining things.

"Am I interrupting something, Jamie Lee?" Parker asks.

"Oh, no. *No!* Griff is just a friend. He stopped by to bring me some strawberry preserves." I look over at Griff who gives me this disappointed look like I've done something wrong. Now, what's up with that? But the look passes and he holds out his hand to Parker.

"Griff Sheldon," he says not exactly friendly, but not too put-offish, either.

"Parker Carrington."

They shake hands and I can't help but notice the difference between the two men. They are both about the same height and probably about the same weight, but that's where the similarity ends. From his precision haircut (which I now notice is highlighted) to his Italian loafers, Parker is all spit and polish with a lot of gold bling in between. He is worldly and exciting and the thought of spending time with someone like him has my heart racing.

Griff, on the other hand, is work-worn and rough around the edges. Dark stubble shadows his jaw and his unruly hair nearly touches his shoulders. Griff is every inch the type of man my mama wants to see me with . . . and where *that* thought came from I'll never know. I'm going off the deep end here. Parker is just passing through and Griff is a friend. What am I obsessing about?

"So, Parker," Griff says, "I don't think I've seen you around here before."

He nods. "I'm a movie producer. I've been searching

for the perfect town to film my next movie and I think Hootertown might be the ticket."

"Really?" Griff sounds curious, but not impressed. "Why Hootertown?"

Parker shrugs. "I don't know. Just a gut feeling. I've been searching for a small town with some character and heart and Hootertown certainly fits that bill."

Griff scratches his chin and then flicks a glance at me that is chock full of *What are you doin' with this guy?* I narrow my eyes a bit, hopefully conveying that he had better back off, but being a guy and all, Griff doesn't catch my drift the way Macy would have. Or maybe he chooses to ignore me.

"Jamie Lee and I were just going to take a little spin around town so I can get some ideas," Parker says very politely, but I know that he is telling Griff to hit the road.

"Is that right?" Griff doesn't budge.

Okay, now I *know* that these two are, like, eyeballing each other and I realize I should put and end to this, but it kinda feels like they are fighting over me and I decide to let it go on a moment longer.

"Yes, that's right," Parker says, still politely but firmly, and then turns to me. "Are you ready, Jamie Lee?" he asks in that smooth, silky voice.

I thought I was, but the look Griff is giving me has me feeling all uncertain, like I'm somehow doing something wrong. Well damn. Talk about bursting someone's bubble. Now, this ticks me off. Here I was all excited and Griff marches in here, unannounced, I might add, and is acting . . .

Like my big brother.

That's it! With a lift of my chin, I tell Griff, "Thanks so much for the preserves." Of course I'm too well mannered to tell him to leave but I sort of let my eyes travel over to the door and this time I know he has to catch my silent plea.

"No problem. I know strawberries are your favorite."

He still doesn't budge. I am hanging onto politeness by a thread. And to think I was lusting after him! I do think the perm fumes are killing my brain cells.

"So, we're on for tomorrow?" Griff asks, drawing a look from Parker.

Now what in the hell is he talking about? I simply blink at him, totally confused. "Oh, you mean the haircut?"

"Yeah, after hours."

"Yes, Griff. We've already discussed this." I'm wondering if the sun has fried his brain and barely refrain from asking this.

"Okay," he says and finally makes his way over toward the door. With a look at Parker, he says to me, "If you need anything, just call my cell, Jamie Lee."

Gritting my teeth, I can only nod. After Griff finally leaves, I turn to Parker and say, "Sorry about that."

Parker grins. "He's totally into you, you know."

"Into me? You mean like sweet on me?"

"Yes. Not that I can blame him."

I shake my head. "Oh, no, you've got it all wrong. Griff is like a big brother. He's always been protective of me. Some habits are hard to break."

Parker walks over to the door and holds it open for me. "Well, he just politely let me know that if I step out of line, he'll kick my ass."

"I'm so sorry!" I tell him as I walk outside.

"Don't be," Parker says as he follows me across my back deck and down the stairs. "I find it quite charming."

I reach the bottom of the steps and turn to look at him. "Charming?" I have to chuckle. "Explain how that was charming."

"Jamie Lee, your friend was defending your honor. You don't see that much anymore."

"I think you're overdramatizing, Mr. Moviemaker, but whatever."

"So there's nothing between you and this Griff?"

We stop at his silver Jag and I give him a firm shake of my head. "I'm telling you, Griff is just a friend. He and my brother have been best buddies forever. I was always a thorn in their side, begging to tag along and usually getting left behind."

He gives me this slow smile that makes me feel all hot and shivery at the same time. The evening breeze plays with his hair and I wonder how the golden strands would feel sliding through my fingers.

"Well if things go the way I hope they will, I'll be in Hootertown for the summer and then some. I just want to make sure the coast is clear."

My heart picks up speed and I ask, "The coast is clear?" My voice goes all breathy and I try not to blush.

"For spending time with you." His smile deepens and ohmigod, there's that dimple again.

"You are one smooth talker," I tell him as he opens the door to the car. I'm trying to be all cool when I really feel like I could melt right into the sidewalk. I slide onto the butter-soft leather seat and take a deep breath as Parker comes over to the driver's side and folds his long legs into the car. His shoulders almost touch mine and, hot damn, the man smells good enough to eat. *Oh, keep your wits about you, Jamie Lee. You are playing with fire here, girl.*

Parker starts up the engine with a quick twist of his wrist and I swear the car sounds like it purrs. "Where to?" he asks me as he presses a button for the windows to silently slide down, letting out the pent-up heat.

I look over at him. "Well, what did you get a chance to see this afternoon?"

"Not much. I had a ton of calls to return and then I have to admit that I fell asleep while reading through the script."

"There's not much daylight left, so why don't we just drive through town and out near Lake Logan? I'm not really sure what it is that you're looking for."

He shifts into reverse and tells me, "Cruising around would be great. Right now I'm still in the development stage. A big studio is interested in the project, but if they decide to pass, I have turnaround rights."

"Meaning?"

"I can take it somewhere else. I'm what you call the executive producer. In other words, I develop the project, but I won't really have much to do with the nuts and bolts or the day-to-day process of producing the film."

"Oh, you mean like you get it organized and then hand it over to someone else?"

He nods. "Pretty much, although it varies from film to film. Once in a while I'll put up my own money to do a smaller project and then I am involved in just about everything from casting the actors to making sure they have hot coffee on the set."

I'm trying to absorb all of this. "So, you're still in the beginning stages of producing *Vanquished*?"

As he pulls out onto Main Street, he nods. "Right. I've got interest and money and a couple of big stars reading the script. It looks good right now, but the market can change. There are so many variables. It can be frustrating to get excited about a project and then for one reason or another have it die." He glances over at me and says, "Sorry. I'm probably boring you to death."

"No, I find it interesting. When I go to the movies, I don't think about how much effort goes into making it. From now on, I'm going to stay and read all the credits."

He laughs, and I wonder if he is laughing with me or at me.

"You must think I'm such a goober."

"What in the world is a goober?"

"Someone who is stupid."

He laughs again. "Hey, isn't a goober a peanut?"

"Yeah, that too."

"Well, Jamie Lee, you are neither stupid nor a peanut."

"How kind of you to say so."

He laughs again. "I do believe *I'm* the goober."

"Goober grape," I tease.

"Goober *what*?"

"You know, the Smuckers grape jelly and peanut butter that comes swirled together in a jar."

"They make it that way?"

"Of course! Genius, if you think about it."

He looks at me to see if I'm serious and I giggle.

"Have you ever even eaten a P B & J?"

"P B & J? Oh, you mean peanut butter and jelly. Sure I have."

I give him a sidelong look.

"Well, when I was a kid. I think."

"Yeah, right."

"Okay, Miss Smarty-Pants, when was the last time you ate a peanut butter and jelly sandwich?"

"I do believe it was yesterday. And did you just call me a smarty pants?"

"I told you I was a goober."

"Yeah, right." I have to laugh. We're cruising down Main Street, and of course I'm well aware that people, many of whom I know, are staring at the slinky silver Jag. Parker is supposed to be eyeing the scenery, but he is mostly focusing on me and I'm eating it up with a spoon. When he pushes the button to roll up the windows, I stop him.

"Oh, no you don't. In Hootertown it's an unwritten rule that you have to cruise on a summer night such as this with your windows rolled down and your radio cranked up."

"Where exactly is the top cruising destination?"

"Why, the Tastee-Freez, hands down, on any given Wednesday in June."

"And on Thursday?"

"The same."

"Friday?"

"Dixie's Dance Hall."

"Saturday?"

"The same. Now, there are other sporadic means of

entertainment like Little League baseball games and church festivals. Our biggie is the Fourth of July town picnic and parade. It's a tradition that dated way back to pre–Civil War days. The whole town attends, including tourists from Lake Logan. There's a pie-baking contest, a picnic-basket auction, and a parade where more people are in it than watching." I glance over at him to make sure he isn't falling asleep at the wheel. "Oh geez, now I'm boring *you*."

"Not at all. Go on."

"Well, of course, there is always Lake Logan, where you can rent houseboats and fish, water-ski, and so forth." I watch him shift and think that he has nice hands. Long fingers.

"So crank up the music, Jamie Lee."

I lean forward and fiddle with the fancy radio, finding my favorite country station. George Strait is singing a love song and I want to sing along, but of course I don't, even though I do have a rather nice singing voice.

"Where's the Tastee-Freez?"

"One street over. Make a left at the stop sign."

He spots the sign sporting a huge ice-cream cone and pulls into the gravel parking lot where young couples and families are licking soft-serve cones and sucking down milkshakes. I look at my watch and see that it's already after ten. Time flies when you're with a hottie.

"Looks like they're closing up," Parker says with such disappointment that I have to smile.

"Not to worry," I assure him as he kills the engine. "I have friends in low places."

He chuckles and I think that if nothing else, I'm entertaining him. We get out of the car and hurry over to the window. Mary Jo Jasper is wiping down the machines and tidying up. She looks up and says, "Well, howdy there, Jamie Lee. I haven't seen you in a coon's age." She shakes her head so hard that her flushed chubby cheeks wobble and her extra chin jiggles. Of course, if I worked at the Tastee-Freez, my rear would have its own zip code, so I'm not one to judge a few extra pounds.

"Are you still open, Mary Jo?"

She gives me a wink. "For you, sugar, anytime. What can I get for you and your fella?"

"I'll have a small chocolate dip-top." I turn and look at Parker, who is studying the menu like it's a wine list.

"What's a dip-top?"

"Vanilla soft serve dipped in chocolate that gets hard like on an Eskimo pie."

"Eskimo pie," he says and ponders this for a moment. "Oh yeah, ice cream on a stick." He gives me this big grin that somehow tugs at my heart. "I haven't had one of those since . . . well . . ."

"Since you had your last peanut butter and jelly."

"Yeah," he says softly. "I'll have one of those . . . what was it called, Jamie Lee?"

"A chocolate dip-top."

"Small?" Mary Jo asks him.

"No, a big one."

A moment later, Mary Jo hands me my small cone and Parker his giant one and I'm guessing that she too has fallen into the smitten category. He pays for them and we walk over to a small picnic table. He starts to sit on the bench, but everyone always sits on the table and puts their feet on the bench. I do this and Parker follows my lead. The night is still warm even though darkness has fallen, so I warn Parker, "You have to eat a dip-top fast or the ice cream will melt out the sides."

"Okay," he says and takes a big bite, sort of savors it, and then says, "Oh, delicious."

"It's best to eat the chocolate off first or it will start to fall off and land on your shirt. In no time you'll have a real mess on your hands."

"Ahh, so there's an art to eating a dip-top." He takes a bite of the chocolate and doesn't know what to do when a whole big piece of it comes off. I come to his rescue and catch the bottom with my fingers.

"Here," I tell him and lift the chocolate to his mouth. He takes it and, ohmigod, his lips feel so warm and his tongue actually touches my fingers. A sizzle of pure heat goes from my fingertips to my toes. For a moment I forget all about my ice cream.

"Jamie Lee," he says in that deep voice, "you're melting."

Boy, am I ever. "Oh!" I feel cool liquid dripping over my fingers and reach for my napkin. I quickly lick the sides of the cone, lapping up the melting ice cream with my tongue. A big piece of chocolate falls off and lands in the gravel. "Well, hell's bells. I hate it when that happens."

He laughs, but then some of his chocolate bites the dust as well. "This is difficult to eat." Tilting his head to the side, he eats the rest of his chocolate dip and works on the big swirl of ice cream.

Mine is to the manageable stage and I polish it off in due time, hoping there isn't any chocolate on my face. I try not to think about the fact that our legs are touching as I dab at my lips with my small napkin.

"That was amazing," Parker says.

At first I think he is joking, but I realize that he's serious. "Don't they have soft-serve ice cream in L.A?"

He shrugs and answers, "I suppose."

I angle my head up at him to get a better look at his face. "I guess you're used to things like tiramisu and chocolate mousse."

"True enough."

He looks down at me and his gaze sort of lingers on my mouth, making me feel all shivery.

"But, right now, I'm thinking that I prefer soft serve at the Tastee-Freez," he says right next to my ear and I swear I feel like I'm going to slither right off of the picnic table.

"You are so full of it," I tell him, trying to hide the fact that I'm getting all hot and bothered. Reaching up, I give him a little shove and he laughs.

"Are you ready to go?"

"Sure," I answer, realizing that we are the only ones left in the parking lot. I hope that when I stand, my legs of Jell-O will hold me up. When Parker shifts to get up from the table, the light from the Tastee-Freez illuminates the fact that he has a bit of chocolate at the corner of his mouth. "Wait," I tell him, putting my hand over his.

"What?"

"You have a bit of chocolate," I point to the corner of my own mouth and say, "right there."

He tries to get it with the tip of his tongue. "Did I get it?"

"No." I giggle.

Parker leans forward. "You get it for me."

Now, if I were a bolder person, I would lean in and lick it right off. *Parker Carrington dipped in chocolate. Whoowee.* My heart pounds at the thought, but I reach up with a napkin and dab at the corner of his mouth.

"Did you get it?"

His voice is low and husky and now I'm really worried about my knees knockin'. What if I have to, like, grab onto him? I can only nod.

Parker stands up and holds out his hand to assist me from the table. I lock my knees and make this display of brushing off my jeans while I wait for my legs to stop being so wobbly. After a moment, I mutter a silent prayer and head (sorta stiff-like) over to the car.

Parker opens the door for me and I slide into the seat. After he gets into the car, he asks, "Do you want to head over to the lake?"

I do, but the moon hanging over Lake Logan is too romantic for me to handle right now. And then, of course, I hear my mother's voice in my head reminding me that Parker is a stranger in town and that I should be careful. "I should get back. I have to work early tomorrow and it's getting late."

"Okay."

He sounds disappointed and that gives me a little rush of pleasure. It must be said that I'm intelligent enough to realize that I'm nothing like what Parker Carrington is used to, and part of the attraction is the difference in our backgrounds. Now, I'm not thinking I'm not good enough or any of that bull, but let's face it. I'm not exactly the type of girl that Parker Carrington would bring home to his mama. So letting this go any further would be real stupid on my part. He'll go back to L.A. and I'll be left pining for him and gain twenty pounds and be real bitchy to everyone, chasing away customers and such. I should probably end this before it begins. Yep, as soon as we get back to my place, I'm going to politely send him on his way and, like, wish him luck or whatever.

"You're awfully quiet, Jamie Lee."

"I'm just a bit tired."

His car purrs up to the front of Cut & Curl all too soon. Killing the engine, he shifts in his seat to face me and says, "I had a great time, tonight."

"I was happy to show you around." This is the beginning of my good-luck speech, but he gives me this crooked grin that stops me in my tracks.

"I can't remember when I've had so much fun. Hootertown is a great place to live. Warm and friendly. You're lucky."

He pauses and I really should jump in with my speech but I'm too busy admiring how good-looking he is.

"I grew up hopping between coasts after my parents split up. My mother lived in New York and my dad in L.A. Mom summered in Europe, and more often than not, I went with her."

"Oh." I'm not sure whether to say that I'm sorry or not. "That had to be hard. You were an only child?"

He nods and then says, "Don't feel sorry for me. I had an interesting and educational childhood."

"But you missed out on being a kid. Things like ice-cream cones and . . ." I lose my train of thought because he's looking at me like he's going to kiss me.

"Jamie Lee?"

"Yes?"

"May I kiss you?"

For a moment I just blink at him like a big ninny.

"I know this isn't exactly a date, but I've wanted to kiss you all night and if I don't, I won't be able to get to sleep thinking about what it would feel like to touch your mouth with mine."

Now how exactly am I supposed to resist a line like that? Huh? I close my eyes, thinking that if I'm not looking at him I'll be able to give him my farewell speech, but my concentration is blown all to hell, and I guess closing my eyes is an invitation, because suddenly I feel his lips, *oh so softly*, on mine.

4

And Then He Kissed Me

It's a gentle kiss, just the slight pressure of his lips against mine. But just when I think it's going to end, Parker cups the back of my head with his hand and threads his long fingers through my hair. He increases the pressure just a little and then the tip of his tongue lightly traces my bottom lip, making me shiver with anticipation.

He pulls away, leaving me wanting so much more. "You are such a player." I try to tease, but my voice has this little hitch in it.

With a low moan, he leans back in his seat and shakes his head. "That was a mistake."

Disappointment hits me smack-dab in my gut.

He looks over at me through half-lidded eyes and says, "Now I'll never be able to get to sleep."

"Parker, you are such a—"

He puts a finger to my lips and then says, "Jamie Lee, I'm not playing you."

It's pretty dark in the inside of the car, with just some

shadowy light from the streetlights, but I look into his eyes and see that he looks sincere. His finger traces my bottom lip, sending a shiver down my spine and making heat pool in places that have been cold for way too long. Now, maybe it's because I haven't felt desire for such a long time, or maybe because this whole day has been sort of surreal. I mean, it started out so normal and now here I am sitting in a silver sports car with a handsome-as-sin man from California who is looking at me like he wants to gobble me up.

Damned if I know.

But suddenly I imagine sliding my hand up his arm, encircling my hand around his, and sucking the finger that is tracing my lip into the heat of my mouth.

But I don't.

"I'd better get going," I tell him in a voice that's shaky. *Before I drag you up upstairs, tear off your clothes, and make wild passionate love to you all night long.*

Disappointment flickers in his eyes, but he gives me a smile and asks, "Will you have time to show me around tomorrow?"

"I work until six."

"Tomorrow evening?"

"Sure," I answer. "Call me." I dig around in my purse and hand him a bright pink business card. "Good night, Parker. You don't have to walk me up." *My willpower might not last.*

"Okay. Thanks again, Jamie Lee."

"My pleasure." Oh, if he only knew. I get out of the car and walk over to the steps to the side of the building that leads to my apartment. At the top of the landing, I look back down to see the silver car glide away into the night. With a long sigh, I put my hands to my warm cheeks and shake my head. "Wow."

I would stand there a moment longer, savoring the sounds and smells of the warm summer evening, but I can hear the phone ringing inside. Fumbling for my keys, I get inside the door and reach for the phone attached to the wall in my kitchen, thinking it's going to be Macy.

"Hello," I answer while reaching inside my fridge for a cold beer.

"Jamie Lee. It's Griff."

"Oh, hey." I twist off the cap and take a long swallow.

"I just wanted to say that I was sorry for being sorta rude to that producer guy."

"That's okay," I say a little stiffly because I'm wondering if he's checking up on me right *now*, and I toy with the idea of letting him think Parker is here. But deep down, I know that Griff is only acting this way because he cares about my safety, so I don't.

"I just want you to be careful, Jamie Lee. You don't know much about this guy."

"He's on the up-and-up, Griff. Macy and I checked him out on the Internet."

Griff sighs and then says, "That might tell you about his professional credentials, but not what kinda guy he is personally."

"Griff, I'm twenty-six years old. You need to quit thinking of me as Luke's kid sister."

"I'm just telling you to be cautious. This guy's from L.A. and—"

"I'm outta my league?" I set the beer bottle down on the counter with a thud, and beer foams out of the top.

"That's not what I meant."

"Damned if it's not."

"Look, I didn't call to piss you off."

"No, just to check up on me."

"So, shoot me for caring about you. I'm sorry, but you can be so trusting and—"

"You mean naive?" I ask through gritted teeth. When will Griff learn that I'm not a child?

"Well, now that you said it, yeah, a little."

"Anything else, Griff? I was just about to go play with my Barbie dolls."

"Jamie Lee . . ."

"Not that I owe you any explanation, but Parker was a perfect gentleman."

"So he didn't try anything, because—"

"Griff! Give it up!" I close my eyes and take a deep breath. "Listen, I've got a beer sittin' here gettin' all warm on me. I'll talk to you later."

"You coming to the softball game tomorrow?"

"You know I will." It's hard to stay angry with him.

"'Kay."

"How's the sunburn?" I have to ask. He might be exasperating, but I do care about him too.

"Better. That aloe stuff helped."

"Well, sleep without a shirt so the heat stays out."

"I always sleep in the buff, Jamie Lee."

"Yeah, right. I bet you're in Spider-Man jammies right now. The kind with the feet in them."

He chuckles and says, "Finish your beer before it gets warm. See you tomorrow."

I hang up the phone, glad that the conversation ended well. I'm chuckling about the Spider-Man jammies, picturing him in them . . . but then a visual comes to me from out of left field. I'm not picturing Griff in the jammies . . . but *without them*.

I close my eyes real tight and try to shake that image from my head, but it takes a minute. Taking a long swig of beer, I wonder where in the hell that crazy thought came from. Thinking that I'm just a bit shook up from the unusual day, I polish off the beer and head to the bathroom to get ready for bed.

I wash up and brush my teeth, but my mind isn't really on the tasks that I'm doing, but rather on the events of the day. After patting my face dry, I gaze at my reflection in the mirror above the sink, wondering if Parker really finds me attractive. I have my mother's rather delicate features, but my daddy's wide-set blue eyes. I consider my nose a bit too perky, but my mouth is nice . . . All in all I'm pretty enough, I suppose, but in a girl-next-door kinda way, not, like, supermodel beautiful or anything.

Before shrugging into my Payton Panthers sleepshirt, I give my body the once-over, backing up to view myself in the mirror. Well, I'm certainly not the reed-thin model type like Parker is probably used to. Nope, I've got curves . . . breasts that have gotten looks since eighth grade, but some junk in the trunk as well. Thank you, J. Lo, for making big butts popular. Instead of being petite like my mama, I got my daddy's long legs, probably my best feature. I'm an outdoor kinda girl, always active, so keeping my weight down has never been much of a problem, especially since I'm usually halfway following whatever diet Macy happens to be on. But I wrinkle my nose and think that by Hollywood standards I'm a blimp.

"Well, hell," I mutter as I tug my sleep-shirt over my head. I realize that I don't really think about my appearance much and then it hits me. "Maybe I should." I walk down the short hallway to my bedroom, flip on the light and slide open the door to my closet. "Nothin' but denim." Jeans of every shape and length hang there. Oh, there's my little black dress sheathed in dry-cleaner plastic for the occasional fancy event and funerals. There are a few sundresses and skirts for Sunday services, but nothing stylish or sexy.

"God, I need some updatin'." I picture myself on a makeover segment of Oprah and the audience gasping and giggling as some fashion-savvy people yank my clothes out of my closet while shaking their heads in disgust. But then I lovingly finger the worn, soft denim of my favorite jeans and I know that if I fill my closet with nice things, I'll still end up wearing my jeans and T-shirts. It's just who I am.

Turning out the light and tugging at the chain to send my paddle fan spinning, I pull back my chenille bedspread and slide beneath the cool sheets. Although I run air-conditioning downstairs in the shop, I rarely turn it on in my apartment. I prefer the night breeze and enjoy the soothing sounds of crickets and bullfrogs.

The beer has made me drowsy and I snuggle into my feather pillow thinking I'll fall right asleep, but I don't. I think about Parker's warm lips kissing mine and with a little shiver I wonder what would have happened if I had invited him up. Would he be in my bed right now making wild love to me? What would those long fingers feel like caressing my bare skin?

So engrossed am I in my sexual fantasy, I about jump out of my skin when the phone rings next to my bed. Reaching over to my nightstand, I pick up the receiver and force my voice not to sound like I've been thinking about Parker Carrington naked in my bed doing delicious things to me with his mouth. "Hello?" There, that wasn't too breathy.

"Hey, Jamie Lee, it's Macy. Hope I didn't wake you."

I push up to a sitting position, tugging my pillow to cushion my back. "No, I was awake."

"You okay? You sound kinda funny. Oh, my God. Parker isn't there, is he?" She whispers this like someone might hear.

"Only in my dreams," I answer with a dramatic sigh. "Good lord, Macy, that man has left me horny as hell. If I had a vibrator, I surely would be putting it to good use about now."

Macy laughs and then asks, "Have you been hittin' the sippin' whiskey?"

"No, only one Bud Light."

"You'd never get yourself one of *those*, would you?" She's whispering again, even though she lives by herself in an apartment much like mine over the hardware store.

I giggle. "No. You know that no matter where I would hide it, somehow my mother would come across it and I would die of embarrassment. Besides, remember when we bought one for Lucy Jackson as a gag gift for her twenty-first birthday?"

"Yeah. It was huge and like, spun around."

"I laughed so hard. Macy, I swear, if I had a big rubber penis in my hand, I'd laugh my ass off. I'd never be able to have an orgasm. No, I think I need a real man for that." I sober a bit. "Therein lies my problem."

"Could you have had Mr. Hollywood's boots parked under your bed about now?"

"You mean his fancy loafers?"

"Whatever. Don't dodge the question."

I hesitate for dramatic effect. "Maybe."

"Just maybe?"

"Okay, probably."

Macy sighs and says, "We made a pact to go after what we wanted, remember? It's our new policy. And a good one, I might add."

I chew on the inside of my lip for a moment. "You know it's not as easy as that. For one, there's the fact that he's a stranger. I have a few standards that get in the way, namely, the voice of my mama imbedded in my brain tellin' me not to fornicate with him. I swear she implanted some sorta moral microchip in my head or somethin'."

"Please tell me you didn't just say fornicate. Ew."

"Hey, I said it was my mother's voice. 'Don't fornicate with men, Jamie Lee'," I mimic in my mother's slow Southern drawl. "And then she'll tell me the tired old expression about giving away the milk for free and not buying the cow or whatever."

"Then get to know him. He's gonna be here for a while, isn't he?"

"I think so." I cross my legs and watch the paddle fan swirl in the moonlight streaming in through my window.

"Go for it slowly, but Jamie Lee, *go* for it."

I take a deep breath of night air laced with the sweet smell of honeysuckle and damp earth like it's raining somewhere close. "But you know what'll happen. I'll fall for him."

"So what?"

"Macy, he'll go back to L.A. and I'll be left here in Hootertown cryin' in my beer."

"Maybe it won't happen that way. Maybe he'll fall wildly, *madly* in love with you and take you back to his mansion. You'll wear big sunglasses and have a little poodle that you carry with you everywhere. You'll have to have a separate closet just for your shoes."

I giggle while she goes on and on. "Macy, I have dark roots and wear cowboy boots. 'Nuff said."

"I'd come out and visit for extended periods, like years, maybe, and we'd turn Hollywood on its ear. Everyone will love us and before you know it, all of Beverly Hills will have dark roots, scuffed cowboy boots, and cutoff jeans. We'll be the toast of the town, or whatever, and make *People*'s Most Beautiful People issue."

"Macy, you've gone off the deep end. I knew that sniffin' perm fumes day in and day out would eventually do it."

"Sorry, I was havin' a moment."

I shake my head and say, "Macy, what are we gonna do?"

"We're gonna go for it, remember?"

"Ah, so you're goin' after Luke?"

Macy is silent for a minute and then says softly, "Yeah. We might eventually be cryin' in our beer, but we'll always have each other. Let's do this thing, Jamie Lee."

I yawn. "'Kay, but I need my beauty sleep if I'm goin' to seduce the very bodacious Parker Carrington. Night, Macy."

"Night, Jamie Lee."

I hang up the phone and scoot back down underneath the covers. My heart is pounding, but I have to smile and very soon I'm asleep. I guess. How do you know when you fall asleep when, well, you're sleepin'?

All too soon, Martina McBride is singing in my ear. I moan and flip over to my back, fumbling for my alarm clock. With a sigh I stumble to the kitchen to start a pot of coffee. I fix a packet of peach-flavored instant oatmeal and eat it while watching some lady do yoga on television. Now, while I don't actually perform the yoga with her, I feel a bit relaxed just watching. Weird, I know, but it's become a morning ritual, and I'm afraid I'm a creature of habit.

After a quick shower and makeup, I head to my closet and once again think about my meager wardrobe. For a minute I consider putting on something other than my usual jean shorts and T-shirt, but the jeans call my name and I pull them from the hanger and slide them on with a sigh.

I'm running a little late, so Macy is already walking up to the door when I enter the shop. I prop it open and she comes rushing in.

"Tell me that you have some Mountain Dew. I'm out, can you believe it?"

"Gotcha covered," I tell her and go over to the little

fridge at the back of the shop. Snagging one, I bring it over to her.

Macy snaps it open with a sigh and takes a long swallow.

"Macy, do you think I need a makeover?"

She wipes a drop of Dew from her chin. "What do you mean?"

"My clothes. I never really dress up and Mama fusses at me all the time about being more professional. Look at you." I point to her white slacks and neatly pressed blue blouse. "You look nice."

"I wear jeans to work sometimes."

"Yeah, nice ones."

"Jamie Lee, it's your place. You can dress as you please."

I start setting up my station. "That's not what I asked."

She takes another swig of her drink. "Do you want to get dressed up?"

"No."

She frowns at me for a minute. "Is this about Parker? 'Cuz you don't have to go changing for a man. When I said to go after him, I didn't mean for you to go changing yourself, Jamie Lee."

She's getting all sassy and worked up with her head boppin' and stuff, so I quiet her down with a reassuring smile. "No. I guess I'm in the mood for something different. I don't know. Sexy."

"Have you ever thought about gettin' your belly button pierced?" She whispers this and then catches her bottom lip between her teeth.

My eyebrows go up. "Have you?"

She shakes her head and her auburn curls bounce. "If I lose twenty pounds, I'm gettin' mine done."

"Shut up."

She takes her last swig of Dew and shakes her head again. "I am." She points to my belly. "You should get it done. All of those college girls who come in here have theirs pierced."

"Yeah, but they're college kids, Macy."

She angles her head at me. "We're not exactly ancient. Come on, I'll go with you."

I lift my shirt and look down at my belly button. "It would hurt like hell."

"Only for a minute." She comes over and looks down at my belly button. "You've got a nice little innie. Perfect for piercing."

"Ya think?" I'm starting to buy into this. I buy into things pretty easily.

Of course my mother takes this very moment to enter the shop even though she isn't scheduled to work for another hour. This is her day to come in and do her regular customers. She sees us staring at my belly and puts her hands to her cheeks and comes flying across the shop.

"You got yourself pierced!"

I pull down my shirt. "Mama, I didn't."

"You did. Let me see! Your daddy is going to just have a fit, Jamie Lee."

"Mama, I didn't. Really."

Of course she has to see for herself and tugs up my pink T-shirt.

"Thank the Lord."

I give Macy this look that says that now I'm really

considering it. See, Luke is the good child and I'm the rebellious one. That's just how it goes.

Mama points a long red fingernail in my direction. "Don't you go gettin' any body parts pierced or tattooed, you hear me?"

"Yes, Mama."

Macy about chokes on the first swig of her second Dew. See, I have this little heart tattooed on my ass that I got in Nashville on the night of my twenty-first birthday when I got rip-roarin' drunk. I'm not quite sure how it got there and there are conflicting stories as to how it all came about. Not many people are privy to this information. I personally think the little heart is cute, but in some circles, namely my mother's, it would be considered a little on the trashy side.

Mama turns her attention from me to Macy and asks, "How was your date with Luke?"

Macy blushes. "It wasn't really a date, Mrs. Carter."

Mama chooses to ignore this minor detail. "So, has he asked you out again?"

I look over at Macy. I've been so engrossed in my own love life, or lack of a love life, that I have completely forgotten to get the details of Macy's evening with my brother.

"Well, the woman he interviewed last night didn't seem like she would work out, so Luke asked for my assistance in looking at a few more candidates."

I give Macy a why-didn't-you-tell-me look and she gives me a you-didn't-ask look right back.

Mama seems pleased. "So, when will this occur?"

"Tomorrow."

Tapping her finger against her lips, Mama nods.

"Wear pale green. Being a redhead myself, I know that you will look your best in green. You do have something in green, do you not?"

Macy frowns for a moment. "I guess."

Mama waves a hand in her direction. "I can see that we need to shop."

Macy's face lights up and she says, "That would be fun. I don't come in until noon tomorrow. We could go early."

Mama is clearly tickled pink and rubs her hands together in glee. "I'll pick you up around eight-thirty and we'll head over to the mall. We won't have nearly as much time as I would like, but we'll make do."

I'm listening to the exchange as I fold towels. Macy's own mother died when she was only ten and my Mama has mothered Macy ever since. You might think that I'm jealous of the relationship, but I'm not. For one, I have no interest in driving some thirty minutes away to the overpriced mall when I can get the same thing at Wal-Mart just a few minutes down the road. But whatever. I'm just glad it takes the pressure off me.

Of course, since I'm anxious for the evening to come, the day seems to drag on forever. To make matters worse, for some unknown reason, hairdressers are like bartenders in that people tend to tell you things you'd rather not know and ask for advice that you're not really qualified to give. And today there seems to be an abundance of this. I do, however, have bits and pieces of knowledge on unrelated topics stemming from my random television-viewing habits, and I can on occasion offer some real advice. But more often than not, I'm clueless.

Another unwritten rule of hairdressing is that you must carry on conversation even when you'd rather simply cut hair and be done with it. Today, especially, my mind is elsewhere, but because Mama is here I do my best to converse with my customers. It's the way of things at a beauty parlor.

At one point, I see the silver Jag go whizzing by the shop and my heart skips a beat, but Parker doesn't stop. Just when I'm thinking that he must have come to his senses and decided not to shoot his movie here in little ol' Hootertown and especially not to see me, my cell phone rings and it's him. I'm in between clients so I take the call outside on a small patio in back of the shop.

"Hi, Jamie Lee," Parker says in that smooth voice that makes me feel all warm and tingly. "Sorry I waited so long to call, but I've been swamped."

"That's okay. I've been busy, too, but I'm on a break right now."

"So are you available tonight?"

I start to say yes, but then I remember that I promised Griff that I'd go to his softball game. My brother plays on the team, too, and I rarely miss a game. Damn, I hate situations like this when you're obligated to do something you really don't want to do. And if you do what you really want to do rather than what you really should do you really don't enjoy said event, anyway. In a word, it sucks.

"Oh, you're busy," he says and sounds so cute and disappointed. "I knew I should have called sooner."

Twirling my hair around my finger I have to grin because I have the solution. "Would you like to see the Hootertown Hell Raisers play softball?"

"Sure," he answers without hesitation. "What time should I pick you up?"

"The field is within walking distance, so if you just come over to my apartment around seven, then we can walk."

"You wouldn't have time to grab a bite to eat before the game?"

I want to, but then I remember that I have to cut Griff's hair after I close the shop. "Sorry, but I can't."

"Oh."

He sounds so disappointed that for a moment I consider calling Griff and canceling his haircut but that doesn't seem quite right.

"Well, I'll see you at seven. The softball game sounds fun and I'm really looking forward to seeing you."

"Me, too," I tell him. After ending the call, I feel like doing a little dance of joy and so I do. I'm in midspin when Mama pokes her head out the door.

"Jamie Lee, what in the world are you doin'? Child, have you taken leave of your senses?"

I abruptly stop my dance and it makes me feel a little dizzy. It's been a long time since I've felt this excited.

Mama frowns at me and asks, "Are you okay?"

"Yes, Mama, I'm fine and dandy."

"Well, get your fine-and-dandy self inside because your five o'clock has arrived."

I nod at Mama and hurry back inside. The rest of the day, thank goodness, goes fairly quickly. After we close, and Mama and Macy leave, I tidy up and throw the dirty towels in the washer. I look at my watch and wonder where Griff is, getting a little ticked that I'm staying over for him and he can't seem to get here on time. Just when I decide to give him a call and a piece of my mind, he arrives.

I'm about to give Griff some grief, but he looks a little tired around the edges and I decide to cut him some slack. It was a hot one today and I know that he's been working outdoors in the heat for hours. He's in his black Hell Raisers softball T-shirt and white baseball pants worn through at the knees. I notice that his hair is wet and curling at the ends. Griff has really great hair, all thick and dark and wavy.

"Sorry I'm late," he says as he sits down, and then gives me a tired grin. "I had to go home and shower first or you wouldn't be able to stand me."

When I lean in to put his cape on, I notice that he smells freshly showered but has dark stubble shadowing his jaw.

As if reading my thoughts, he rubs his chin with the palm of his hand. "I didn't have time to shave," he says looking at me in the mirror. "I didn't want to keep you waiting."

"Don't worry about it. That scruffy look is the in thing, Griff. Sexy," I tease.

"Ya think so?"

Okay, he says this with a grin, but I swear when I meet his eyes in the mirror, I get the weird feeling that he's asking *me* if *I* think he's sexy. "Sure," I tell him and run my fingers through his hair, checking the length. "You'll have all the girls in the bleachers cheering for you, Griff."

"That's the plan," he says lightly.

I gaze in the mirror at him, but he's looking down at

his hands. Oh, okay, so I was wrong. What was I thinking? This is Griff, for goodness' sake. Now, there was a
time when I had this big crush on him back when I was
about a junior in high school, but he made it abundantly
clear that I shouldn't go there.

Picking up the spray bottle, I wet his damp hair down
and then ask, "How short do you want it?"

"What?" He seems to be lost in thought.

"How short do you want you hair, Griff?"

"Oh, uh, a trim. Whatever you usually do."

"Okay," I tell him and start snipping away. He's kind
of quiet, but Griff tends to be that way. "Who you playing tonight?"

"The Panthers, I think."

"They any good?"

"Yeah."

"Bend your head so I can trim you hairline. You can
beat those guys."

Lifting his head, he grins at me in the mirror and
says, "Always the cheerleader."

"What can I say? The Hootertown Hell Raisers are
my team." I trim around his ears and then ask, "Short
enough?"

"Looks good."

Picking up a fat brush, I dust the hair off of his neck
and then remove his cape. "All done, then."

Griff swivels the chair around and then stands up.
Looking at his watch, he says, "Hey, we have a little
while before the game. Wanna grab a burger?"

"No thanks. I need to get cleaned up first."

"You look fine."

"I'm bringing Parker to the game."

"Oh," he says with an annoyed edge to his voice.

Tossing his cape into the dirty laundry, I turn to him and ask, "You have a problem with that, Griff?"

He hesitates a minute and then says, "I don't trust the guy, Jamie Lee."

"That's not fair. You don't even know him."

"And neither do you," he says firmly, like I'm a little kid. "Listen, he's real smooth and I'm sure you're flattered by the attention he's giving you, but—"

"Oh, let me finish. Parker Carrington, Hollywood producer, couldn't possibly be interested in a girl like me." I jab my thumb into my chest for extreme emphasis and it sorta hurts, and I want to say *ouch*, but that would totally ruin the whole effect.

Griff frowns. "What do you mean, a girl like you?"

I put my fists on my hips. "Small-town. A redneck."

"You're not a redneck," he says quietly.

I thrust my chin upwards. "Damned if I'm not. But that's okay. I'm proud of who and what I am."

"As well you should be."

"Ha, obviously you think I'm not good enough, Griffin Sheldon."

A little muscle is jumping in his clenched jaw. "That's not what I was goin' to say."

"What, then?"

He looks at me for a long moment, swallows, and then says, "Forget it."

"What do you mean, forget it?"

"You heard me."

I put a hand on his arm because he seems so upset. "Tell me, Griff."

"It doesn't matter." He reaches in the back pocket of

his baseball pants and draws out his wallet. "How much do I owe you?"

"Owe me? You know I don't charge you."

"You should."

I try to laugh but I can't because this is getting too weird. "Griff, you do so much for me. The least I can do is cut your hair."

He pulls out a twenty and thrusts it towards me.

"I'm not taking that."

Griff slaps the money down on the front table. With a little growl, I pick it up and hurry towards him, catching him before he can get out of the front door. I hook my finger in his back belt loop and I shove the twenty way down in his side pocket.

Griff tries to get away from me, but my hand is shoved too far down in the pocket of his tight pants, sorta stuck. So, here I am plastered to him and he's dragging me outside the front door. Of course, there's Rose Jenkins wheeling her clothing rack inside of her shop and turning to wave at Griff only to see me with my hand very near groping his . . . *you know*, and wow, have to wonder if he's wearing a cup or . . .

"Howdy, Griff, uh, and Jamie Lee." Angling her head, she is clearing trying to decipher what I'm doing and I try in vain to tug my hand out of Griff's pocket.

Rose's cheeks turn rather pinkish so I feel compelled to explain. "He won't take my money. His money. I— I'm tryin' to give it to him." Now that didn't sound at all right.

"Take the damn money," Griff growls.

"You've always been free and I'm not about to start charging you now!"

Rose Jenkins' eyes widen and she hurries back inside. Oh, great.

"Get your hand out of my pocket."

"It's stuck! Your damned pants are too tight and my watch is hooked on something. If you could just hold still!"

"Let's get back inside. People are starting to stare."

We hobble back inside and Griff stands very still. "Get your hand out of my pocket," he says tersely.

I tug and wiggle trying to avoid his, well, his *penis* but I keep rubbing against it.

"Good God, what are you doin'?"

"I told you that my watch is hooked on the fabric!" God, Parker is going to show up any minute and find me looking like I'm copping a feel and heaven help me, *I am*. Not meaning to, of course, but still. *I am*. And I know that Griff isn't tryin' to but he's gettin', holy cow, *hard*.

My boobs are pressed up against his back but I can't help it. "I'm sorry, Griff, I'm not meanin' to—to . . ."

"You're goin' to have to take your watch off," he says tightly.

"How? One hand barely fits. I'll never be able to get my other hand in your pocket too. You're gonna have to take your pants off."

"Well, fuck." He gives me this really pissed-off look.

"Hey, this is your fault!"

He glares down at me and I notice that there is sweat beaded on his upper lip. "You're the one who shoved your hand down my pants!" He starts heading for the stairs leading to my apartment and of course I must follow. "We'd better go upstairs before someone else sees you groping me."

"I'm not groping you!" I feel the hard evidence nearly wedged inside of my hand and my face feels like it's on fire. "Okay, I'm not trying to—"

"Shut up, Jamie Lee."

Once inside my apartment, Griff takes a deep breath and asks, "Where do you want me to take off my pants?"

I don't want Parker to walk up to my door and see me in this predicament, and the bathroom is too small, so I say in a very small voice, "My bedroom."

Griff curses under his breath and heads down the hallway, dragging me with him. Once inside the room he stops, tosses off his shoes, and begins to unbuckle his belt and then unzip his pants. I don't know what to say so I remain silent and so does he, leaving the sound of our breathing hanging heavily in the room.

Griff starts to ease the fabric over his hips and I have to follow from behind as he pushes the tight baseball pants past his thighs to his ankles. The pants pool at his feet and I'm going to have to tug them over his ankles to be totally free. Griff's back is still to me and I get a very up close and personal view of his muscled thighs and tush clothed in white boxer briefs.

"Sit down on the bed so I can pull your pants off." I'm startled at the husky timbre of my voice and I suddenly realize with a rush of heat, that I am, well . . . getting rather hot and bothered.

Griff sits down on the edge of my bed and I avert my eyes from his near-nakedness while tugging on his pants, which are rather twisted around his ankles. He doesn't say a word, but I can feel him watching me wrestle with his pants. Just when I finally get them free of his feet, I hear the doorbell chime.

"Ohmigod." I scramble to my feet and head toward the bedroom door.

"Jamie Lee," Griff says. "Stop."

"What?" My voice is sort of breathless from my recent tug-of-war with his pants.

Griff points at me. "You might not want to have my pants dangling from your wrist when you answer the door."

I look at my hand and gasp. "Good Lord." I tug at the pants but my watch is still all tangled up in the pocket.

Mumbling under his breath like this is all of my doing, Griff gets up from the bed and comes over to assist me. The doorbell rings again and I get all agitated.

"Hurry."

"I'm tryin'." He finally gets my watchband unbuckled and the pants fall to the floor.

"Thank God." I start to hurry from the room, but then I decide I should apologize for being so testy. Stopping, I turn back and say, "Griff—"

"Don't worry. I'll stay hidden until you leave. Wouldn't want to cramp your style." He looks up from where his dark head is bent over the pants while he attempts to unhook my watch.

Something flickers in his brown eyes and I'm about to explain that I wasn't going to say that, but the doorbell chimes again.

"Go," Griff growls, but the look in his eyes is telling me something different.

All of the sudden I feel emotional like I might start

crying. I turn so he won't see my eyes get misty and start to walk away. Before I get out of the room, Griff says, "Jamie Lee, watch yourself, you hear?"

I nod without turning around and I have to fight back tears as I approach my front door. Now don't that just beat all? What in the world is getting into me?

5

Promises, Promises . . .

Closing my eyes, I take a deep, shaky breath with my hand poised on the doorknob. With a little groan, I realize that I haven't gotten the chance to spruce myself up, but it's too late to do anything about that. My jean shorts and pink T-shirt will just have to do. Plastering a smile on my face, I swing open the door just as Parker is about to ring the doorbell again.

"Hi," I say, embarrassed that my voice is a little husky from my recent trauma that resulted in near tears. I'm not a crying kinda person, but when I do, holy cow, I just wail. I'm that way with most things. Whatever I do, I go all out. So you can see how I really wanted to keep my tears at bay.

"Hi, Jamie Lee," Parker says with one of those thousand-watt smiles. He's wearing tan cargo shorts and an expensive-looking blue button-down shirt open at the collar. He's got some sort of woven leather sandals on and I notice that he has very nice feet, all like, groomed and everything. He looks at me closely and his smile dims a bit. "Are you okay?" he asks as he enters.

See, now, that's another problem that I have. I wear my emotions on my sleeve. Some people can remain calm and collected when they're upset. My brother Luke is an expert at this but unfortunately I'm not. Clearing my throat, which is still tear-clogged, I nod and say, "I just had a bit of a rough day."

"We don't have to go to the game," he offers. "If you'd rather, we could drive up by the lake and kick back with a nice bottle of Merlot."

The only wine I've ever consumed came from a box with a spout on the end and gave me the mother of all headaches the next day, so I politely decline. "No, I'll be fine." A slight thumping noise comes from my bedroom and I suddenly remember that Griff is still here. I know that he promised that he would stay hidden, but I don't want to take any chances, so I grab my purse and smile. "Let's get goin'." I say this a little loudly so Griff will know that in a minute the coast will be clear.

"Okay," Parker says and follows me out the door and down the side steps to the street.

"The ballpark is just a few blocks away. I hope you don't mind walking?"

He slides on a sleek pair of sunglasses and says, "No, not at all. In fact, I walked from the Mid-town Inn over to your place. I could use the exercise. I haven't jogged in two days and I've been eating tons of fattening foods."

Before I can stop myself, I chuckle.

He stops in the middle of the sidewalk, angles his head at me, and asks, "What?"

"Nothin'"

"Jamie Lee . . ."

I look up at him and shake my head. "Oh, it's just that I never heard any of the guys I know use the term *fattening foods*."

He grins. "Oh no, I'm being a goober again, huh?"

"Not at all. I do wish the men in Hootertown would figure out that some foods are not meant to be consumed every day of the week, like bacon, for starters. Way too many of them are sufferin' from Dunlap's disease."

His blond eyebrows rise above his sunglasses. "Dunlap's disease?"

With a giggle I link my hands over my belly. "Done lapped over the belt."

He throws back his head and laughs . . . a deep rich sound that I thoroughly enjoy. You know some people sound really stupid when they laugh. Like me, for example. When I laugh really hard, I snort. I can feel the snort coming on, but I just can't help it. But like I said, I tend to go overboard with just about everything, including laughing.

I have to laugh with him, but thank God I refrain from snorting. "Parker, you *are* different than the type of guy that I'm used to, but I'm sure you think the same about me."

"I'll give you that."

"Bein' with you makes me feel like Julia Roberts in *Pretty Woman*, except for, you know, I'm a hairdresser, not a hooker." Even though Rose Jenkins might think it's my side job. After I say this I feel sort of embarrassed and I look down at the sidewalk thinking he must think I'm a dork but he reaches for my hand like it is the most natural thing in the world to do. We start walking toward the ballpark hand in hand. I try to remember when I last held the hand of a guy and I think it must have been in high school. It feels good. Sweet and romantic, especially on a warm summer night such as this.

"You may not be a hooker, but you are a pretty woman, Jamie Lee," he teases.

"You are so—" I start to say, but he suddenly tugs at my hand, pulling me into a small passageway between two buildings. Before I can catch my breath, he threads his fingers through my hair and kisses me. His mouth is warm and gentle, sweet and sexy. The touch of his tongue against mine sends a zing of desire through me that has me wrapping my arms around him. I can feel the heat of his skin through the silky texture of his shirt and I want to tug it free of his pants and slide my hands up his bare back. I am just about ready to give in to this notion when he ends the kiss with a lingering lick across my bottom lip.

With a grin, Parker looks down at me and says, "I thought I'd better get that out of the way before we get to the ballpark."

Right about now, I'm not sure that I want to proceed to the ballpark. I'm thinking that I would like to drag him back to my apartment and have my sweet way with him. Good Lord, am I turning into a hussy or what?

"Jamie Lee, quit looking at me like that," Parker says while running his index finger down my cheek.

"Like what?"

"Like you want me to kiss you again."

Oh, if he only knew.

Parker takes my hand and says, "We'd better get going."

"No, wait!" I peek out from between the buildings to see if the coast is clear. I don't want to have tongues wagging any more than they already are, especially after the hand-in-Griff's-pocket incident.

Parker chuckles, obviously knowing what I'm doing.

"Okay, we can go," I tell him after glancing left and right. "Hurry."

We slide from in between the brick buildings and begin walking down the street. The shops are all closed down, so it's pretty quiet except for a few people heading to the ballpark and an occasional car full of teenagers cruising by with music blaring. The sun is sinking lower in the sky but it's still warm and humid. As we approach the softball complex I can smell grilled burgers and hot dogs and my stomach reacts with a loud rumble.

Parker grins at me. "Hungry?"

"Starvin'."

"Me too. I didn't get a chance to eat. Is the food good here?"

I shrug. "It's typical concession-stand fare."

"No veggie burgers?"

"You're kidding, right?"

"Yeah."

"Just about everything on the menu is high-fat, high-carb. Burgers, hot dogs, nachos, soft pretzels, and candy bars. Although the burgers are mostly filler, so in a way, they're like veggie burgers." I give him a sideways glance. "Have I enticed you yet?"

"You know you have."

I feel my cheeks heat up. I'm not usually the blushing type, but the look he's giving has me blushing all the way to my toes. "Parker, that's not what I meant."

"Oh, but it's what I meant." His grin is a bit wicked and he leans sideways to snag a quick kiss that leaves me breathless. Okay, until now, I thought the whole breathless stuff was a bunch of bull. But I swear, if I spend much more time with this man, I just might need an inhaler . . . really. My breath is coming in short little gasps like I've just finished jogging. Not that I ever jog. I just don't get the point of running for no reason. Well, of course there's the whole fitness thing, but I at least have to have a ball in my hand or be walking a dog or something to be moving. But that's just me.

The gravel parking lot is crammed full of cars and pickup trucks. Smack-dab in the middle of the complex is the big concession stand surrounded by picnic tables. There are three ball fields, and right now all of them are occupied with softball teams. It's noisy but in a good way. People are cheering, and music is blaring from speakers at the concession stand.

"This is a busy place," Parker comments as we head to the front gate.

"Another Hootertown hot spot." I sneak a look up at Parker, thinking that this atmosphere must be totally foreign to him, but he seems to be enjoying himself.

About half the town is here, young and old alike. Children are scurrying around, laughing, and weaving in and out of the crowd. There are families with strollers and young couples clinging to one another. Of course, I know most of these people and I have to pause to introduce Parker to many of them, so by the time we finally get to the concession stand my stomach is gnawin' on my backbone.

"I'll have a hot dog and a Bud Light," I tell the bored young guy behind the window who is chewing a huge wad of bubble gum. Parker is, of course, studying the menu.

"What is a brat?" he asks.

"A naughty kid."

"No," he says, pointing to the menu. "That."

"You pronounce it like it's short for bratwurst, you know, the German version of a fat hot dog."

"Oh, bratwurst! I know what that is."

He seems pleased at his knowledge and it occurs to me that he would feel more at home in Germany than Hootertown.

Parker turns back to the bored guy, who has blown a bubble as big as his head, and says, "I'll have a bratwurst with sauerkraut."

After popping the bubble and sucking the gum back into his mouth, he answers, "We don't have no sauerkraut."

"Oh." Parker gives me this sheepish, so-very-cute look that has me wanting to kiss him senseless, but then everything about him makes me want to do that. After a moment, he says, "I'll have what she's having."

After he pays for the food we head to the condiments table where he loads his hot dog up with mustard and relish. "I'm impressed that you know how to dress up a hot dog," I tell him. "I like mine the same way."

"Remember, I spent half of my childhood in New York City with my mom. Hot dog vendors are on every street corner."

"I've never been to New York," I say, and I'm surprised at how wistful my voice sounds. "It's on my list of places I want to see." I take a bite of my hot dog. God, is it good.

"I'd love to take you there," Parker says, but gets this funny look on his face like maybe he really didn't mean to say that out loud.

This hurts just a little because it has me wondering if he'd be embarrassed to have me on his own turf. But then, maybe I'm analyzing things way too much. Macy says I do this all the time. I take a swig of my beer and then say, "We'd better get over to the field. The game's already startin'."

Parker is in the middle of a bite of hot dog, so he does the polite thing and merely nods. We make our way over to the bleachers and I see Macy, who waves at us from about ten rows up, right behind the plate, our usual spot.

I've been coming here ever since I was a little kid, first to watch my daddy play softball while Mama kept me and Luke happy with Popsicles and red licorice sticks. Daddy was quite a good athlete, which is where I guess Luke got his talent. But I couldn't hit the broad side of a barn, but I sure do like watching, and of course giving my two cents about how the game should be played and, more importantly, how the umpires are calling it. I think I mentioned that I go a little overboard in most things that I do and cheering for my team is no exception. I make a mental note not to ride the umpires too hard in front of Parker and to keep my language clean, not that I talk like a sailor or anything, but I tend to get a bit colorful after a beer or two.

"I been gettin' some dirty looks from people who

wanted your seat," Macy says as she scoots over to make room for Parker and me. "Where've y'all been?"

"We took our time walkin' over here," I tell her. "What inning is it?"

"Bottom of the first and we're losin' by three runs. Griff is pitchin' and he seems a bit preoccupied. Walked the first two batters, and he hardly ever does that. Luckily, Luke made this amazin' catch and threw a rocket home to get a double play, gettin' us out of an ugly inning." Macy lets out a big sigh and then says, "Oh, hey there, Parker. How's it goin'?"

Parker opens his mouth to reply, but whatever he said is drowned out when Jake Brisco hits a line shot to center field for a stand-up double and Macy and I, of course, have to jump up and yell our appreciation. Sticking my thumb and pinkie in my mouth, I give a loud whistle and shout, "Nice hit, Jake!"

"Move him over," Macy yells when Griff heads up to the plate.

Griff looks up into the stands and grins, but when he sees me, his grin fades and I'm hurt when he doesn't tip his cap like he usually does. Instead, he sorta scowls. Now, what is up with that? Oh, but when Krista Brown, who is always throwin' herself at Griff, stands up and yells in that squeaky voice of hers, "Smack that ball, Griff baby!" he gives *her* a big grin and a tip of his cap! *Well!*

I turn to Macy, who shrugs her shoulders. "What's that all about?" she asks me kinda low in my ear, but I'm afraid Parker might hear. "Did you and Griff have a fight?"

I give her this little jerky shake of my head, which tells her not to go there right now.

She mouths, "Okay, tell me later."

Our attention is grabbed by the loud smack of Griff's bat connecting with the ball. Macy and I both jump to our feet with everyone else. "I think that one might be outta here!" I yell and jump up and down when the ball sails over the center fielder's head and over the fence. Macy and I do a chest bump and then a high five, which is our home-run ritual.

"Wow," Parker says. "He killed that ball."

"He sure did," I agree, and watch Griff and Jake trot around the bases. The rest of the team comes out, giving them swats on the butt and thumps on their helmets. Griff looks up into the stands and I start to yell, "Nice hit," but I'm totally ticked off when he waves his hat at that hussy Krista who has the nerve to blow him a kiss!

I turn to give Macy a we've-got-to-have-a-meeting-in the-bathroom look, but Luke is up at bat and her attention is solely on him. Luke takes the first pitch for a ball and then just about smacks the cover off the ball, but it lands just foul.

"Straighten it out," I yell, but the next pitch is way too low to hit. The pitcher obviously doesn't want to give Luke another hittable ball. The next pitch is way inside and although Luke tries to lean back out of the way, the ball smacks him on the upper thigh, bringing a collective moan from the hometown crowd. Luke, being all manly-like, doesn't even flinch, but I know it's gotta hurt like hell. This might be softball, but it's fast-pitch and at that speed those balls are anything but soft.

Macy jumps to her feet, cups her hands around her mouth, and shouts, "You big jerk!"

This draws a shout from some mean-looking woman rooting for the other team, probably the big ugly pitcher's girlfriend. "Aw, sit down and shut yourself up!"

Of course, Macy doesn't sit down or shut up. "You just try and make me!" She shouts this with her little head-bopping, finger-pointing thing, making matters worse.

"Macy, chill," I hiss. "That woman looks like she could kick your ass with one hand tied behind her back. She's the size of a refrigerator." I glance at Parker, who looks confused, as if he is trying to decide whether or not he should get involved. Smelling disaster in the air, I tug on Macy's shirt, but she stubbornly remains standing with her chin jutting out. Holy cow. Of course she has that McCoy blood in her. Watching her it's clear how the whole feud got started.

Thank God the woman does this dismissive wave of her hands and sits back down, probably realizing it wouldn't be much of a fight, thus no fun on her part. Macy, however, thinks she's all big and bad, so I don't voice my thoughts on the matter, being merely relieved that she isn't rolling around in the dirt with the woman/refrigerator. I hear Parker sigh and realize he's been holding his breath.

"I woulda shown her a thing or two," Macy says as she sits down.

"Damned straight," I lie and give Parker a little nudge with my elbow. He starts to laugh, drawing a glare from Macy, and tries to disguise his chuckle with a cough.

Macy looks at Luke, who is standing on first base, absently rubbing his thigh. "He's gonna have a bruise the size of a grapefruit," Macy says and glowers at the pitcher.

"Luke's used to it, Macy," I assure her, patting her on the leg. "He'll be fine." It hits me how much she cares about Luke and I really hope that something sparks between them. She would be great for my brother, kind and loving and loyal, all of the things his ex-girlfriend was not. Luke was always so focused on sports that he just sort of dated the women who chased him instead of the other way around. Although women are constantly flirting with him, and Luke, being Luke, is always nice right back, it's been forever since I've seen him out on a real date. I glance at Macy, who is still mumbling under her breath about the nasty pitcher, and I just know that she would be so good for him. Luke has had such a rough time of it the past few years, but now that he's back on track and back in Hootertown, it would be awesome to see him totally happy the way he deserves.

The rest of the inning is uneventful, with two fly balls and a strikeout to send the Hell Raisers trotting back out to the field.

I hear a familiar gruff voice yell, "We need some defense, boys," and I grin when I see Miss Irma looking real nice with her not-too-curly perm, sitting two rows over. She spots us and waves. "Hey there, Macy, girl, I got yer back!" She gives us a thumbs up and then gives Parker this flirty little two-fingered wave.

Macy mouths, "Let's go to the bathroom."

I mouth, "Okay," and turn to Parker. "We're goin' to the ladies' room. Save our seats, 'kay?"

He doesn't look too comfortable with the whole saving-our-seats thing, but nods his agreement.

"Can I bring you back anything?" I politely inquire.

He mulls this over for a moment but I guess he can't think of anything he wants from the concession stand. "No, thanks."

Macy and I make our way to the bathroom, stopping only a few times to chat with friends, mostly about Luke getting smacked by the mean pitcher and how Macy almost had it out with his ugly girlfriend. Of course in the retelling the story will take on a life of its own, and after a few beers it will get worse. After we pee, we take our time washing our hands until we have the two-stall room to ourselves. I apply some shiny pink lip gloss while Macy fluffs her curls and we discuss the non-tipping-of-Griff's-hat episode.

"What was up with that, Jamie Lee? Something musta happened to tick Griff off."

I pause, not sure of how much I want to tell her.

"Spill," she tells me, so of course, I do. I'm weak that way. I could never work for the CIA.

Leaning against the sink, I say, "Well, first of all, Griff made it clear that he doesn't approve of me seein' Parker."

Macy's auburn eyebrows go up. "You think he's jealous?"

I shoo this notion with a wave of my hand. "Naw, he's just bein' overprotective. Old habits die hard."

Macy's not quite buying this. "I don't know, Jamie Lee. Sometimes I catch Griff givin' you the once-over.

Maybe he's got a thing for you." She leans forward and says, "You had it bad for him, if you do recall."

I push up from the sink and say, "Macy, that was when I was *seventeen*, and Griffin Sheldon made it quite clear what he thought of me. Said he thought of me as a sister. God, I was mortified. I will never make that mistake again! Now, he's a fine-lookin' guy, no doubt, but I don't think of him in that way!"

Macy puts her hands in the air. "Whoa, back down! Didn't mean to hit a nerve."

"You didn't hit a nerve!" But of course she had.

"Well, then, what's his big problem? Huh?"

I shake my head. "Danged if I know. But he got all weird on me and wanted to pay me for his haircut." I feel my face grow warm and turn to hide it, but you can't hide nothing from Macy.

"There's more."

"There's not."

"Liar."

"Okay, I got my hand stuck down in his pants and sorta copped a feel even though I wasn't tryin'."

Okay she wasn't expecting this and her mouth forms a big *o*. She recovers and sputters, "What? You . . . you had your hand down his *pants*? Explain yourself."

I go through the whole story rather quickly because Parker is waiting and Macy just stares at me forgetting to blink until I remember that Rose Jenkins saw a portion of the hand-in-the-pants thing and then Macy starts to laugh. She just snickers a little at first, but then really gets going and of course I join her and soon I'm snorting. We have to cool our faces with wet paper towels.

I am about to divulge that I got a bit turned on by the

whole incident, but I don't want her to think that I have a thing for Griff anymore because I don't. He's just got a really nice build and I haven't had sex in a long, long time.

"Griff is probably a bit embarrassed by the whole thing, Jamie Lee. Maybe that's why he's bein' such a shithead."

"You got me." I shrug, thinking we had better get back to Parker. I'm guessing he's only used to being in places where the seats are numbered, thus not knowing the fine art of saving seats for an extended period of time.

As we are quickly repairing our laughed-away makeup, I very casually ask, "You don't think Griff is gonna date that hussy Krista, do you?"

"Would that bother you?" Macy keeps her voice casual too, but she eyes me sharply, like if she looks at me closely she'll get the truth.

"Well, of course it would. Krista is nothin' but a home-wrecker. Had an affair with Jess Steward and his real nice wife Mary Lou up and left him." I have to shudder. "You don't think Griff's gonna hook up with the likes of her, do you? She's always been pantin' after him."

Macy shrugs, still eyeing me. "Naw. Griff's smarter than that."

As we head out the door, I say, "Yeah, but guys don't always think with the head *above* their shoulders, Macy."

Macy laughs and gives me a little shove. "You are so bad."

We start walking toward the stands, but just before we get there, Macy stops me with her hand on my arm.

"Hey," she says softly near my ear. "You're pretty into this Parker guy, aren't you?"

"Yeah," I whisper back.

"Then you remember our handshake promise, right?"

I swallow and then nod.

"So you're going after him, then."

I hesitate and she gives me a nudge with her elbow.

"Yeah, okay." I nudge her right back. "But then you have to set your sights on Luke, Macy."

She gives me a quick nod. "I'm nervous as all get-out, how 'bout you?"

I spot Parker in the stands and he waves to us. "Shakin' in my boots, but that's not gonna stop me. Macy, let's make this a summer to remember."

6

A Little Less Talk and a Lot More Action . . .

Of course, Macy and I have always been real good at talking the talk. It's walking the walk that we suck at. So after the game, as I'm walkin' home with Parker, I'm talking a blue streak like I usually do when I'm nervous. The game turned out to be exciting, with the Hell Raisers winning with a walk-off home run in the bottom of the ninth inning. Griff hit the homer and even though I was still ticked at him, I did the polite thing and applauded.

So now here I am in front of Cut & Curl, blabbering on about nonsense. Right in the middle of talking about the tanning beds I'm going to put in, I just shut myself up. Just like that. Zip.

"You stopped talking right in the middle of a sentence," Parker says as we approach the side steps leading to my apartment. By now it's dark out but I left the outside light on and the small bulb is casting a soft glow like a beacon leading up the steps.

"I thought you might be getting sick of my nonsense."

Leaning one shoulder against the corner of the brick building he says, "I could never get tired of listening to you, Jamie Lee. I think your Southern twang is sexy as hell."

"Y-you do?"

He reaches out with his hand and runs one long finger down my cheek. "Yeah, I do." His hair is fluttering in the breeze, making me itch to run my hands through it and see how silky it is. I just bet he uses real expensive products.

Go for it, a voice in my head croons.

Taking a step closer to him, I say, "I think your voice is sexy as hell, too. Whiskey-smooth."

"Like Kentucky bourbon?"

"Yeah, like that."

"You have any upstairs?"

"Do I look like the type of girl that would have whiskey in her cabinet?"

His answer is a slow grin that makes my heart thud, but the look he's giving me makes my nervousness evaporate like summer rain on a hot sidewalk. I swear he looks like he wants to gobble me up and it makes me feel so damned sexy. Bold. Tilting my head to the side with what I hope is a saucy grin I ask, "You wanna come upstairs for a little nip?"

"I was so hoping you would ask."

"Well, I'm askin'."

"Then I'm coming."

With a shake of my head I say, "I won't touch that

line." Tugging on his hand, I lead him up the back steps and fumble for my house key.

"Let me help." His mouth is next to my ear and his warm breath sends a shock right through me. He's standing behind me, so close that I can feel the heat of his body and smell the spicy scent of his aftershave. Wrapping his hand over mine he slides the key in the lock and together we open the door.

We enter my small kitchen and I toss my purse and keys on the table. Gesturing toward the adjoining living room I say, "Have a seat and I'll bring you your drink. Do you want it neat or on the rocks?"

"On the rocks," he answers and settles his long frame on my couch.

After locating the bottle of Maker's Mark on my lazy Susan, I fix us each a generous shot of bourbon on ice and add just a splash of water. I take off my sandals and pad on my bare feet over to Parker and hand him the glass. "I hope you're not too warm. I rarely turn on my air-conditioning. I like the sounds and smells of summer to soothe me to sleep." I walk over to the front window, open it wider, and then tug the chain of the paddle fan. "Cool enough?"

He nods. "I'm fine. Come over here and sit by me, Jamie Lee." He pats the sofa as he's taking a sip of his bourbon. "Mmm, this is smooth. You have good taste."

"Why, thank you." I sit down on the sofa, tuck my feet under me, and take a sip of my drink. The iced bourbon is cold going down my throat, but heats up as it hits my belly. "You want to watch some TV?"

"No."

"Music?"

"That would be nice. Put on whatever you like."

"That would be country," I warn him as I pick up the remote from the coffee table and turn on a music-only cable channel. A moment later Kenny Chesney is singing a love song. A fragrant breeze billows the lace curtains, cooling the air a bit. The only light is coming from the three-quarter moon and the soft glow of the TV screen that changes colors with the music, sending shadows dancing on the walls.

Parker looks at me with a slow smile that does funny things to my insides. "This is the most relaxed I've been in a long time," he tells me.

"Everybody needs some downtime," I tell him. "I guess producing movies is pretty stressful." Setting my drink down, I get down on the floor and unbuckle his sandals and slide them off. "Put your feet up on the coffee table."

"Jamie Lee, you're an angel," he says as he stretches out his long legs.

Of course, the thoughts I'm having about now are anything but angelic. The heat of the bourbon is melting away my inhibitions. I'm thinking I'd like to swing my legs over his lean hips and give him a little ol' lap dance, but I sit back down on the sofa and stretch out my legs beside him. "Tell me about yourself, Parker Carrington." Pointing the remote at the TV, I mute the music so I can listen to him.

We both lean our heads back against the cushions and after a moment he begins to talk.

"I think I told you that I grew up hopping between coasts and parents. My mother was a Broadway actress and my father started his own production company. It's

funny because the very thing that brought them together, the love of the theater, was what drove them
apart."

"Do they still see each other?"

Parker takes a sip of his drink and then answers,
"Yes. They're a classic example of two people who
can't live with one another, but who can't quite stay
apart. They love each other passionately, but, unfortunately, fight with just as much passion."

"How romantic, in a sad sort of way," I say with a
sigh.

"Ahh, so you're a romantic soul."

I give him a dismissive wave of my hand. "Naw, I
don't go for all of that hooey. I'm a pretty down-to-earth
kinda gal. You're wrong, Parker. I'm not into wine and
roses." I say this, but it suddenly hits me in my gut that,
well, no one has ever sent me flowers or uncorked a bottle of wine for me at a fancy restaurant. I've never been
what you'd call wined and dined. "Who needs that
stuff?"

"So if you don't want wine and roses, what do you
want?"

This makes me a little uncomfortable, so I say,
"We're supposed to be talkin' about you."

"We can talk about me later. Tell me what *you* want,
Jamie Lee."

Go for it. "Eventually, I want a hardworkin' man with
a good heart who'll treat me right. I wanna give my
mama and daddy some grandkids, live in a nice house
with a little bit of land." I shift on the cushion to face
him. "But right this very minute?" I pause for a moment
to gather my courage. "I want you." My heart pumps

double time while I wait for his reaction. Part of me can't believe I just said that to him, but I'm glad I did.

Parker drains the last of his drink and sets the glass down on the table. He shifts on the sofa so he's facing me. "Jamie Lee, I don't—"

I stop him with my fingertip to his lips. "Macy says I analyze things way too much. I don't want to think or talk. Right now, I just want to feel."

With a groan, Parker leans his head back against the cushions. "You're making this hard to resist. Let this go on record that I tried. Jamie Lee, the last thing I want to see in those beautiful eyes of yours is regret." He puts a hand over his eyes and does this sorta painful chuckle. "I don't know why I'm suddenly being so noble." Taking a deep breath and blowing it out, he says, "Yes I do. It's because I like you so much. You're sweet and honest and have this vulnerable edge beneath your feistiness." He rubs his finger down my cheek, a gesture that's becoming familiar to me. "I don't want to take advantage of you."

"No regrets, Parker," I promise him. When I push up to my knees and swing my leg over his lap to straddle him, his eyes open in surprise. My heart is thumping and my fingers are a bit shaky as I begin to slowly open the buttons on his silky shirt, exposing his very fine chest. With a little sigh, I let my hands explore his smooth, warm skin, graze over his nipples and trail over his abs. His stomach quivers in response. Sitting up straighter, I push the shirt over his shoulders and he lets me remove it and toss it to the floor.

I drink in the sight of him. He's lean with well-defined pecs. Tawny hair lightly covers his chest and narrows to a line to his belt buckle. I'm glad that he's not one of those guys who shave away all of their hair because I like a man to look and feel like a man, and that includes chest hair.

Parker reaches for my shirt, but I shake my head and push him back against the cushions. Where I'm getting this nerve, I'll never know, but hot damn, I'm loving it. "No, let me play for a while. I love the feel of your skin," I tell him and let my hands rub over his collarbone and down his arms, pausing to admire his biceps, which are hard and bulging like baseballs. Very nice, indeed. Still holding onto his muscles, I lean in and flick my tongue over one nipple and then the other.

"God, Jamie Lee . . ."

"You smell sooo good," I murmur as I bury my face in the crook of his neck and lick where his pulse is racing. He moans, threading his fingers through my hair, and his reaction to me gives me a sense of feminine power making me even bolder. "You taste good, too . . . salty, sweet." I nibble on his earlobe and then let the very tip of my tongue trace his jawbone. The abrasive texture of his five-o'clock shadow is rough and tickly on my tongue, making the soft fullness of his lips seem even softer when I lean in and press my mouth against his.

He lets me stay in control and I take my sweet time, giving him a deep, long, delicious kiss. He tastes of whiskey and man, heat and excitement, and I'm melting against him. From out of nowhere, I'm morphing into this sex kitten, tasting and nibbling as I please until with a groan Parker grabs my bottom with his hands and moves me against the heat and steely hardness of his arousal. I feel so sexy and full of feminine power that I've managed to put him in this state. This makes me want to test my allure and make him crazy with desire.

I rock my hips very slowly while my tongue plays with his bottom lip, licking back and forth, but I refrain from kissing him.

"God, Jamie Lee, kiss me," he growls.

"Say pretty please," I tell him, wondering where in the hell I learned to be such a tease, but it's coming sorta natural. I know I'm playing with fire, but I always was a daredevil.

"Pretty *damned* please," he says with a frustrated growl that has me giggling. I give him a sweet kiss and then nibble on his neck and earlobe and anywhere else that strikes my fancy.

He doesn't seem to mind my enthusiasm. Not at all. Suddenly we are kissing like there's no tomorrow, long and lazy. I guess I should have warned him that when I do things, I go all out, and sex is no exception.

And it's been such a long, long time.

After the never-ending kiss, I pull back and tug my shirt over my head, tossing it over my shoulder. Luckily I've always loved frilly underwear and I'm wearing this peach-colored satin bra that barely contains my breasts. Parker sucks in his breath, making me smile. Now someday I know my boobies will be sagging to my knees like Granny Carter's, but at the moment, they are bodacious.

"Show me," he says in a low breathless voice.

Okay, I know I've been on a roll here, but I suddenly get this attack of you're-being-such-a-bad-girl that has me pausing. It's that damned brain-chip thing. Of course, after my sex-kitten behavior, Parker thinks I'm just messing with him, and with a quick flick of his wrist, my bra is unhooked and flung across the room. I'm thinking this is going too far and I'm about to voice my concern when he reaches up, cups my breasts, and does this magical thumb-flicking thing over my nipples and, well, being a bad girl suddenly seems like the thing to do.

Parker keeps doing this until my head is lolling to the side and I'm crazy with desire. My eyes, of course, are shut and so I don't know he's gonna take me in his mouth until suddenly his hot tongue is laving one breast and then the next. Holy cow, then he tugs on my nipple, just hard enough to send me into orbit, and I'm wantonly moving against him like a little sexpot.

"Jamie Lee?"

"Hmmm?"

"Tell me that you have protection."

"What?" My brain is only responding to sexual sensations. Conversation is beyond me.

"A condom."

"C-condom . . . ? Ahhh . . ."

"Jamie Lee, do you?"

"What?"

"Have. A. Condom?"

My brain waves swim through the sex-induced haze, and suddenly go on full alert. "Oh." I blink at him in the dim light. "Um, well." I search my brain, trying to think if there is any possibility of finding a condom in my apartment. There isn't. "No," I answer in a small voice and then ask hopefully, "Do you?"

He gives me a shake of his head and at first this

pleases me, making me think, *Good, he's not the fooling-around type*. But then it hits me. We can't have sex without one. Well, we could, but that would be real stupid.

"Is there a convenience store close by?"

"No. Everything in Hootertown shuts down about ten o'clock. The closest place is the Wal-Mart about twenty minutes away." Which, of course, means a forty-minute round trip, not counting the purchasing of the rubbers and whatnot.

Parker makes this odd noise that is like a laugh-groan-moan sound of pure frustration.

In situations such as these, namely hopeless, I think it's best to keep a sense of humor, and well, make the best of things. "We could, um, you know, do other stuff." I feel a full-body blush after suggesting this. In the heat of the moment I was a go-getter, but this is all of a sudden like a splash of cold water and I'm getting rather self-conscious sitting here on Parker's lap, half naked. I feel like putting my hands over my bare breasts, but it's sorta stupid after what I just let him see and do, so I muster up as much dignity as I can and say, "Parker, I do believe I let myself get a little outta control."

"Me too," he says and I find this so endearing. He could, by rights, be all pissed off, but he remains a gentleman . . . and I'm thinking that I really like this guy.

"I'm sorry," I tell him and I mean it.

"It's not your fault. I pushed for an invitation, Jamie Lee, when I knew full well I would have a tough time keeping my hands off of you."

Of course, this admission has me getting all hot and bothered all over again, so I do the safe thing and remove myself from his lap. Looking around the room, I hope to spot my clothes. My pink shirt is dangling from a lamp shade, but my bra is missing in action, so I tug my top over my head, take a deep breath, and turn to face Parker, who is buttoning his shirt.

He gives me this smile that tugs at my heartstrings. All the sudden I'm wondering how old he is and true to form, I ask him. "How old are you, Parker?"

He stops buttoning and seems rather amused at my question. "How old do think I am?"

I angle my head at him. "Well, you're so worldly and sophisticated and that makes you seem, you know, older. But when you smile you are so . . . kinda cute and boyish, it had me wonderin' just how old you really are."

"I just turned thirty last week," he admits and pushes up to his feet and slips on his sandals, not bothering to buckle them.

"That's pretty young for bein' such a big shot." I have to look up now that he's standing and I'm in my bare feet. His shirt is open halfway and I'm thinking how I'd like to . . . *no*, don't go there! He takes two long-legged strides toward me and my heart starts a-thumping all over again.

"I don't want to leave," he tells me and my God, I just want to grab him and kiss him. "Don't look at me like that, Jamie Lee. The Wal-Mart is too far away." He chuckles as he closes the gap between us, snags me around the waist and gives me this sweet, lingering kiss that has me going all weak-kneed.

"Good night, Jamie Lee."

"'Night, Parker."

He walks toward the door and I follow on my wobbly legs, wanting the whole time to drag him down the hallway and toss him into my bed and, well, you get the picture. The no-condom thing is a problem and, well, now that my bourbon buzz has worn off and my inner sexpot has gone back into remission, I refrain. Barely.

Parker opens the door and I hate that he's leaving. I'm also so pathetically hoping that he'll ask to see me again . . . like tomorrow, but he turns and gives me a quick kiss on the cheek and steps out into the night. I stand there for a second, giving him ample opportunity, but he starts down the steps. *Damn.* Maybe my whole act turned him on . . . and then turned him off, you know? He didn't even bother to lie and say that he'd call me. How humiliating.

Putting my hands to my cheeks, I groan. It shamefully occurs to me that all Parker wanted was a quick roll in the sack and good Lord, I was more than willing to oblige.

But wait a doggone minute. Isn't this what I wanted? A summer fling? Some excitement? A no-holds-barred affair so hot that it will leave me a little singed around the edges? So what am I beating myself up about?

Throwing my hands up in the air, I all but shout, "Why in the hell don't I have any condoms? Note to self: go to Wal-Mart and purchase a huge box of rubbers. A giant economy box. It is a Southern woman's responsibility to always be prepared, and tonight of all nights I was not. Damn, damn, *damn!*" I stomp my foot so hard I think I might have sprained my ankle. Well, damn again.

Limping around my apartment, I'm suddenly getting all fired up about men and sex and everything else I can think of. How dare Griff not tip his hat to me! How dare Parker not ask me out again after I showed him my bare boobies! How rude! I limp-stomp around in a circle and say, "I'm gonna swear off men for good and . . . and . . . become a lesbian!" I think about this for a minute, sorta picture it in my head and, well, naw, that's not gonna happen.

I take a big breath and blow it out. Now what? I'm way too keyed up to go to sleep. Spotting the bottle of Maker's Mark still sitting out on my kitchen counter, I hobble over and pour myself a shot. Then I decide I really don't want it, but I can't bear to dump it down the drain, it bein' such good stuff, so I tip the glass up and start to take a sip and then with a what-the-hell shrug I just toss it back. Yeow. The bourbon goes down smooth, but leaves a trail of fire down my throat and lands with a hot splash in my belly.

Okay, now I'm blinking back tears and it's a little from the bourbon, but mostly from frustration. Refusing to cry like a ninny, I limp (just slightly . . . the bourbon musta helped) over to the back sliding door leading to my deck. As an afterthought, I pick up my cordless phone. The door slides open with a soft *whoosh* and I step out onto the wooden deck that Griff constructed for me last summer. With a sigh, I flop down on my lounge chair and push on the armrest to lean back at an angle so that I can gaze up at the moon and the stars.

The deck butts up against a wooded area that has trails that lead to the city park. I can hear the scurrying sounds of nocturnal critters, the hoot of an owl, and the *rib-bit, rib-bit* of bullfrogs. Closing my eyes, I inhale the scent of damp earth, pine, and honeysuckle, and I begin to relax. Someone needs to make an aromatherapy candle that smells like a warm summer night.

I'm just about half asleep and would have woke up with dew on me in the morning when the phone rings, making me just about jump outta my skin. Fumbling with the phone, I finally say, "Hello?"

"Jamie Lee, it's Macy."

"Oh, hey."

"So, give me the scoop."

I don't hesitate since I know she will badger me until I tell all, and this *is* Macy, who will keep my business under her hat, so I spill. "I invited Parker up for a drink and proceeded to throw myself at him."

"So, did you do it?" Her voice is low and excited.

"I don't see how this is your business, Macy McCoy."

"Tell me or I will beat this information out of you."

"Things got a little out of hand and well, we would have probably, *you know*, but I didn't have any condoms." I put one hand over my eyes and say, "My God, Macy, I was like a woman possessed. What has gotten into me?"

"Did you get naked?"

"Halfway."

"What half?"

"Macy! Don't you see the gravity of this situation? I

threw myself at that man and showed him my bare breasts! I've turning into a strumpet."

"What the hell's a strumpet?"

"I don't know. Somethin' my mama would call me. A hussy . . . a . . ."

"No! Stop it right this here minute! Get over your guilt trip. You were two consenting adults. This is goin' to be our summer when we go after what we want, remember? We did the handshake and everything. You're goin' to buy some condoms, right?"

I swallow. "I don't know. Macy, in the heat of the moment, it seemed like the thing to do, but now I'm having some reservations. Besides, oh, and this is the truly awful part. Parker didn't ask me out again or say he would call or anything. He must think I'm a—"

"If you use the word strumpet or hussy again, I'm hangin' up this phone! Good God, the man is from L.A. The fact that you showed him your boobies is hardly shocking. At least yours are the real deal. He's probably never seen anything but big ol' implants."

I gaze up at the inky black sky dotted with so many stars they look like glitter. "Well, the fact remains that he didn't ask to see me again, so it's a moot point."

"So go after him."

I sit up straight and say, "I do have my pride!"

Macy sputters, "Now weren't you the one who gave me this almighty speech to go after Luke? Huh?"

"And did you?" I cross my legs and twirl my finger in my hair.

"That's not the point."

"Answer me."

Macy sighs and then says, "Well, after you left with

Parker, I went with the rest of the team and some girls up to Dixie's for a few beers. I fully intended to approach Luke, but then Jess Hanson cornered me for like half the night, buyin' me beers and sweet-talkin' me."

I grip the phone tight and it's hard to talk because my teeth are grinding. "Macy, that man is a fixer-upper and we both swore off of those kind."

She sighs again and says so low that I almost can't hear her over the bullfrogs, "I know."

"Was Luke there?"

"Yes, but Tina Lane was hangin' all over him and damn she is so pretty. Long-legged and so skinny."

"So you settled for the likes of Jess Hanson?"

"Yeah." She sounds so defeated that it makes me sad.

"Well, you *are* goin' with Luke tomorrow to interview the cheerleading coach, right?"

"Yes."

"And Mama is takin' you shoppin' in the morning, right?"

"Yes." She sounded glum.

"Then perk up, girl. There's hope for you, yet. So what else was goin' on at Dixie's? Did I miss anything excitin'?"

"No. That bitch Krista was glued to Griff's side, though. Made me want to puke."

I check out my fingernails and casually ask, "Did they leave together?"

"Would it bother you if they did?"

"I'm just curious."

"They walked out together, but Griff might've just been leavin'."

"Well, it's his life," I say, but can't quite keep the anger out of my voice. "It's getting late, Macy. I'll see you tomorrow. Don't let Mama boss you around tomorrow, ya hear?"

"You know that I will. I enjoy it. Good night."

I have to chuckle. "'Night."

After pushing the OFF button, I lean back into the plastic chair and gaze up at the sky, hoping for a shooting star, my all-time good-luck sign. Of course, I don't see one. With a groan, I start pondering the evening and I must admit that I'm totally confused. In so many ways, my life is just the way I want it. I have friends and a loving family. A job that I enjoy. But there's this big gaping hole in my life right about now and I'm not sure how to fill it. I'm getting the scary feeling that life is passing me by.

Emotion wells up in my throat and I give my tear-filled eyes an angry swipe. To hell with Parker Carrington and Griffin Sheldon and, well, men in general. Tomorrow night, I'm gonna pour myself into my tightest jeans, tug on my favorite dancin' boots, and have me a good ol' time at Dixie's. I'm gonna flat-out ignore every single guy who approaches me. Yep, I'm gonna snub them all . . . flirt and tease and leave them pantin' for me and then just walk out the door with my hips swayin' and my head held high.

Alone.

On that angry note, I start to push up from the chair, but just as I'm about to get up, I see a shooting star out of the corner of my eye. Before I can stop myself, I make a wish to find the love of my life to come knocking at my door.

Slapping myself on the thigh, I wonder why in the hell I had to go and wish *that*? Am I pathetic or what? Chastising myself under my breath, I about jump a foot in the air when the phone I'm clutching in my hand rings.

7

Be Careful What
You Wish For . . .

"Hello?" I finally manage after almost dropping the phone.

"Jamie Lee, why won't you answer your door?"

"You're at my front door?"

"I . . . I think so. Yes. Yes I am."

"Griff, are you drunk?"

"Naw."

"Then go home. I'm tired and still pissed at you. And if you're checkin' up on me, Parker's not here. So you can go home."

"'Sss . . . a long-ass walk."

"Where's your truck?" I ask as I slide open my back door and enter my kitchen. Flicking on the light, I head over to the front door, but I don't open it.

"Dixie's. I couldn't d-drive the damn thing, now could I?"

I roll my eyes. "So you *are* drunk." I swing open the door and glare at him.

Griff puts his thumb and index finger an inch apart.
"Tiny . . . bit."

I almost grin when he does his best to look sober but
the whole swaying-on-his-feet thing gives him away.
Griff likes to tip a few with the boys, but he doesn't usually get plowed. This is unusual for him, and I would
find the situation amusing if I weren't so mad at him.

"You don't want me here," Griff slurs and manages
to look hurt. He tries to turn around on the small landing. His legs get tangled and he starts to fall, barely
managing to catch himself with the railing. He grunts
when his shoulder slams into the top post.

"That's it," I tell him as I grab his shirt and yank
hard. "Get your ass in here."

Griff stumbles inside, almost knocking me over.

"Sorry," he says, holding my shoulders to keep me
from falling backwards.

I stab my finger in the air toward the sofa. "Go sleep
it off, Griff."

"'Kay."

Shaking my head, I grab a bottle of water for him
from the fridge. Turning, I watch with more interest
than I should as Griff tugs his black Hell Raisers T-shirt
over his head. His back is to me and I can't help but admire how his muscles bunch and flex as he completes
his task. My mouth goes a little dry when he toes off his
Nikes and then proceeds to peel his baseball pants off
and kick them out of his way. For the second time that
night, I'm looking at Griff in his boxers.

And liking it.

I must still be keyed up from my near-nakedness with
Parker. Yeah, that's it. To play it safe, I decide to sneak

out of the room and drink the water myself, but Griff turns and pins me with his gaze.

"That for me?"

I nod, walk over, and hand the cold bottle to him. "I'll get you a blanket and pillow."

"Thank you." He weaves a bit and flops down onto the sofa.

I give him a small smile since I'm finding it hard to stay mad at him. After getting a pillow and afghan from the hall closet I ask, "Wouldn't anyone drive you home from Dixie's?"

After a long swallow of water, he answers, "After I got rid of Krista, who was all over me like white on rice, I went back in and made the mistake of switchin' from beer to bourbon. Big mistake."

Ahh, so he wanted to get rid of Krista. I'm getting less and less mad at him.

"Why'd you go doin' that?"

He shrugs and looks a bit uncomfortable. "Felt like it." He pins me with another look. "So, how was your date with that Parker guy?"

"Okay," I answer, but avoid his gaze.

"You sleep with him?"

Okay, my pissed-off meter suddenly soars into the red zone. "I did not! Not that it's any of your damned business." Now, why did I deny it? I should have left him guessing.

"What do you see in him, Jamie Lee? Don't ya know what he's after?"

I angle my head at him and say, "What *he's* after? Maybe it's what I'm after."

Griff narrows his eyes at me. "And just what is that?"

"I don't know," I almost shout. "Some excitement, maybe."

"Oh, so you need Mr. Hollywood to give you that. A small-town hick isn't good enough for you?" He swings his hand in an arc, sloshing water down his chest. "I didn't think you were the type of girl to be swayed by smooth talk and a flashy car."

"Maybe I want to be treated like a woman and not somebody's kid sister." God, I can't believe I just said that . . . *no*, shouted that. It sort of echoes in the room for a minute while Griff blinks up at me.

"I can treat you like a woman."

I snort and take a step to leave the room, but my heart is beating wildly. "Yeah, right." I turn my back on him so he can't see how he's getting to me.

But then suddenly Griff's standing close and says low in my ear, "Try me."

I stand perfectly still while my heart is practically jumping out of my chest. I can feel the heat of his big body and the tickle of his breath on my neck. I know I'm playing with fire, but I slowly turn around. The water he splashed on his chest is now trickling down and I have this urge to lick it off. Instead, I look up at him.

"Did he kiss you, Jamie Lee?"

I can only nod.

"Well, let's just see if this ol' boy can give you more excitement than he could. In fact, I know I can, because . . ."

"Because why?"

He doesn't answer, but lowers his head and slants his

mouth across mine. I think that because he's been drinking, he'll be sloppy and I'll want to push him away.

I am oh so wrong.

Parker's kisses had made me go all soft and melting, but Griff . . . God, Griff sets me on fire. His mouth isn't coaxing, but demanding. Hungry, wild, hot, deep. He steals my breath. Still kissing me, he lowers me to the sofa. I've wanted Griff for so long, suppressing my feelings because he always kept me at arm's length, and now all those feelings are bubbling to the surface.

"Take your clothes off for me, Jamie Lee," he says in my ear and leans back against the cushions so that I can.

I wiggle and tug until I'm completely naked.

"Let me look at you."

I let him gaze his fill and let me tell you, I've never felt more like a woman. His brown eyes are dilated with desire.

"You are absolutely beautiful," he says and it makes my eyes tear up.

How long have I waited for him to say that? I've loved him for *so* damned long. God, my breath catches when his big hands, calloused from hard work, caress my feet, my calves, my thighs, and then he makes my back arch when one long finger sinks into my heat.

"God, you're so hot, so ready."

"I've been ready for this for a long time, Griff. What took you so long?"

"Damned if I know," he growls and then shucks his boxers before coming back on top of me.

Ahhh, skin to skin, Griff rocks back and forth while kissing me with an all-consuming passion. He moves his mouth to my neck, then I moan when he feasts on my breasts, hot, loving, just short of rough. Desire is curling in my belly, sinking lower, slowly unfurling. His hands, his mouth, are everywhere.

"I've got to taste you."

Before I have time to register shock, he scoots to the edge of the sofa and puts his head between my thighs. The heat of his mouth, his wet, probing tongue, tasting, licking, is making me wild. He seems to be savoring me with each lick, each nibble, until I'm arching shamelessly against his mouth.

And then I shatter. Burst into a million pieces while running my hands through his hair.

Oh. My. God.

For a moment I'm sort of stunned. While my eyes are closed, smaller ripples of pleasure wash over me and I feel like my insides have turned to warm jelly oozing all the way to my fingertips and down to my toes. My heart is seriously slamming against my ribs and my breath is all shaky. Finally, I feel like I'm sort of floating back into my body and I say in a throaty voice that doesn't even sound like me, "Griff?" My fingers are fisted in his soft brown hair and he is all tangled around me with his head on my belly. "Griff? My God . . . that was . . . well, just amazing." I wait for him to respond but all I get is the sound of his breathing and it suddenly hits me that he is asleep.

Oh God. Reality check. Griff isn't sleeping; he's passed out. And he's damned heavy . . .

And what the hell have I just done? I'm shameless. No, I *was* shameless a minute ago, and now I'm bursting *with* shame. I mean I'm not a prude about sex or anything, but I'm not a nympho either and yet just a short while ago I had almost had sex with a man barely more than a stranger and now with a man I've known almost all of my life. What's wrong with me?

Still pondering this, I scoot my naked self from beneath Griff and on shaky legs I search around my living room for my hastily discarded clothing. I shimmy into my bra and panties and locate my jeans and shirt, holding them in a bundle clutched to my chest.

I'm about to scurry from the room, but I pause to look over at Griff. His long legs are draped over the sofa and his tanned, muscled body looks incredibly masculine against the floral print. His head is resting on a fringy throw pillow facing me and he looks peaceful, younger with his features relaxed in sleep. I know I should leave the room, but I can't help but gaze at him for another moment. A kind of longing steals over me and if I wanted to be real honest I would remind my sorry self that my feelings for Griff run way deeper than *just friends*. But I don't want to be honest because I'm afraid that Griff will forever think of me as being Luke's baby sister. He showed up here tonight in a misguided effort to protect me from Parker. How I ended up naked is beyond me.

Well, okay, not really. I mean, I know I just threw my clothes across the room at his mere request, it's just that I can't believe that I let myself feel instead of think, something I swore I'd never do again with Griff. With a pathetic little intake of breath I swipe away a tear. "Well, Griff," I say softly, "Parker Carrington doesn't hold a candle to you. Why'd you go on having to prove that to me? Huh?"

Okay, now I'm pissed. I handed my heart to Griffin

Sheldon once before and I'm not about to do it all over again. Where does he get off giving all of these damned mixed signals anyway? I glare over at him. First he gives me the cold shoulder and then he has the nerve to show up on my doorstep and give me an earth-moving orgasm! The jackass!

Well, enough! I'll fix him breakfast in the morning and act like nothing exciting happened. With a twist of sadness, I realize that he probably won't even remember in the morning anyway due to his drinking binge and if he does I'll pretend like it's no big deal. I mean, maybe it wasn't. Maybe any guy with a tongue could make me feel the same way. I've just never let a guy do, you know, *that* to me before, but a tongue is a tongue, right? A mouth is just a mouth, I think to myself, but this thought has my eyes drifting to Griff's mouth, making me recall his hot, demanding kiss, and I know I'm only fooling myself.

With a groan, Griff rolls to his back, trying to make his big body comfortable on the small sofa. He flings one arm over his head causing a ripple of muscle that has me staring in fascination like I've never seen a dog-gone male body before. Good God almighty. I need to get a grip on myself.

Turning on my bare heel, I head for my bedroom wishing that I could call Macy but it's way too late. After scrubbing my face and brushing my teeth I tug on a sleep-shirt and flop into bed but instead of falling asleep, I toss and turn trying to make some sense of my crazy evening. Of course there's no making sense of something that doesn't make any sense so I just stare at the paddle fan with a sleepy frown, trying to forget that

Griff is sleeping on my sofa, having done to me intimate things that no man has ever done before.

Macy is gonna have a field day with this one . . .

A loud thump has me opening my eyes wide while jackknifing into a sitting position in bed. What the . . . ? I swing my legs over the side of the bed and stumble into the living room still groggy from a fitful night's sleep. I'm not exactly what you'd call a morning person anyway and I'm halfway across the room when I remember that Griff is sleeping on my sofa. This makes my heart thump a bit harder and I'm instantly awake.

"You okay?" I ask when I realize that the loud thump was Griff falling off the sofa. He's absently rubbing his head and looking real confused from his position on the floor. "Griff, you okay?" I repeat when he fails to answer me.

He seems startled at the sound of my voice and gazes up at me. "This might be a stupid question, but what in the hell am I doing here?" His voice is all gravelly and I'm thinking that he looks pretty damned sexy all sleep-rumpled in his boxers.

"You tied one on last night."

He frowns and rakes his fingers through his hair, making it stand up on end. With a glance at the sofa he looks back at me. "So, I slept on the sofa?"

"Your questions aren't gettin' any smarter," I try to joke but Griff's frown deepens and I wonder how much, if anything, he remembers. "How 'bout some coffee?" I ask, trying to divert his thoughts but he's looking at me in a funny way and I feel the heat of a blush warm my cheeks.

"Did I come on to you last night, Jamie Lee?"

I sort of shrug.

"God, I'm sorry. I'm such a jackass." He pushes up from the floor and sits on the edge of the sofa, resting his arms on his knees.

"It's no big deal, Griff," I try to say nonchalantly, but my voice is kind of shaky.

"It is a big deal. Here I was worryin' about the Parker fellow making advances and I end up bein' the one out of line." He looks down at the floor with his head in his hands.

"Why is it such a bad thing that you came on to me, Griff?"

His head snaps up. "You should be able to trust me."

"I'm not seventeen anymore."

This statement hangs in the air between us and his brown eyes turn stormy.

"You made it damned difficult, but I did the right thing back then and I'm going to do the right thing now."

"What the hell's that supposed to mean?"

He stands up and starts yanking on his clothes. "I'm not going to be your summer fling because you're bored."

I gasp. "That's what you think of me?" I wanted to shout this but my voice is a flimsy squeak.

"You as much as said so, Jamie Lee. You said that you needed some excitement."

Okay, this hits a nerve because it's pretty much true, but coming from Griff's mouth makes it sound so tawdry. This of course makes me get defensive. "So you came here last night to save me from Parker Carrington's evil clutches . . . to offer yourself to me instead. How noble of you, Griff."

He flushes and says, "It seemed like a good idea after too much bourbon."

"But not now." This seems to surprise him and I wish I hadn't said it. Avoiding looking at me, he looks around for his shirt. "Well, Griff?" I press, making a muscle jump in his clenched jaw.

"No. I won't be your summer-fling boy toy. I've got more pride than that."

Seeing red, I take a roundhouse swing at him but lucky for him he bends down to retrieve his shirt so I come up with nothing but air. I'm very close to crying but I'll be damned if I'll let him see how much he's hurting me. Pointing to the door I croak, "Go."

"Jamie Lee . . ."

"Go!" I give him a shove.

"No, that didn't come out right. Let me—"

"Get out of here." My voice cracks and my pointing finger is shaking, making me sound more pathetic than pissed even though he has me royally angry. If I had a gun I'd shoot him! Okay, maybe I'd just shoot his hat off or make him dance while I shoot at his feet, you know, just to scare the bejesus out of him! But I don't have a gun because quite frankly guns frighten the hell out of me, but I sorely wish I had something to . . . to throw at him at least.

"Jamie Lee . . . listen!"

I spot my sandal on the floor and after snatching it up I wing it at him. He ducks just in the nick of time and it lands on the floor with a loud *thwap*. I throw the other one, and it whacks him in the shoulder.

"Ouch!"

He has the sense to start backing toward the door but I follow, throwing anything I can get my hands on. A pillow hits him in the head and I look around for something more life-threatening.

"Stop!"

"No!" A candlestick sails past his head.

"You're crazy, woman!"

"Is that right? Well, you're a jerk." I'm seriously considering throwing the table lamp at him but he's already out the door. Not nearly finished, I follow him to the landing and down the steps. "Just for the record, I—"

"M-morning, Jamie Lee," says Rose Jenkins as she rolls her sale rack outside her store. She can't see me at first since she isn't much taller than the metal clothes-laden rack but her mouth forms a big *o* when she spots me with Griff.

Gawd, I'm in my sleep-shirt, barely reaches to midthigh, and Griff is barefooted, his Hell Raisers shirt is on backwards, and his hair is sticking straight up. But I try to redeem the situation. "Uh, Griff just for the record," I repeat, "Your bid to uh, install my, uh, tanning beds is a tad high. Thank you for stopping by *this morning* to discuss the terms with me."

Griff blinks at me like I've sprouted another head. I give him an encouraging widening of my eyes meaning *work with me here* but he just keeps blinking at me. "The tanning bed stalls, Griff," I repeat slowly.

"Oh, uh, okay." He reaches in his pocket and extracts his truck keys but of course he's forgotten that his truck is over at Dixie's Dance Hall.

Rose Jenkins is pretending to arrange her merchandise but her beady little eyes keep darting to us. I know she isn't buying any of the bull I'm shoveling for her benefit but I feel compelled to save the last shreds of my tattered reputation.

"Thanks for stopping by this morning. Get back to me after you sharpen your pencil."

Griff blinks at me, clearly confused, and I know he has yet to remember where his truck is located. A kinder person would have offered a ride to Dixie's, but I'm not feeling at all kindly toward him at the very moment. So, with as much dignity as I can muster, which is very little, I pivot and march up the steps to my apartment.

8

What Was I Thinking?

I really want to slam the door to let off some steam, but the way my luck is going I would just break something and since Griff is the person who fixes everything that I break, I refrain . . . but just barely. Desperately in need of caffeine, I stomp over to the fridge and snag a Diet Coke since brewing coffee would take too long. After snapping the top back I slurp the overrunning fizz, take a long slug, but then screw up my nose. Diet soft drinks really blow but Macy has me recently convinced that the real deal is full of evil sugar so I now have a fridge full of diet drinks that gag me.

I drink it for the caffeine jolt and then let out this little unexpected burp that normally would have me giggling but I am *so* not in a giggling mood. In fact, I may never giggle again. "Oh God, what was I thinkin'?"

I moan and then flop into a chair at the kitchen table, setting down the half-empty Coke can with a loud clunk. I mull over my sorry situation for a few sulky moments, wishing I could call Macy, but she's shopping for something green with Mama so that leaves me to mull on my own. I don't know that I would fully divulge my interlude with Griff to her anyway. It's just too embarrassing. With a sigh I acknowledge that the bonemelting kiss and the earth-shattering orgasm isn't my main concern, even though I'm really hoping that Griff doesn't recall the whole thing. Since he was having trouble remembering the location of his truck, I think I'm safe on that score. No, my real concern is my feelings for him. God, I really do need to discuss the situation with Macy and I don't think I can hold out until noon when she's due in at the Cut & Curl.

Finally I give in and call Macy on her cell phone. I figure that even if we can't have a full conversation with Mama in the background, at least I can convey some of my dilemma to her.

Leaning my hip against the sink, I take a sip of Coke while I wait for Macy to answer. I'm about ready to give up when she answers, "Hello, Jamie Lee."

"Having any luck shoppin'?" I ask, trying to sound casual.

"No, but your mama is relentless. I've been in this here dressin' room for forty-five minutes and she's out there huntin' for more green clothing."

"So you're alone?"

"For the moment. What's wrong, Jamie Lee?"

"Nothin'."

"Yeah, right. Spill."

Cradling my hand around the cold can of soda, I respond, still in a casual manner, "Griff showed up on my doorstep last night drunker than Cooter Brown."

"No . . . really?"

I hear the rustle of clothing and demand, "Macy, do I have your full attention?"

"Of course!" The rustling ceases.

I swallow and then begin, "There is a possibility that I might . . ." I can't get the words out.

"What?"

I take a shuddering breath. "Well, I think I could be . . ." Oh, I just can't continue.

"Pregnant?" Macy squeaks.

"No, for pity's sake!"

Of course Mama takes that particular moment to enter the dressing room. "Who is pregnant?"

"No one," Macy quickly responds.

Good girl. I let out my held breath.

"Who are you talkin' to?"

Shit.

"Um . . . Jamie Lee called to see how things are goin'."

I hear Mama gasp when the words pregnant and my name collide in her head. Suddenly, she's on the phone. "Jamie Lee! Are you in the family way?"

"Of course not," I answer.

"Did you just take one of those tests in a box? Have you been fornicating with that flashy Hollywood producer person? I *knew* that man had trouble written all over him. He's from *California*!" She says this like he's from outer space.

"Mama, I am not pregnant! Calm down and give Macy her phone."

Another gasp is followed by, "Macy, are *you* with child?" She sounds so horrified that I have to chuckle.

"Why *no*, Mrs. Carter."

Mama's sigh of relief has me chuckling once again.

"Jamie Lee, are you amusing yourself at my expense? Someday you are goin' to give me a heart attack."

"Macy just misunderstood what I was sayin'. Sometimes cell-phone reception gets fuzzy, you know?"

"Oh, yes, of course I know that. I have my own personal cellular phone, mind you."

I shake my head. Cell phones are as much of a mystery to her and Daddy as computers are. She carries one around with her but never turns the danged thing on and has no clue as to how to retrieve messages. If she does have the phone turned on, finding the thing in her massive purse full of unnecessary items is impossible and it causes her such panic that I rarely call her or Daddy on their cell phones. The funny thing is that whenever someone else's phone rings, Mama thinks it has to be hers only to dig into her purse to find her phone turned off or with a dead battery. I sigh and say, "Would you please give the phone back to Macy?"

"Certainly. Now don't go wastin' her minutes," she says with the authority of someone who knows nothing about cell phones.

"Good one, Macy," I hiss into the phone. "Now why on God's green earth would you think I was *pregnant*?"

"I don't know! You just couldn't seem to spit out what you were tryin' to say."

"Are Mama's ears perked up?"

"Of course."

I sigh. "This is so not a good time to discuss this. You will never be able to maintain your composure."

"I will!"

I hear Mama tell her that time is a-wastin' so I say, "We'll discuss this later."

"Jamie Lee!"

"Everything okay?" I hear Mama ask.

"Fine, Mrs. Carter," she answers sweetly and then hisses into the phone, "Please! I can't wait."

Mama chimes in, "Oh, do you have to use the bathroom, dear?"

"No, Mrs. Carter," she says, all sweetness, and then hisses at me again, "Tell me!"

"I think I'm in love with Griff."

Of course Macy gasps but then disguises it with a cough. "And you know this *how*?"

"He kissed me and it curled my toes." And a helluva lot more, but I leave that other part out.

"Yes, but—"

"I know, I know! There are complications that we can't discuss with Mama hovering in the background. We'll talk when you come in, okay?"

"Okay . . ." Macy responds in a tone that says that waiting is going to just kill her. Her tone also conveys her concern for my well-being. She fully knows my history of heartbreak with Griff and my subsequent wild behavior that resulted in hooking up with a jerk of a boyfriend and then a string of Payton College frat boys that Mama dearly hated.

I sigh. I'm too old for frat boys and keg parties. But then a thought hits me. I'm no longer too young for Griff. Maybe, just *maybe*, I can get him to stop playing the big-brother role and think of me as a woman and not Luke's kid sister always in need of rescuing.

I head out onto my back deck to soak up a bit of sunshine. The aroma of sweet honeysuckle makes me close my eyes and suck in a deep, somewhat shaky breath. I've tried so hard not to think of Griff in any other way other than as a friend that I almost had myself convinced. The big question is: how does Griff feel about me? I really don't want to open my heart up to rejection from him again but I'm not quite sure how to find out how he feels in a subtle way. Subtlety is not my strong suit.

I hope that Macy will have some intelligent insight regarding my situation. Macy can be really smart as long as she can remain in control of her emotions. She is the levelheaded one in this friendship until she gets worked up and then she becomes a loose cannon, imagining far-fetched scenarios that suck me right in.

I finish off the last of the soda and head inside to get ready for work. Saturdays in the summer are usually a bit slow since the college kids are mostly gone and everyone else is doing summertime-related activities rather than having their hair done. Macy and I finally decided to shorten our hours in the summer, much to my mother's dismay. What we really wanted was a vacation, specifically a singles cruise, but Mama was so appalled at the notion of closing the Cut & Curl for a week that we gave up on the idea. Like someone might need an emergency haircut! I really think that Mama was more opposed to Macy and me leaving the country to sail into foreign waters than to closing the shop.

After a long hot shower, I decide to put on a pair of white cuffed shorts and a nice yellow scoop-neck blouse, since Mama will likely stop in when she drops off Macy. I take extra care with my makeup just in case Griff stops in to try and make things right between us. I mean, after all, last night was entirely his fault. Of course, I didn't have to be so compliant, but that's not the point.

While I make my way down the stairs to the shop, my brain is still buzzing with thoughts about the night before. Beneath the flash and the bling, Parker turned out to be such a nice guy and his kisses did make my heart go pitter-patter. Okay, I didn't melt like with Griff, but maybe I was just, like, all worked up from my earlier encounter with Parker?

Another thought stops me in my tracks and I actually have to sit down on the steps. I don't want to lose Griff's friendship. Griff has been there for my family and me so many times over the years that I've lost count. He drove me to the hospital when Daddy had his heart attack. I cried on his shoulder when my jackass boyfriend dumped me, and most importantly he brought Luke back to us when he was on the path of destruction.

I just know that when friends become lovers there's no turning back and the thought of losing Griff's friendship makes my stomach clench. Plus, I remember the pain of handing him my heart on a silver platter only to have it handed right back to me. Granted, I was seventeen, but I don't think the pain of rejection lessens with age.

"Well, horse-fuck-pucky. Just what am I gonna do?" I really need Macy here to hash this out but she isn't due in for another hour and that's if Mama doesn't keep her at the mall late.

A rapid knock at the front door interrupts my musings, so I push myself up from the steps and then cringe when I see who is standing on my doorstep. "I am *so* not in the mood for this," I mutter but then paste a big fake smile on my face as I open the shop.

9

Too Close for Comfort

"Well, hello, Dinah." The smile on my face is stretchy and fake.

"Hey there, Jamie Lee," Dinah answers. She enters the shop with her baby boy balanced on her hip. What the hell is his name? I rack my brain. Starts with a *d*. David? No, too normal. Dillon? No, too yuppie.

"Dallas, say hi to Miss Jamie Lee."

Dallas? Oh, horrors, now I remember the story about how he was conceived in Dallas, hence the name. I can't remember just how I came to be privy to this information. I'm sure alcohol was a factor. Dallas wrinkles up his nose and buries his face in Dinah's neck. I must admit that he's very cute.

"He's shy like his *daddy*."

"Oh, how sweet." I have to concentrate on not narrowing my eyes at her comment. After all she *is* holding a child. See, Dinah's husband is Dirk Dunlettie, former Hootertown Hornets quarterback who became third-string quarterback for the Payton Panthers. That's right, *third string*, and Dinah still prances around like she is queen of Hootertown.

I made the very poor choice of accepting a date from Dirk after my big rejection from Griff. I shudder at the memory of Dirk's beefy hands and sloppy lips. When I refused another date with him he turned to Dinah, who formed the misconception that she stole him from me. She still uses every chance she can get to rub it in my face, along with the fact that she beat me out for homecoming queen. To this day I believe that there were some behind-the-scenes shenanigans going on with the votes.

Anyway, in the state of mind that I'm currently in Dinah is the last person I want to deal with and from the looks of it, I'm going to have to cut baby Dallas-conceived-in-Dallas' hair. I want to tell her that Dirk isn't shy, but just can never think of anything intelligent to say. But of course I don't. I pride myself on being professional and so I stretch my rubber smile a bit bigger. "What can I do for you today?"

Dinah shifts Dallas up higher on her hip and announces, "He needs a haircut. Dirk is complainin' that Dallas looks like a girl with all these blond curls."

"Okie-dokie," I say with false brightness and lead mother and son over to my station. I get the big board that goes across the arms of the chair and serves as a booster seat. Patting the board, I say, "Have a seat, Dallas." I show Dinah a red lollipop, the safe flat kind with the rope handle, to offer to Dallas and thank God she shakes her head yes. I hand it to Dallas who smiles and pops it in his mouth. Ah, so far, so good.

I drape the cape over him and fluff his soft blond

curls. Taking out my scissors, I turn to Dinah. "How short?"

Dinah's mouth trembles and for a moment I think she might start blubbering. After swallowing, she says, "Uh, a little-boy cut, you know, up over the ears. Dirk says to make him look like a boy and not some sissy."

Dirk is a jackass, I want to say, but I just nod and start spraying his hair to dampen it. Some kids start to wail at this part but Dallas is content to suck on his cherry candy. I'm halfway though cutting his hair without incident when Dallas suddenly spots himself in the mirror. I hold my breath and keep snipping. He watches with interest in his big blue eyes and I let out my breath.

"We've been potty trainin'," Dinah says as if I want to know this information.

"Isn't he kind of young?"

Dinah's chest puffs out with parental pride. "Just turned two but he's real smart for his age."

I just nod and keep snipping.

"It's so cute when he pees. I just have to laugh because his aim is off because his . . . his . . ." She puts her hand to her mouth and blushes.

"Penis?" I dryly supply.

Her eyes widen and she looks at Dallas to see if he has heard the *p*-word.

"We call it his *winkie*," she whispers.

I blink at her for a moment. This is coming from a woman who as I recall from our senior year knew exactly what a penis was and what to do with it. She stands there looking all plump and rosy-cheeked and motherly. I recall my rather unseemly actions of the night before and I feel heat in my own cheeks. Before I can dwell on this further, Dallas starts to whimper. Knowing that a full-blown cry is on the way, I hurry to finish cutting his hair but not before he's wailing. Soon snot is running from his nose, collecting snips of blond hair. He looks at his reflection, down at the hair on the floor, and then accusingly at me. I want to say, "Blame your daddy for this, not me," but I just keep cutting.

"You look like such a big boy, Dallas," Dinah croons soothingly but he continues to wail. Her lips start to quiver and soon she's crying too. Not noisy wails like Dallas but tears and pathetic little hiccups. "He . . . he looks so *old* with his hair like that." She too gives me an accusing look in the mirror like it's my fault.

"It's what you asked for, Dinah," I say with just a bit more bite than intended. "He looks cute," I add with a smile.

"I suppose." Dinah nods and then swipes at her tears.

I'm starting to feel a little emotional myself. But then she says, "It's just that they grow up so fast, you know?" I nod with a sympathetic smile, but then Dinah covers her mouth for a moment and then says, "Oh, you *wouldn't* know. I'm so insensitive!"

Okay, that busted my give-a-damn all to pieces. "Oh I'm not ready to settle down yet if that's what you're gettin' at." I say this a bit too loudly.

Dinah pats my hand. *Pats my hand!* "I heard you've been walkin' a bit on the wild side with that Hollywood movie man, and we're just a bit concerned is all."

"Concerned? We? We . . . *who?*" I put the scissors down as a safety precaution. Dallas's bangs are a bit crooked but I don't give a fig. I peel the Velcro from his little neck and shake the hair from his cape. Picking up the big fat brush, I swipe at the hair on his neck, and he stops crying and giggles.

Dinah shrugs and then picks up Dallas. "Just, you know . . . *people.*"

As I walk over to the register, I say, "People should just mind their own business in this town."

"Oh, Jamie Lee, don't get so riled up. We're just worried about you."

"I'm not riled up." Unfortunately I say this way too loudly to sound unriled.

"The right man will come along." Dinah croons like she's talking to Dallas. "You just need to protect your reputation."

"Protect my reputation?" I'm so angry that I'm sputtering like Daffy Duck.

"Tongues are waggin', Jamie Lee." She does this little tisk-tisk thing while shaking her finger at me.

I really, *really* want to smack her.

"Parading around with that flashy man in his fancy car has people talkin'."

"Some people have small minds and big imaginations," I respond tightly. I give her a pointed look that says that I include her in this particular category. I close the register drawer a bit too hard and it springs back open. Frustrated, I do the same damned thing again.

"I'm only tryin' to give you some friendly advice, Jamie Lee."

I swallow the scream that's bubbling up in my throat. I love Hootertown, but sometimes living in a small town just bites the big one, this being one of those times. I take a deep breath and I'm about to say something smart-ass when the bell on the front door tinkles, drawing my attention. My comeback dissolves on my tongue like cotton candy when I look up to see Griff enter the store, looking hot, tired, and hungover. There's a smudge of dirt on his white T-shirt and his worn jeans are ripped at both knees. His dark hair is mussed like he's run his fingers through it a million times and yet the sight of him standing there makes my heart leap into my throat.

Our eyes lock and there's this vibe in the air between us. Dinah must have felt it too because she refrains from saying anything and just watches the interaction. Even baby Dallas looks at us with his big blue eyes like he can feel something going on. He squirms and wiggles in Dinah's arms and although I can tell that she wants to hang around and see just what's going on between Griff and me, she hikes Dallas up on her hip and says, "Looks like it's nap time. You take care, Jamie Lee." She nods to Griff. "You too, Griff."

Griff, who is usually very polite, nods absently in Dinah's direction while his attention remains on me. I feel like I need to squirm much like baby Dallas but I raise my chin a notch and ask, "What brings you here, Griff?" I was so hoping for a nonchalant tone but my voice has this stupid little hitch in it.

Griff's brown eyes go all stormy and he takes a step towards me.

I barely refrain from taking a step back but I stand my ground. "I'm not in any need of rescuing right now. I'll call you on the Batphone if I need you."

"Jamie Lee, I'm sorry about last night."

My Frosted Mini-Wheats do a little tap dance in my tummy while I wonder just how much of last night he remembers. "It's no big deal. You can go now. I'm really busy." I look around for something important to do. Picking up a broom I start sweeping Dallas's blond curls into a pile. That takes all of about two seconds. Picking up the small cape I take it over to the wicker hamper at the back of the shop but I can hear the heavy clump of Griff's work boots on the tile floor as he follows me.

"Jamie Lee!" His deep voice sounds low and urgent so I feel compelled to turn and face him.

I wait but Griff seems to have lost his voice. His brow furrows and he runs his fingers through his hair. Finally he clears his throat and says, "I've been having these fuzzy memories . . . images really and I don't know whether I was dreamin' or if—"

"Forget about it, Griff. We've already been down this road. You made a pass . . . so what?" I tell him in a rush. I really want to stop this train of thought before he remembers . . . *God,* what he did to me. "Your intentions, however misguided, were noble in a weird way so just forget about last night. I *get it* that it didn't mean anything."

"*What* didn't mean anything?" His eyes widen a fraction.

Oh crap, why do I always put things the wrong way? I decide to give him enough information to get him off my back . . . but not everything. "The . . . kiss."

He looks so horrified that my heart does a painful little twist. "It was just a kiss, Griff," I say softly. "People do it all the time."

He continues to frown. "So we didn't—"

"No!" I squeak and then have to mentally calm myself down. "Look, you thought you were protecting me from Parker or some such stupidity. Just forget about it."

"Are you seeing him again?"

"Why does it matter so much?" I lift the lid of the hamper and toss the cape inside so I can turn away from his probing gaze.

"I . . . care about you."

Ahh, but not in the way I want. Not in the way that I need so damned much. Unreasonably angry now, I whip around, place my palms on his chest and shove. "Go, Griff. Just . . . go!"

The force of my unexpected shove has Griff stumbling backwards and he catches himself from falling by grabbing the sink with a hand that I suddenly notice is bandaged. His hiss of pain has me rushing to his side.

"What's wrong with your hand?"

"Banged my damned thumb with my hammer."

"Let me see."

"No, it's no big deal. I've done it a million times."

"Let me see!"

With a sigh he unwraps the gauze, revealing a purplish black thumbnail and split skin at the tip that's oozing blood. Oh God. I hate blood. I feel a bit woozy. "That needs ice," I advise him rather weakly.

"You okay?"

"Sure. I'll just go get that ice." I make the mistake of glancing at the swollen thumb and it feels like all the blood in my body drains to my toes.

"Jamie Lee, are you gonna hurl?"

"No . . . *of course not* . . . okay maybe. I'm just a

bit . . . light-headed, uh . . . weak-kneed, oh God . . . a bit queasy.

"Here." Griff puts an arm around my waist. I swallow and lean heavily against him.

"Breathe deep through your nose," he instructs.

I do as ordered, feeling a bit foolish that he's the injured one and I'm being such a wuss. I drag in a deep breath and my head is filled with the musky spice of his aftershave and a hint of the outdoors. His body feels warm and solid beneath the soft cotton of his shirt.

"Better?" His voice sounds gruff and so damned sexy.

"A little." I know that this is bad on my part but I milk this a bit. It just feels so good to be pressed against him. Oh, how I want to turn into his embrace and tilt my face up for a kiss. Would Griff kiss me if I did? Or push me away in horror? Or kiss me and then push me away in horror? Should I go for broke? I'm thinking yes. I mean, Macy and I *did* make this pact to go after what we want and right now I really want a kiss. I really *need* a kiss. A kiss would confirm my intense attraction to him or dispel my bone-melting reaction as a mere fluke. Okay, this needs to be done.

I decide to twist around in his arms in an effort to gain maximum kissing position, namely having my breasts crushed to his chest, but I unfortunately catch an up-close and way-too-personal glance at his injured thumb. I shudder and do this girly moan.

"Let's get you over to a chair."

"'Kay." I lean heavily against Griff as we walk and then ease myself into my station chair.

"Can I get you anything?"

"A Coke, maybe. Not one of those diet things. I need the real deal."

Griff knows his way around the shop and in nothing flat he has a cold Coke in my hand. I take a sip and start to feel better. Realizing that I'm acting like a spoiled Southern diva, I say, "Oh, you need some ice on that thumb."

"I'll get it," he insists when I start to push up from the chair.

"There are some plastic perm caps in the cabinet that you can dump some ice in."

Griff nods and walks in that direction. I watch him, admiring the way his wide shoulders stretch the cotton of his shirt. Angling my head, I let my gaze linger on his butt . . . nicely rounded and firm. When he reaches up into the cabinet I'm treated to a few inches of tanned skin. Yes, as Miss Irma put it, Griffin Sheldon is one fine specimen of a man. I haven't allowed myself to think of him in that way in so long it's like seeing him with fresh eyes . . . and I'm liking what I see.

Griff fills the plastic cap with ice and ties the ends together. He grabs a towel and then comes over to sit in Macy's station next to me. I cringe when I catch a glimpse of his thumb as he gingerly places it on the ice pack and then wraps it in the towel, probably to keep it hidden from me.

"Does it hurt?"

"A little."

Okay, I know in guy talk this translates to hurting like hell. "I'll get you some Advil and some clean gauze."

"I'm fine. Stay there, Jamie Lee. You look a little flushed."

Now, just what would he say if I would tell him that my flushed state is from sitting here admiring his very fine attributes? He would probably think that I was just kidding around and laugh because in his mind we're merely friends and I'm just Luke's kid sister who still needs looking after. "I'm feelin' much better," I falsely assure him, hoping I won't wobble when I stand up.

While I fumble around for the first-aid kit I feel his gaze on me and I wonder what he's thinking. Is my panty line showing? Did I remember to shave my legs? Does he think my butt is cute or huge? "What did Macy do with the danged thing?" I tend to blame all misplaced items on Macy. I would feel guilty about this practice, but she does the same thing to me.

"Forget about it, Jamie Lee. I'll live."

"Ah, here it is!" I turn to him with a triumphant smile that immediately fades when I notice that he's cradling his hand in his lap. "Do you think we should take you to the emergency room?"

Griff rolls his eyes.

"Men," I grumble as I pop open the Advil and shake two of them into my palm. Walking over to Griff I give him the pills and my Coke to wash them down. When our fingers brush I feel a tingle of awareness but he just takes the pills and guzzles some Coke. I sadly wonder if this attraction will always be one-sided.

While he's tipping the coke back I notice that his elbow and forearm are scraped raw. "You hurt your arm too."

"Huh? Oh," he says as he examines his elbow. "Yeah,

after I smashed my thumb I cursed a blue streak and fell sideways into some loose lumber."

Clicking my tongue against the roof of my mouth I pop the lid of the first-aid kit and rummage around for some salve and bandages.

"What are you doin'?"

"I'm about to patch you up."

"Without fainting?"

"I do think that I can handle the scrape. It was the open wound dripping blood that got to me." I shudder just thinking about it.

"It's a little cut, Jamie Lee, not an open wound."

"I just can't do blood. How did you manage that anyway?"

Griff shrugs but doesn't meet my eyes when he says, "My brain was a bit preoccupied. I guess I lost my concentration."

Normally I would make some joking comment like friends do but I'm too busy wondering if *I* could have been on his mind. But after last night and the episode this morning there's a weird tension between us so I stay quiet. Glad to have something to do, I tear off the end of the packet of antiseptic lotion. "Hold your arm up for me so I can rub this on."

"This isn't necessary, you know."

"Do it."

"Okay, okay!"

"This might sting."

He sighs and raises his arm. After squeezing a dollop of the lotion onto my fingertip I gingerly rub it over the skin that's been scraped raw. When he sort of sucks in a breath I pause and look at him. "Sorry, does it hurt?"

Griff blinks at me for a moment like he's having trouble understanding my simple question. I show him the glob of lotion on the tip of my finger and repeat, "Does this stuff sting?"

"Oh, uh, not really."

"Good." I start to smooth the rest of the medicine gently over the scrape.

"Jamie Lee, you never did answer my question. Are you gonna see him again?"

"While your *brotherly concern* is touching and all, I'll remind you that I'm a big girl, Griff. And just for your information, Parker is a really nice guy."

"You're too trusting."

"You're too nosy!" I turn away to grab a towel so he can't see how close I am to tears. I rummage around in the first-aid kit for some gauze. Keeping my eyes on my task, I lean in and start to bandage his arm. He remains silent while I perform my task, way too damned aware of him while I stand between his long outstretched legs. I can feel the heat of his body and when I turn to reach for the scissors to cut through the gauze, my bare thigh brushes against soft denim and hard muscle. It's all I can do not to jump back when I realize that I'm way too close for comfort. When I tape the edges of the bandage together I sneak a look at him through my lashes, wondering if my close proximity is having any effect on him at all.

"Jamie Lee . . ." His voice is low and sounds unsure.

I look at him, holding my breath. He swallows and opens his mouth, "I want to make my—"

The opening of the front door stops him in midsentence. Macy rushes in with a shopping bag in each hand.

She stops in her tracks when she sees me standing between Griff's legs. Since I'm no longer bandaging him up it must look like we've been caught in an intimate moment of some sort.

"Oh," Macy says and then is at an obvious loss for words . . . a rare occurrence.

Feeling guilty for no good reason, I take a quick step backwards, trip over one of Griff's big work boots and suddenly find myself on my ass. Now, what it is about seeing someone fall on their ass that makes people laugh I'll never understand, but Macy has the nerve to snicker. I give her a glare and she shuts up. Griff looks dangerously close to laughing but politely refrains or perhaps it's because I'm within striking distance. Refusing his outstretched hand with a scowl, I push up to my feet. I really want to rub my smarting cheeks but I don't. The only saving grace is . . . well, there really is no saving grace.

"I should be going," Griff says in a we're-not-finished-with-this tone. He stands up, gives me a funny look that I can't read, and starts for the door.

"My God, what happened to your hand?" Macy asks, abruptly dropping her bags.

Griff shrugs. "Hit my thumb with my hammer."

"Oh, so Jamie Lee was patchin' you up?" Macy sounds a bit disappointed that we weren't caught in a compromising position.

"Yeah." Griff looks back at me and grins. Now the man has grinned at me a million times over the years so just why is a flash of white teeth and dimple turning my insides to jelly? "She's a regular Florence Nightingale."

Macy's eyebrows shoot up. "Really?"

"He's makin' sport of me. There was a bit of blood involved and you know how I am around blood." I shiver at the sudden vision but say, "Keep the ice on that thumb of yours, okay?"

"I will." Griff's grin fades a bit. He nods at Macy and leaves the shop.

Macy immediately fires questions at me like a machine gun until I hold up my hands in surrender.

"My God, girl, one at a time."

Macy takes a deep breath. "So, do you really think you're in love with Griff?"

10

Ripe for the Picking

Before I can formulate an answer Macy just keeps right on talking. "Now, hear me out," she pleads, as if I have a choice in the matter. Her hands are waving like she's preaching at Sunday services. "See, I'm thinkin' that, you know, maybe you're reading a bit too much into a little kiss. I mean, Griff had been drinkin', right?

I open my mouth to answer but she just keeps right on going.

"So, he wasn't really aware of what he was doin' and I'm thinkin' that he wouldn't have kissed you otherwise."

"Macy don't you get it? It's about my *reaction* to his kiss."

"But you had been foolin' around with Parker earlier. Maybe you were still in a state of arousal, you know?"

"Macy McCoy! Are you tryin' to talk me out of my feelings for Griff because you're havin' this fantasy that we'll end up in Hollywood livin' in the lap of luxury?"

"Of course not! It's just that your infatuation with

Griffin Sheldon has fucked up your love life for so long
that I hate to see you do the same thing all over again."

"Tell me how you really feel, Macy. Don't hold
back."

Ignoring my sarcasm, Macy glances at the front door
and then comes closer to me. "You said yourself that
you almost, you know, *did it* with Parker! I just wonder
if you were thinkin' straight when Griff arrived."

"So, just what are you suggestin'?"

"Jamie Lee, you're just gonna have to get Griff into
bed. That way you'll either get the man out of your system or know once and for all that he's the one."

"Don't you think that dating first might be in order?"

Macy shoves her shopping bags to the side and flips
the little red sign on the front door over to say, BE BACK
IN 30 MINUTES. "Dating is for getting to know one another. Name one thing that you don't already know
about Griff."

I sit down in my station chair and ponder this. "There
are things . . ."

Macy rolls her eyes. "What's his favorite color?"

"Red."

"Favorite food?"

"Hot wings."

"Brand of beer?"

"Bud Light."

"Brand of truck?"

"Ford."

"Favorite sports team?"

"UK Wildcats and the Tennessee Titans."

"Boxers or briefs?"

"Boxers . . . okay, *okay,* I get the picture." I swivel

my chair to face her. "But we both know that if I sleep with Griff there's no turning back to just friendship. Losing that is downright scary."

"Is that what you're really afraid of?"

I swallow the emotion clogging my throat and whisper, "No, not entirely. I'm afraid that he will always view me as Luke's little sister and not . . . *want me*. Macy, I don't know if I can take rejection from him again."

"Oh, so you'd rather spend the rest of your born days comparing every man you date to Griff."

"I don't do that!"

She crooks one eyebrow at me.

"Okay, I suppose I do." I sigh. "I've buried my feelings for him for so long that when my lips touched his I was in shock that he could make me feel that way. God, I sound so damned sappy."

"You've got to settle this thing with Griff. I just wonder if this thing about him protectin' you from Parker isn't more a jealousy issue."

Hope blossoms in my chest. "You think?"

"It could be." Macy taps her finger against her cheek while nodding. "You might want to play the jealousy card, too."

"That wouldn't be fair to Parker."

"Love isn't fair. We need to pull out all the stops. We need—"

"Whoa, Macy, you're spinnin' out of control."

She flops down into her chair. "I know. I just want to see you happy. You're goin' to have to risk your heart if you want to see this through. You know that, right?"

Swallowing, I nod.

"Then let's do this thing."

"I'm gonna be the doin' person," I remind her dryly.

"Yeah, baby." She wiggles her eyebrows.

Covering my suddenly warm cheeks with my hands I say, "Aw, Macy, I don't know if—"

"Shush! Don't you make any backin'-out noises." She does the head-bopping finger wave at me.

With a groan I nod slowly but my heart is hammering a million miles a minute. On the same page now, we both spring up from our chairs and do our secret handshake.

The phone rings but we both ignore it. Sometimes there are more important things than business. "Macy, maybe we'd better open up. What if Mama comes by?"

"She went home to fix lunch for your daddy. She said that if she didn't he would eat nothin' but junk and she still worries about his heart." Macy sighs. "Aw, Jamie Lee, do you *ever* think we'll find the kind of love that your mama and daddy share?"

I'm startled for a minute. I don't really think of my mama and daddy of having a soul mate kind of love, but I remember the stricken look on her face when he suffered his heart attack. They've stuck by each other through thick and thin and well, I guess I have to agree. "Picturing them in bed together is beyond me but I'd like to find the kind of lasting love that they have. Yes, they tend to bicker over the goofiest of things but I have to say that they do adore each other."

Macy goes all misty-eyed on me. "Okay," she says with a sniff, "just how are you gonna get Griff's boots under your bed?"

"We're gonna have to take this slow, Macy."

"The hell you say!"

"I'm likin' this less and less . . ."

Macy takes a deep breath and blows it out. "Just think about it. It's the only way you'll ever *know*."

I swivel my chair back and forth for a minute. "This could all blow up in my face. Then what?"

"Jamie Lee, we're like two plump plums ripe on the vine. If we don't do somethin' real soon, we'll just shrivel up like nasty old prunes. I don't know about you, but I don't want to be a prune, now, doggone it."

I giggle at her analogy. "Oh, and don't think you can put all the emphasis on me. It kinda creeps me out to say this, since Luke's my brother and all, but you need to get that boy's boots under your bed, too."

Macy squirms in her chair. "You're much further along in this whole process than me. How about if we got all gussied up tonight and head on over to Dixie's and just start feelin' our way through this thing?"

"Okay." We would have discussed this further, like what to wear and so forth, but there's a banging at the door and we have to actually get back to work before Mama hears that we've been shutting down the Cut & Curl in the middle of a Saturday afternoon.

We're surprisingly busy for the rest of the day, which makes the time pass in what seems like the blink of an eye. I'm a little miffed though that Parker hasn't called me. Even though I've decided to set my sights on Griff, I did show the man my boobies. Is a phone call asking too much?

As we're cleaning up for the day I ask, "What are you wearin' tonight, Macy? Somethin' green, I guess?"

Macy pauses in her task of folding towels. "I do believe I'll wear white capri pants and a sleeveless dark green shell that your mama spotted on the clearance rack at Talbot's. I have these little strapless sandals to match. You wearin' jeans?"

"How'd you guess?"

"Cowboy boots?"

"Right again."

"Hmm, and let me go out on a limb and guess that you'll have on a white tank top." She flashes me a crooked grin.

"Now *now,* I'll dress it up with a silver necklace and my least battered cowboy hat. Besides, the boys like the little white tank top, just like the Dierks Bentley song says."

Macy's grin fades. "I wish I had the figure to wear a skin-tight tank top."

"Yeah, and I wish I was taller and my butt was smaller and that I had those big juicy Angelina Jolie lips." I pucker my lips up and Macy laughs.

"You do not."

"Do so," I insist with my lips still all puckered up.

"Save that pucker for Griff."

My stomach does a little flip at her comment.

"Don't you go givin' me that deer-in-the-headlights look, girl." Her head bops, making her curls bounce.

Before she can get all riled up, I head over to the front door and open it for Macy. "I'm gonna eat a little somethin' and take a power nap. You're comin' here and we'll just hoof it over to Dixie's, okay?"

Macy nods. "Sounds like a plan."

After Macy leaves I button up the shop and head upstairs. I pop a frozen low-carb something or other in the microwave and pour myself a glass of sweet tea from the pitcher I always have in my fridge. This is the same ritual I perform just about every night after work, which is really kind of lame since I'm a pretty good cook. Granted, sometimes Macy and I go out and I eat at Mama and Daddy's most Sundays, but by and large this is it: a frozen dinner, a glass of tea, and me at my little kitchen table.

I've gotten myself into a rut . . . a boring rut.

"Well hell!" I bang my fist onto the Formica so hard that my low-carb rubber chicken and veggies jump in fright and my sweet tea wobbles. "There's gotta be something more than this," I mutter, looking down at my shriveled chicken breast swimming in icky orange sauce.

I think about defiantly tossing the chicken into the trash but I'm hungry and there's nothing better in the fridge so I take a bite. Not so bad, I think, but then this pisses me off too. *Not so bad* could describe my life, but I'm suddenly sick of *not so bad* . . .

Okay, I know I'm getting way too worked up about nothing in particular. I suppose it has something to do with the arrival of Parker Carrington that's turned my way of thinking on its ear. I'm so deep in thought that when the phone rings I yelp, jump, and toss a bite of chicken in the air. I almost knock over my tea as I reach for the cordless phone. "Hello?" My tone is laced with my current state of discontent.

"Jamie Lee?" Parker's silky deep voice has me sitting up straight in my chair and smoothing back my hair as if he can see me. I cringe when my fingers find the bite of chicken. Ew.

"Oh, Parker. Sorry to have barked in your ear."

He chuckles like I've said something funny. "I had to go to the airport and pick up Jessica Hanes, one of my producers for *Vanquished*. I drove around all day showing her Hootertown and I lost track of time or I would have called sooner."

"Oh."

"I was wondering if you'll be at Dixie's Dance Hall tonight. That's where all the locals go, right?"

"It's the place to see and be seen," I tell him, a bit amused. "I know the bouncer so I can get you in."

"Great. Can you get Jessica in, too?"

"Parker, I was kiddin'."

"I knew that," he says but I know that he didn't. I have to smile.

"I'll be there around eight o'clock."

"That early?"

"This is Hootertown, Parker. Last call is at one."

"Oh. What should I wear? I want to blend in."

I chuckle thinking that there's not much chance of that. "A cowboy hat, cowboy boots, Wrangler jeans with a Skoal ring in your back pocket, a belt with a big silver buckle and a Western-cut shirt if you want to get dressed up, or a T-shirt if you're feelin' casual."

"How come I never know if you're serious or not? And just what is a Skoal ring?"

"Parker, just come as you are. You're not likely to blend in no matter what you do."

"Can I pick you up?"

"No, Macy and I are goin' to walk since it's such nice weather."

"Okay." He sounds disappointed enough to feed my ego.

"I'll see you there." I smile as I hang up the phone. My mood is a bit lighter but I can't help but wonder what this Jessica Hanes is going to be like. Will she be warm and friendly or stuck up and bitchy? I guess I'll just have to wait and find out.

11

A Hollywood Hussy Blows into Hootertown

When Macy arrives at my place, I'm still fussing with my hair so she comes into the bathroom and sits down on the toilet lid. "I like that color of green on you. Mama was right."

"You think so?"

"Yeah. I think I might buy me a dog."

Macy wrinkles up her nose. "What brought this on?"

I unplug the curling iron and eye my hair critically in the mirror. "I just feel like I'm in a rut. For example, what did you have for supper?"

Macy's cheeks turn a rosy shade of pink and she has the grace to wince as she confesses, "A cheeseburger from Fred's Diner."

I think about giving her grief over the matter but her mouth wobbles and she says, "I eat all the wrong things when I'm nervous."

I turn and lean against the sink. "Just what are you nervous about?"

"Your brother."

"Oh Macy, you are so much better than the Barbie dolls Luke's dated. Don't you see that?"

"Yeah, I'm more like Midge."

"Midge?"

"Barbie's not-as-pretty friend." Macy tries to smile but her mouth does the little wobble thing. "Jamie Lee, when I was ridin' with Luke in his car just the smell of his aftershave had me all a-flutter. Then, when he would shift gears, the muscles in his arm would flex and ripple. Oh, I just wanted to purr." She pokes me and actually makes a purring sound.

I try to purr but all I do is spit. "How'd you do that?"

"It's all in the tongue."

I try again and fail. Thinking that I'm never going to feel the need to purr, I give up.

"If I would *ever* get his boots under my bed, I'd turn that man every which way but loose."

"Then do it!"

Macy jumps up from the commode and gives me a high five. "Let's go!"

We talk about the shop and various unrelated subjects including my recent decision to purchase a dog as we walk to Dixie's. "It's already getting crowded," Macy remarks and I nod in agreement. Dixie's is a big brick building that was a warehouse until the early 1960s when the Johnson family bought it and converted it into a dance hall. Dixie was the Johnson family dog, a shepherd-collie mix that would dance on her hind legs to Johnny Cash music. My brain is full of useless Hootertown trivia.

"This place is hoppin' tonight," Macy remarks as we pay our three-dollar cover charge. This isn't just a hangout for the young crowd but is a mixture of everyone of legal drinking age.

"You got that right." The twang of an electric guitar has us looking toward the big stage at the opposite end of the huge dance floor. "Look, Wet Willie's Barnyard Band is warming up." I grin at Macy. The Barnyard Band plays some popular country cover songs to please the young crowd but they have a rockabilly sound to their own songs that the older folks enjoy.

To our left is the main bar that runs about half the length of the room. Wide and sturdy, it's big enough to dance on and before the night is over someone *will* until one of the good-ol'-boy bouncers drags them down. Once a month they have Coyote Ugly karaoke night when women are allowed to parade around up there while dancing and singing and of course this more often than not includes me. Macy, bless her heart, is totally tone deaf but she *is* quite the dancer being a former Hootertown cheerleader and all. We're heading over to a big tub of iced-down longnecks when we spot Luke and Griff. Macy sucks in a big breath and I whisper in her ear to *get a grip*.

"Hello, ladies," Griff says. He smiles but there's something almost tangible in the air between us.

"Can I get y'all a beer?" Luke asks.

We both nod. I must admit that I'm a bit nervous too. We'd been though this same exchange countless times but now that Macy and I have our secret agenda everything is the same and yet completely changed.

There's a sort of weirdness hovering in the air that Luke picks up on because he frowns and says, "Is there something up that we should know about?"

I find his choice of words amusing and almost choke on my beer. I so want to say *not yet,* but Macy gives me a look of warning so I refrain. "I'm thinking about gettin' a dog," I blurt out, successfully changing the subject.

"You don't have a yard," Luke points out.

"That's what I said," Macy chimes in.

Griff frowns at me. "Why do you suddenly want a dog?"

"She says she's lonely," Macy answers for me and I give her an I-could-kill-you glare.

Griff gives me a funny look that I can't read. "Is that so, Jamie Lee?" His eyes narrow a bit and he asks, "Or do you feel the need for some protection for some reason?"

I'm about to vehemently deny my state of loneliness or my need for protection when a sort of a hush falls over the noisy crowd. I look in the direction of the door and in walks Parker Carrington with a blond bombshell who has Luke and Griff staring with their mouths gaping.

Macy leans in and hisses in my ear, "Just who is that hussy?"

"Her name is Jessica something-or-other." I whisper back with my mouth close to Macy's ear. "She's a producer for the movie. Parker's been showing her around town." I glance in Jessica's direction and venture, "Maybe she's nice?"

Macy rolls her eyes. "Pul-ease. Take a look. The woman has *bitch* written all over her."

I think that this is rather unfair on Macy's part but

then again Macy tends to form an instant opinion of skinny women and it's not usually flattering.

As Jessica and Parker make their way toward us I see that she's wearing a flirty floral skirt that will twirl around her legs while she dances. Her blouse is a soft pink that fits snugly in all the right places and shows a good two inches of tanned torso. Macy pokes me with her elbow when we see the glitter of a belly-button diamond.

"Told ya we need one of those," Macy says.

Jessica's hair is her most amazing feature—long, straight, and Paris Hilton blond. She looks as if she's stepped right out of a fashion magazine, leaving me feeling like the redneck hick that I am. This is fine with me until I notice that Griff seems to be quite taken with her Hollywood beauty. My heart feels like it's sinking all the way to my toes.

"Those boobs can't be real." I say this loud enough for Griff to hear but he seems oblivious to my existence. This hurts so much that I wonder why I want to set myself up for another fall.

I paste a smile on my face when Parker and Jessica-the-hussy reach our little circle even though I really want to give her a hard shove. I know that what I'm experiencing is jealousy and it confirms that my feelings for Griff are real but, from the look of things, once again one-sided.

"Hi," Parker says to the group in general. "I'd like to introduce a colleague of mine, Jessica Hanes." He turns to me first and says, "Jessica, this is Jamie Lee Carter."

"Parker's told me a lot about you, Jamie Lee. It's nice

to know that I'll have a place to get my hair done while I'm here in town."

"Hi Jessica." I smile, hating that she seems rather nice, and offer her my hand to shake.

"This is her friend and associate, Macy McCoy," Parker continues.

Macy, minding her manners, shakes Jessica's hand as well, but has a prim little set to her mouth that almost makes me giggle.

Parker hasn't met Luke so I step in. "This is my brother, Luke Carter, and my . . . my *good* friend Griff Sheldon."

Jessica shakes Luke's and then Griff's hand and it may be my imagination but Griff seems to hold her hand a bit longer than necessary or maybe it was the other-way around . . . *whatever,* it's too damned long. Oh, and then she says, "Well, hello, cowboy. Love the hat."

"Uh, thanks," Griff says and he blushes just a bit. Now I'm thinking that *I've* certainly never made Griff blush unless you count the other day when I had my hand caught in his pants but that doesn't count. I have to admit that Griff's hat is pretty sweet. It's a black one and gives him a bit of a bad-boy look. I notice that he hasn't shaved and has sexy dark stubble shadowing his jaw and I have to wonder if it's because of the comment I made while cutting his hair. His teeth flash white in his tanned face and his dimple is so damned cute.

But he's not smiling at me . . . he's smiling at *her.*

Instead of his usual T-shirt, Griff is wearing a Panhandle Slim Western-cut dress shirt in burgundy, tucked into Wrangler boot-cut jeans. The first four pearl snaps are open, giving Jessica a nice view of a tanned chest.

The sleeves are rolled up almost to his elbows, showing off his muscled forearms. I notice that his thumb is bandaged, and I'm about to ask him how it's healing when Jessica beats me to the punch.

"Oh Griff, what happened to your thumb?"

He gives her a shrug. "Banged it with my hammer."

"That had to hurt." She gives him a pout. "Let me buy you a drink to make it feel better."

Griff holds up his beer. "I've got one but I'll be glad to get you whatever you want."

"Well that's an offer I can't refuse," she says with a suggestive grin. I'm beginning to not like her at all. "Deal. Do they make a good appletini here?"

I barely refrain from rolling my eyes at Macy but she's too busy looking at Luke who, like a jackass, is looking at Jessica-the-hussy. Oh why does he go for the Barbie-doll types?

Parker chuckles while shaking his head but it seems to me that he's finding her high-maintenance thing sort of endearing. With a sigh he says, "Jessica . . . let me go—"

"The bartender's a friend," Griff interrupts. "I'll see what I can do." He offers her his arm. "But you'd better come with me because I'm not sure Gus will know how to make your . . . what was it?"

Jessica tucks her slim arm through Griff's and gives him a sultry smile. "An appletini. It's a sour-apple martini. Makes my mouth pucker." Of course she has to pucker her plump, shiny lips for demonstration. "You should try one."

Griff flashes her another dimpled smile and looks at

her from beneath the rim of his hat. "I'd never hear the end of drinkin' one of those girlie drinks."

Parker chimes in saying, "Oh, don't be fooled. Those babies pack quite a punch." He gives Jessica what I think is a don't-overdo-it look.

Jessica turns her pout on Parker for a moment and I swear that something passes between them but she turns on her spiky heel and says to Griff, "Come on, cowboy. I'll give you a taste of mine."

I don't realize that I'm staring after them like a ninny until a moment later when the band starts playing and Luke turns to Macy and asks her to dance. This is a bit startling because Luke isn't usually much on dancing unless he's had one too many. I look at Macy, who is blinking at Luke like she doesn't know what to say. I give her a discreet nudge with my elbow.

"Oh, uh, sure." Macy gives me a bit of a panicked look so I nudge her again and she hands me her beer bottle.

They head off together, leaving me standing there with Parker. I take a sip of my beer and almost sputter when Parker says, "So you're into him after all."

I cough and then ask, "Who?"

Parker shakes his head while giving me a crooked smile. "Your *friend,* Griff."

"There's nothin' between us except friendship, Parker."

"Ah, but you *want* there to be something between you." He's standing close so that I can hear him over the band. To those watching—and believe me there are people watching with interest—we must look like we're having an intimate conversation.

"Am I that doggoned transparent?"

Parker sighs. "To me. I think I made it clear how interested I am in you, Jamie Lee. I even made a trip to Wal-Mart for some . . . uh . . . essentials, so you've got to be up front with me on how you feel about this Griff fellow."

I put my hands to my cheeks. Just when did my simple life get so complicated? Oh yeah, when that silver Jag rolled into town. "Parker—"

"Oh, okay, I think I'm about to get the 'about what happened between us' speech." With another sigh, he says, "I need a beer. You need another one?"

"Sure."

Tapping my foot, I pretend to watch the band while Parker goes after our drinks but I'm really scanning the crowd for Griff and Jessica. I spot them at the end of the bar and sure enough Jessica has a martini glass in her hand. I didn't even know that Dixie's *had* martini glasses. She leans her blond head in close to him and says something that makes him laugh and *then* . . . Griff puts his hat on her head! Now cowboys are particular about their hats so this move is significant in my book. Jessica laughs and strikes a pose for him, making me want to march right over there and put the hat right back on Griff's head where it belongs.

"So, you spotted them, huh?" Parker presses a frosty, wet bottle into my hand.

I don't even try to deny it. "Yeah," I admit glumly. "Looks like they're hittin' it off." Jessica looks so cute in his hat that it totally gripes me. I take a long pull off my beer and then turn away. I have to smile, though, when I see Macy and Luke doing the Texas two-step on the dance floor. Parker sits down on a bar stool at a tall round table and I join him.

"That looks like fun." Parker points his beer bottle at the dance floor. "It seems as if they're gliding."

"The steps are slow, slow, quick, quick. Four steps to six beats of music. Luke can only do the basics."

"Explain the system out there."

"Well, one side of the dance floor is reserved for line dancin'. The other side is for freestyle and the outside circle is for two-steppin'. Under no circumstances are these lines to be crossed. Honky-tonks have their own particular rules of etiquette."

Parker chuckles. "Like what?"

"Well, hard-core line dancers take it very seriously. Don't ever tell locals that they're doin' a dance wrong because every club has their own versions, even of classics like tush push or boot scoot boogie."

Parker takes a drink of his beer and nods. "Go on."

I tap my chin. "Well, *never* take your drink or cigarette onto the dance floor. Let's see, um, don't stay on the floor to chat. Once a song ends exit or start dancin'. Oh, and don't be showin' off for beginners, but by the same token don't go out there and try a dance if you don't know what the hell you're doin', because it messes up the whole rhythm of the dance and some of them are pretty darned complicated. Oh, and here is an important tip: don't ever cross the dance floor to go to the bathroom or the bar or whatever. Always go around, or you could find yourself in an unpleasant situation."

Parker frowns. "How do you learn if you don't go out there and try?"

"You come early for the lessons."

"They have lessons?"

He seems so eager that I have to laugh. "You don't seem like a line-dancin' sorta dude, but then again I notice that you're drinkin' a Bud Light. I would've thought you were a foreign-beer drinker or maybe into fancy cocktails like Jessica."

Parker shrugs those very fine shoulders of his. "When in Rome . . ."

"Ah, so you're gonna ditch that preppy polo, designer jeans, and fancy loafers and get some Wranglers, a Stetson, and some Justin Boots?"

His gaze flicks over to Griff and Jessica. "Maybe I should."

"Oh, okay . . ."

"What? That was a loaded *okay*?"

I scoot my stool a bit closer to his. "So you can catch Jessica's attention, too?"

He twirls the top of his beer bottle between his thumb and middle finger. "That's not what I meant."

"I think it is."

Parker chuckles but squirms a bit. "You've got it all wrong, Jamie Lee. I'm just a bit protective of her. She looks so polished and sophisticated but she's too damned trusting. There's a vulnerable side that not many people see. Sure, Jessica and I are friends and we go back a few years, but that's all. Besides, mixing business with pleasure is a recipe for disaster."

Eyeing him over my beer I have to ask, "So, you've thought about it that much?"

He shrugs. "Maybe once or twice."

"Ha."

"Okay, maybe a few hundred times." He takes a swig

of beer. "Jessica flirts with guys wherever we go. She's not into me at all."

"Maybe she's tryin' to make you jealous?"

"Maybe Griff is trying to make *you* jealous."

"You think? No . . ."

"Who the hell knows?" Parker gives me a slow grin. "I say let's fight fire with fire."

I clink my beer bottle with his. "Now that's the Hootertown spirit. You're catchin' on." I take a long swallow but then have to ask, "Just what do you have in mind?"

"I think we should get cozy, maybe slow dance. What do you say?"

"Macy advised me to play the jealousy card."

"Oh, so you were going to use me?"

I knock my knee with his under the table. "No! I would have spelled it out for you. But since we're on the same page, that's a moot point."

"Let's do this, then. A slow dance is coming on. Are there any rules about slow dancing?"

"No."

"Good."

"Wait a second. I want to polish off my beer so it doesn't get warm."

Parker chuckles but then does the same. I've got a little buzz going from downing my beer so fast. When Parker stands up and offers me his arm I get a sudden rush of nerves. "You don't think this plan might blow up in our faces, do you?"

"No, of course not," he scoffs. "What could possibly go wrong?"

When Wet Willie starts singing a pretty good version

of George Strait's classic hit "If I Know Me," we head
up to the dance floor. I feel everyone's eyes in the place
on me with Parker . . . well everyone's but Griff who is
still chatting up Jessica. They seem oblivious to anything but each other.

I'm hoping that Luke is slow dancing with Macy but
I spot them heading over to where Parker and I were sitting. We sway to the music and I know that before the
song is over my mama will have been informed of my
dance with Parker. Griff and Jessica, however, continue
to ignore us and I'm pissed when I spot Griff taking a
sip of a fresh appletini.

"They're not watchin'," I tell Parker right next to his
ear so as to be heard over Wet Willie's crooning.

"Maybe they just don't see us."

"Dance over that way but slowly so as not to be obvious." I realize that to onlookers it seems as though
Parker and I are whispering sweet nothings in each
other's ears instead of plotting this stupid scenario that
doesn't seem to be working at all. There is one bright
spot, though, when we almost bump into Dinah and
Dirk Dunlettie. I see Dinah look at Parker with longing
and I feel like the belle of the ball. Too bad my Prince
Charming is with another woman.

Not that it's any hardship dancing with Parker. The
man dances like a dream and he smells good enough to
just eat with a spoon. It's kind of fun, too, having all the
women in the joint wishing that they were me. My new-
found glory is diminished, however, when I see Griff
spot us on the dance floor. He gives us only a passing
glance, then turns his attention back to Jessica. She
playfully flips her amazing hair over her shoulder,

knocking off Griff's hat, which she's still wearing. With a giggle she leans down to pick it up and I just know that Griff is eyeballing her cleavage.

"Horse-fuck-pucky," I mumble under my breath.

"What did you just say?"

"I said that this isn't workin'."

"Well, let's step it up a notch."

"To my absolute surprise, Parker lowers his hands from a gentlemanly place at the small of my back . . . *to my ass!* I'm about to tell him to remove his hands, not because I mind, really, but because Rose Jenkins is eyeing me with she's-at-it-again horror and I just know that one of my mama's friends is speed-dialing her with the news that Mr. Hollywood has his hands on her daughter's ass in front of God and the good people of Hootertown, the latter being the most important. I refrain because I finally have Griff's attention . . . uh, make that a glare of disapproval.

"Griff looks pissed," I tell Parker. "That's a good thing, right?"

"That's the plan. You don't think he's going to kick my ass, do you?" Parker says this with a joking inflection, but I'm not one hundred percent sure that this won't occur. "Uh, Jamie Lee, you haven't answered my question."

"Well, I don't think so."

"Not that I'm worried. I'm in pretty good shape," he assures me as we dance.

"Oh, I know you could hold your own." I bite back a chuckle. Guys are all the same, whether they're from L.A. or Hootertown. They might come in different packages but deep down they're all cut from the same cloth. Although Parker is in amazing shape, I seriously doubt that he's ever thrown a punch. While Griff isn't much of a fighter, I've seen him get into a few scuffles, mostly to come to Luke's aid during his dark days when his football career ended and his girlfriend dumped him and Luke was just spoiling for a fight. Yeah, Griff most definitely can throw a punch. I decide that we'd better not push the issue so I decline another dance with Parker.

On our way back to the table Irma Baker gives me a thumbs up and mouths, "You go, girl," as I pass by her table of rowdy senior-citizen friends which is sort of like the Hootertown version of the Red Hat Ladies. I have to shake my head when I hear Irma's gruff shout for a round of purple hooter shooters for the silver-haired posse.

"Oh my God." Parker jumps about a foot in the air.

"What?"

"One of those ladies pinched me on the butt!"

"I'm not surprised." We turn to look at Irma's group in time to see them high-five and I have to giggle. My mood is lifted a bit as we weave our way back to our table and I find myself singing along with Wet Willie who is belting out "Save A Horse, Ride a Cowboy." Of course just about everyone else is singing along as well, making Parker laugh while shaking his shaggy head.

Macy and Luke are discussing cheerleading . . . well, make that *Macy* is talking about cheerleading and Luke is listening, but he seems interested, nodding his head and interjecting a question now and then. I see Parker scanning the room and I give him an elbow and say,

"Don't look for them. Let's just have some fun. Hey, you want to ride the mechanical bull?"

Parker's eyebrows shoot up and he grins. "They have one of those here like in the movie *Urban Cowboy*?"

I jab my thumb over my shoulder. "Over there is the billiards room and the bull is over in the far corner."

"Have you ever ridden it?"

I flash him a grin. "Now, just what do you think?"

Parker laughs and I think to myself how much I like this guy.

"Hey," says Macy when she sees me grab Parker's hand. "Where y'all goin'?"

"To ride the bull."

Macy frowns. "Aw, Jamie Lee, the last time you rode that sucker you hurt your neck and couldn't cut hair for a week."

I give her a look. "Macy, I was challenged by Dinah Dunlettie. I simply had no choice in the matter."

Parker tugs on my hand. "Hey, you don't have to do this. I don't want you to get hurt."

Luke chimes in and says, "Jamie Lee, I smell disaster."

I wave a dismissive hand at them all. "What are y'all worryin' about? It's mechanical, not the real deal. I'll tell Bubba to go easy on me. Really, I will. Now come on, you bunch of wussies."

We're heading in the direction of the billiard room when a sultry voice stops us all in our tracks. "Hey, where are you guys going?"

We all turn around to see Jessica and Griff directly behind us. Although Jessica's no longer wearing Griff's hat, her arm is linked with his and she's leaning into him so that her breast is pushing against his bicep. I, on the other hand, am holding Parker's hand, which makes me feel like a schoolgirl. Griff has the grace to look a bit embarrassed when our gazes lock but makes no move to disengage his sorry self. His gaze then travels to where my fingers are entwined with Parker's. Something flickers in his eyes that makes me want to tell him that Parker is just a friend who will soon go back to L.A. and forget all about me. But just when I think that Griff is jealous, he turns his attention to Jessica and my heart feels like it was just snapped with a rubber band. As if sensing my distress Parker squeezes my hand and I have this stupid urge to cry.

Macy, bless her heart, breaks the sudden silence. "We gonna ride that bull or not?"

I grin over at her. Macy wouldn't ride the bull unless she had a gun to her head and even then she would probably talk her way out of it. Macy tends to be all talk while I tend to be all action. She raises one eyebrow and I just know that she has a devious plan in mind. "Hell yeah," I say, "let's do it!"

12

Desperate and Dateless

"Aw, it's kind of cute," Jessica says as we lean against the orange railings that separate the mechanical bull from the rest of the pool hall. Wet Willie's Barnyard Band's next song drifts into the room, accompanied by the sound of balls smacking together. Parker smiles over at Jessica but she's looking up at Griff. "I'm going to ride. How do you sign up?"

"Jessica . . . maybe you should just watch," Parker warns her.

"You know me better than that." She wrinkles up her nose at him and flips her amazing hair over her shoulder.

Griff points to the mechanical bull anchored to the floor by a big pole that spins and whips in a pretty accurate imitation of the real thing. "Parker has a point, Jessica."

She waves a French-manicured hand in his direction. "Yes, but look, the floor is cushy. Even if you fall you can't get hurt. It looks like a big balloon."

Macy shakes her head. "Oh come on boys, let Jessica have some fun. I'll go sign her up . . . my treat."

Luke remains silent but gives me a disapproving shake of his head while Macy goes over to Bubba Baker, who happens to be Irma's twin brother. A grin lights up Bubba's weathered face while Macy pays for Jessica to ride.

While Parker and Griff try to talk Jessica out of the whole thing, Luke comes over next to me. "Just what the hell are you two cookin' up?"

"Nothin'." This *is* the truth. I really don't know what Macy is up to so I'm really innocent thus far even though I've made no attempt to stop whatever Macy's doing and I'm guessing she's telling Bubba to give Jessica a wild ride. "I didn't drag Jessica over here or anything. She's the one who wants to do this so who am I to stop her?"

Luke narrows his eyes like he doesn't quite buy my story but then grins. "Whatever, little sis. I'm just gonna sit back and watch."

I angle my head to where Parker and Griff are *now* giving Jessica instructions about how to ride the bull. "She sure has Griff turned inside out. How come you're not over there fawning over her?"

"She's a looker all right but I've had my fill of high-maintenance women."

I see my opening and pounce. "You and Macy sure looked good out there two-steppin'."

"Don't go gettin' any ideas, Jamie Lee. I was just bein' polite."

This comment is disappointing and I'm not quite buying it but I don't want to appear pushy so I simply nod. Macy gives Bubba a wink and then comes our way. Luke and I look at her expectantly.

"I signed you up, too, Jamie Lee."

"What?"

"Just trust me."

I barely suppress a shudder. Whenever Macy utters those three little words disaster strikes like lightning to a tree. I don't have time to ponder the matter or ask any more questions because Bubba calls Jessica's name to come on down and ride.

With a delighted little squeal, Jessica scampers over to the gate . . . yes, *scampers*, there is just no other way to describe it. She nods while Bubba gives her instructions and then heads into the ring. Bubba cups his hands for Jessica to step into them and hoists her up onto the big bull. Macy and I exchange a guilty look but then I notice a big crowd of guys who were previously content to play pool come over to the ring. This is kind of early for bull riding since it's usually the sort of thing that happens after you've had a few drinks and are feeling bulletproof, but Jessica sitting atop the big bull with her floral skirt hiked up to her ass is creating quite a stir. Griff, Parker, and even Luke are glued to the sight.

My guilt evaporates and Macy and I exchange a wicked grin. "Bubba's gonna throw her, right?"

Macy nods. "I gave him a big tip to give her one helluva ride. You, on the other hand will look lovely . . . graceful even, as you ride at a much slower pace."

The bull starts spinning in a circle while bucking a bit. Jessica has one hand in the air as per her instructions to help her balance while holding on with the other. Macy and I exchange a what's-up-with-this glance when the bull continues to move in what seems like slow motion. Jessica smiles and waves while the guys in the crowd whistle and applaud like she's performing some incredible feat. Luke joins in on the whistling and I jab him in the side with my elbow.

"Did you tell Bubba to go *easy* on her?" I hiss onto Macy's ear. "The penny horse at Meijer goes faster than this!"

"No, of course not. I already told you that I gave him an extra five dollars for him to shake her like a Polaroid and to go easy on—" The rest of Macy's comment is lost in the roar of the crowd as Jessica gracefully dismounts the bull and gives them a beauty-queen wave.

And then my name is called.

I have the whole situation figured out when the bull starts whipping me around so fast that the crowd is just a blur. I realize that Bubba got his wires crossed. To my credit, I hang in there while the bull bucks and turns me every which way but loose. It's pretty much out of sheer terror. I've done this bull thing before but never at this warp speed and never while sober. At one point my hat goes flying off my head and the crowd starts cheering for me! *Hey, this is pretty cool after all.* I must look like quite the expert next to Jessica's wimpy little show. I feel like I'm getting my groove on—buck and spin, buck and spin, buck and spin . . . I let out a whoop and I'm rewarded with a cheer from the crowd but just when I'm feeling all confident and cocky the damned thing swings sharply in the opposite direction and does this really high buck that sends me flying over the horns and onto the floor so hard that even the cushy padding can't keep the air from leaving my lungs in a whoosh when I crash-land with a loud splat. The two beers I've consumed swish like a tidal wave in my stomach and threaten to come up. I swallow hard and pray that I don't upchuck right here in front of everyone.

The cheering crowd does a collective gasp and then groan . . . oh wait, that's me groaning. I'm dimly aware of Griff hopping the fence and then kneeling down beside me on the blue cushy floor that still really hurts when you hit it.

"You okay?"

"Well, hell no," I try to answer but can only wheeze. I also realize that I'm lying there with my arms and legs spread out like I'm ready to do a snow angel except I couldn't flap around if my life depended on it.

"Can you get up?" He asks this gently and I'm thinking that maybe this fiasco might still work to my advantage. I'm pondering whether to milk this or act like I'm fine even though I'm not quite sure if I'm fine. My voice still won't work so I nod even though I don't really know if I *can* get up. Bubba has the nerve to come over and peer down at me and I really feel like flipping him the bird but I don't.

Griff offers his hand and helps to tug me to my feet. He bends over to retrieve my hat and puts it back on my head and the crowd cheers. I give them a weak little wave of my fingers and bounce over the cushy flooring with Griff's arm around my waist.

Everyone is looking at me all bug-eyed, so I try to give them all a reassuring smile but it wobbles a bit at the corners.

"That was amazing," Jessica says but has a look of concern on her face. I suddenly feel like a real jerk since

this could have been done to her. I know that this was
Macy's doing, but she often acts without thinking and I
knew what she was up to and did nothing to stop her, so
in effect I got what I deserved.

Parker looks concerned too. "You look a bit shaken,
Jamie Lee. Would you like me to take you home?"

I nod but I can feel Griff stiffen. "My truck's parked
close. I'll take her home."

Macy looks so upset that I dig deep and muster up a
smile. "You stay and have some fun. I'm fine, really.
Parker, you should stay too and keep Jessica company. I
don't want to see everybody's night end early on ac-
count of me." I turn to Luke and say, "Macy and I
walked. You see her home safely, okay?"

Luke nods. "Sure thing."

Griff's arm stays around my waist and I don't protest
since I'm still feeling a bit shaky. It helps once we're
out in the fresh air. I suck in a big gulp of sultry-but-
sweet night breeze and Griff tightens his hold on me as
we head over to his truck. Now that I can breathe I'm
feeling a bit better and able to enjoy leaning against
Griff.

"You're limping," Griff says with concern but I detect something else in his tone, too.

"Oh, I guess I twisted my ankle a tad."

"You want me to carry you?"

"Oh, I . . . *no*," I protest, but I'm so flustered by the
thought of him carrying me that I stumble in the clunky
gravel.

"Well, too bad because I am." He scoops me up in his
arms. I'm relieved when he doesn't grunt or anything.

Looping my arms around his neck I protest rather weakly. "Griff, I can walk."

"Stop squirimin'."

"I thought your truck was close."

He shrugs. "It's not too far."

But it is . . . almost to the edge of where the gravel turns to grass. He carries me seemingly without effort and of course I'm wishing I could bury my face in the crook of his neck. He smells so good that I groan.

"You okay?"

Embarrassed, I say, "Yeah, my ankle is throbbin' a bit."

"We're almost there."

Well damn.

"Here we are," he says when we reach his pickup. It's a beat-up black Chevy Silverado given to him by his daddy right before he died of lung cancer going on ten years ago. Griff and Luke just keep patching the truck together because Griff can't bear to part with it. After opening the door Griff gently puts me on the seat and heads over to the driver's side.

With a flip of his wrist he starts the engine. "You have to open the window. Air's on the blink."

"I like the night breeze anyway so it doesn't matter."

"I figured as much." He nods and then goes all quiet on me until we reach the Cut & Curl just minutes later. He pulls into the driveway and kills the engine and I'm about to ask him up for a beer, hoping that he'll stay instead of heading back to Dixie's, but he's got this firm set to his mouth that screams trouble. I wish I could see his eyes but the top half of his face is shadowed by his cowboy hat.

"So are you goin' to tell me just why you pulled that stunt back there?"

"What stunt?"

"Riding that bull like you were goin' for the PBR National Championship. Were you that desperate to impress that Parker fellow?"

"D-*desperate*?" I sputter.

"Oh, come on, Jamie Lee. You had Bubba give Jessica a tame pony ride so you could show off."

I swallow the hurt squeezing my throat. "So you think you have me all figured out, huh, Griff?"

Tipping his hat back he chuckles without humor. "Come on, it was pretty damned obvious."

"Is that right." See, here is when I wish I had the courage to tell him what really happened and how I really feel but I'm too afraid so I resort to anger. "I'm outta here."

Griff puts a hand on my arm. "Now, don't go gettin' all pissed. I just don't want to see you get hurt. Even if this guy films the movie here in Hootertown, he'll eventually leave, Jamie Lee. You're just settin' yourself up for a fall. Can't you see that?"

"Yeah well I've been there, done that, and bought the T-shirt. I'm not going to make that mistake again. Go on back to Dixie's. Sorry to have cramped your style." I wrench my arm free and yank on the door handle.

"Jamie Lee! Let me help you up the stairs."

"I'm fine!" I toss over my shoulder but he's already getting out of the truck. I hurry to try to get a jump on him out the door but of course I have to humiliate myself further by stepping down on my tender ankle which lands my ass on the sidewalk. "Ouch! Dammit!" is my

very loud, very unladylike response. Of course Rose
Jenkins just happens to be taking out the trash and hears
me plain as day and does this little tisk-tisk thing with
her tongue. I swear she has a Jamie Lee Carter radar that
shows her how to find me in my least becoming moments, this being right up there at the top of the list.

"You okay?" Griff asks for the second time in less
than thirty minutes.

"I'm fine!" Slapping his hand away I push up to my
feet. My ankle hurts but I think I can force myself to
walk like it doesn't. "You can leave now." *Jessica might
be missing you,* I want to add but that might make him
think I'm jealous so I point to his truck. "Go!"

"Quit being a baby."

"Quit being a jerk!"

"I'm helpin' you up those stairs."

"The hell you say!" To prove my point, which is another tactical error on my part, I grit my teeth and start
walking. Step, hurt, step hurt, step hurt. The side stairs
leading up to my apartment look like Mount Everest.

"You're limping, Jamie Lee. Let me help you up the
damned steps before you fall and break your neck."
He's standing right behind me, making me want to lean
my weight against him. Would he wrap his arms around
me if I did?

Pivoting on my good foot, I push at his chest. "I don't
need or want your help."

Griff grabs my wrists. "What the hell has gotten into
you? I'm just being a friend."

Closing my eyes I swallow and say softly, "Yeah, I
know." A friend.

Clearly confused at my behavior, Griff frowns, and

I'm feeling that all is lost, but then his gaze lingers on my mouth. For a heart-pounding moment I think he's gonna kiss me. I hold my breath when he leans closer . . . just a fraction. I feel this more than see it when he inches even closer and then closer still. I wet my lips with my tongue, wanting them to be moist . . . but just like that he straightens up and takes a quick step backwards.

Instead of a kiss I get disappointment slapping me in the face. Thinking that it will forever be this way with Griff, I turn back towards the steps.

Forever is a long damned time.

Disappointment has a way of pissing me off so of course I plan on stomping up the steps which isn't a good idea with a twisted ankle but I've totally forgotten that my ankle is tender since I'm too busy dwelling on how I love Griff and he doesn't love me back. I stomp with my right foot but when my left foot hits the step pain shoots up my calf and my knee sort of gives out.

Griff saves me from a fall by hooking his arm about my waist but then he has to go and ruin his kind gesture by saying, "Dammit, Jamie Lee! Let me help."

"I don't want your help." I bump him sideways with my hip but his arm remains firmly hooked around my waist.

"Knock it off or I'm gonna toss you over my shoulder like a sack of feed."

"You just try it!" As soon as the words are out of my mouth I know it's the wrong thing to say. A nanosecond later I'm swept off my feet and hefted over his shoulder. "Hey, my hat fell off!"

"Too bad." He starts up the steps.

"Put me down . . . you . . . you . . ." I can't think of a word vile enough to call him so I decide to pound him on the back with my fists.

"Stop it, Jamie Lee."

Of course I only pound harder, provoking him to smack me on my jeans-clad ass. "Put. Me. Down!" I shout.

"Hush, or Ms. Jenkins will call Sheriff Cooper."

Of course this shuts me up.

"Where's your key?" he asks when we reach the top landing.

"It's unlocked."

"You shouldn't go off leavin' your place unlocked."

"Crime is scarce in Hootertown, Griff, although this might qualify as . . . as . . . assault and battery!" Ignoring me, he fumbles with the doorknob, which tends to stick when the air gets humid. Meanwhile the blood is going to my head. "That's it, I'm callin' Sheriff Cooper and tellin' him to toss you in the slammer. He's related, you know. I can and will have this done. Where's my cell . . . oh yeah in my purse." I twist around to try and get my purse, which is dangling behind me.

"Hold still!" Griff orders and finally gets the door to pop open, sending us into my kitchen sort of off balance. It's dark inside except for the moonlight streaming in the windows but he knows his way around and heads into the living room toward the couch.

Releasing his hold over my upper thighs he shifts my weight and eases me slowly off of his shoulder—I'm guessing so I don't land hard on my ankle. I put my hands on his shoulders for balance and his hands are spanning my waist and I'm thinking that surely he's gotta be feeling *something* of what I'm feeling as I slide downward. I try to sneak a peek at his face but his black hat hides his eyes. This is sort of irritating so I snap, "Put me down already."

"I can't. We're stuck."

13

Oops, I Did It Again

"What?" I try to wiggle away but the thin leather strap connecting the silver medallions on my concho belt has looped over his big, round, silver belt buckle. "Lift me up higher," I suggest but we're still caught. "The leather must somehow be hooked on the back of your buckle."

"What the hell . . ." he growls, as if this is my fault! "My arms are getting tired, Jamie Lee."

"Sorry to be such a load. I *am* on Macy's low-carb diet."

"I didn't mean it that way."

"Sure you didn't." I wiggle and fiddle with the belt but it's difficult since we're sort of intimately connected and rubbing together and such, making me more than a little flustered.

"Come on!"

"I'm tryin'! Back up and sit down on the couch."

With an exasperated sigh he sits down. I have to straddle him as I reach between our bodies to try to unhook my thin belt from his big buckle. "Suck in your gut so I can get my fingers behind the buckle where it's caught."

"I don't have a gut." My boobs, which are sort of squished in his face, muffle his protest. "Good God," he says in a sort of strangled voice.

"Your damned hat is in my way."

He tosses it to the floor. "There."

I slide my fingers behind the silver buckle. "I can't figure out how it's hooked." Of course my fingers are fumbling a bit because although I'm trying to concentrate, the fact that Griff's face is up close and very personal with my boobs has me a bit distracted. The moist warmth of his breath permeates the thin cotton of my tank top. His mouth is dangerously close to my nipple, which is threatening to pop over the edge of my bra because of all my damned wiggling coupled with the angle of my upper body. I'm getting a bit hot and bothered, which is making me more than a little frustrated. "Damn it all to hell!" I pull my hand out, deciding that I need to come at this thing from a new angle, and I cop a major feel. Apparently I'm not the only one getting all hot and bothered. "Sorry!"

"It's an involuntary reaction," he says through gritted teeth. "Just like the last time."

This really pisses me off. "Gettin' my hand stuck in your pocket wasn't my fault, and neither was this! So sorry to keep turnin' you on."

"You're not turnin' me on!"

"Yeah, well right back at ya!" I yank and wiggle and *oh God* both my nipples pop over the edge of my bra. Judging by his sharp intake of breath Griff is privy to this new development in our predicament. Not turned on, my ass.

"Stop. You're making it worse."

I'm not sure if he means the hooked-together belts or my exposed nipples or our collective state of denied arousal in general.

"Calm down and let *me* try."

Now, just why is it that men think that they always have the answers? "Go for it."

Griff slides both hands between our bodies and fiddles with the big buckle. "Ah, so there's the problem. Your leather strap is caught up underneath where my buckle connects to my belt. There's a hook there."

I already knew this. "So now what?"

"I don't know." He wiggles and pulls downward. "It's sort of jammed tight from all the tugging."

"I hear blame in your tone."

"You hear frustration. I can't believe we've managed to do this. I mean"—he tugs hard—"what are the odds that we'd get connected like this again?"

Kismet? Fate? Full moon rising? Maybe the odds are in our favor, Griff. Of course I'm too much of a wimp to say what I'm thinking. "I dunno, a million to one?"

"Okay, don't take this the wrong way but I'm gonna have to flip you over to your back. That way I can get some leverage to tug the leather free."

Oh, heaven forbid that I should take his intentions the wrong way. "Okay."

"Here we go."

Griff eases up and moves me over to my back. Bracing his hands on either side of my shoulders he says, "I'm gonna sort of jerk my hips upward. . . ."

"I know, I know, *don't* take it the wrong way. Gotcha."

But when Griff rocks his hips sharply it's so sensual that I really want to move in the rhythm with him. Fisting my hands against the couch cushions I try to suppress the longing generated by his *accidental* erection rubbing against me.

"Jamie Lee," he says in a gruff kind of breathless voice. "Try to get a hold on your belt and pull downward while I tug upward, okay?"

Huh? What? "Oh, sure . . ." I hold, he tugs once, twice, and God help me I'm getting so worked up that I think I might . . .

"Whoa!" Griff shouts as we go tumbling off the couch and onto the floor, rolling twice, almost taking out an end table before coming to a stop with me on top of him. Still connected at the waist, we're nose to nose and Griff says, "God, I'm sorry. Are you *okay*?"

"I'm gonna have bruises in strange places but yeah, I think so."

"This is completely insane," he growls and yanks at the belt.

This sort of ticks me off. "Sorry about your luck."

Griff leans his head against the floor. "I realize that most guys would be takin' advantage of the situation, Jamie Lee."

"Doesn't it get kind of boring being such a saint?"

A couple of heartbeats tick by. "Yeah, come to think of it." Threading his long fingers through my hair he raises his mouth to mine. The touch of his lips sends a jolt of heat singing through my veins. Opening my mouth, I offer him more. His mouth is so hot; his lips are so soft and yet firm ... demanding. When his tongue touches mine I moan as pent-up passion explodes in an open-mouthed kiss that is so intense, so deep that my mind reels. When he traces my bottom lip with his tongue I shiver and then melt against the solid length of his body.

I'm about to tell him that the kiss rocked my world and that we should explore these feelings further ... like in my bed, but I can feel the tense set of his shoulders and there's this little muscle ticking in his jaw.

"I'm sorry, Jamie Lee. I lost my head."

"Another involuntary reaction?"

"I'm only human. You goaded me into it."

I feel as if he's slapped me. "I'm not seventeen this time, Griff. I know I made you feel guilty as hell when I threw myself at you back then and we almost . . . you know. It was a mistake then and it was a mistake tonight. Mama always said I had to learn the hard way."

"Jamie Lee . . ."

"I will *never* throw myself at you or goad you or any of that stuff ever again." I tug hard on my belt but of course the leather is way too strong to snap. "How the hell are we goin' to get apart? Huh?" I wiggle and tug like a crazy person.

"Stop!"

"Go to hell!"

"We're going to have to get a knife and cut through the leather."

"I paid a hundred bucks for this belt."

"I'll get you a new one."

"I don't want anything from you *ever* again. Never

not in a million years ever . . ." I swallow hard so I don't start crying.

"Jamie Lee . . ."

"And you can get your hair cut at the mall."

"Don't do this."

I think about telling him to go to hell again but I just know that my voice will crack and I'll start crying.

"We're going to have to get out to your kitchen so we can get a knife."

"We're not gonna ruin my belt!"

"We're out of options."

Of course I know this but I feel the need to be difficult.

"We're gonna have to get up and make our way into the kitchen. Think you can do that?"

"Well, as you said, we're out of options."

"I'm . . . I'm gonna have to sit up so you'll have to straddle my waist and then I'll stand."

Oh goody. More humiliation.

"Then I want you to wrap your legs around me and I'll carry you to the kitchen."

"No way. You're not gonna carry me. I'm walkin'."

After drawing in a deep breath and then exhaling, he says, "Given your twisted ankle and the fact that we are connected at the waist, that would be a tad difficult."

My answer is a growl.

He sits up and I do as instructed trying to ignore the fact that I'm wrapped around him like a rubber band and his hands are cradling my ass as we head to the kitchen to ruin my favorite belt. We both blink when I flip on the overhead light. "There is a really sharp paring knife in the top drawer, or you can try scissors."

He pulls open the drawer and takes out the paring knife. "I think this will do the job."

I wince when he slices through the side of my belt and then tugs the leather and silver medallions through my belt loops. He sets me down and takes a step back looking a bit goofy with my belt dangling from his buckle. After unhooking his own belt he works the thin strap from the back of his buckle. "Sorry," he says and hands me my ruined belt. "It was really jammed in there."

I shrug.

"Where'd you get the belt?"

"I ordered it online, and you're not gonna buy me a new one. It wasn't your fault."

There's a moment of uneasy silence.

"Let's get some ice on your ankle."

I shake my head. "I can take care of myself, Griff. I'm really tired so you can go on about your business. Why don't you just head on back to Dixie's? The night is still pretty young."

"I don't mind stayin'."

I swallow thinking that this statement is so much different from "I want to stay." Mustering up what I hope is close enough to a smile, I say, "I'll be fine."

"Let me just get an ice pack . . ."

"I'll be *fine*, Griff. I'm going to change into some sweats and a big old T-shirt first, anyway." I do a shooing with my fingers. "Go and enjoy your Saturday night."

He hesitates. "Jamie Lee . . . we exchanged some words. . . ."

"Forget about it."

Of course the kiss isn't mentioned but it's hanging there in the air. I'm still feeling a bit emotional about the episode and there's still the very real danger that I'll burst into tears at any given moment, so I say more firmly this time, "Go, Griff."

He nibbles on his lip for a moment like he wants to say something. I hold my breath and wait but he finally just nods and then says quietly, "Okay. I'll let myself out but you lock the door behind me."

I roll my eyes but then nod.

After he leaves I hobble to my bedroom and change into some Payton Panthers sweats. My ankle is a little swollen but not too bad. Hobbling back into the kitchen I grab a bag of frozen peas and then locate a bottle of water from the fridge and head into the living room to watch some television, trying not to feel sorry for myself, but as soon as I sit down on the couch I burst into noisy tears. In between hiccups and sobs I mumble things like "I'm so pathetic" and "I hate my life" and other similar thoughts. I remember that Griff had called me desperate . . . *desperate* and I'm not even a housewife . . . just desperate and dateless.

"Jamie Lee?" I squeal and jump about a foot off of the couch when Parker's deep voice interrupts me wallowing in my misery. "I'm sorry, but when you didn't answer the door I got worried and since it was open I took the liberty of coming in. I hope you'll forgive my boldness. I found your hat lying outside . . . you know you should really lock your door . . . hey, have you been crying?"

"No." I try to smile but fail.

"Yes you have." His eyes narrow. "I found this lying

on the floor." He holds up my ruined belt. "Has that cowboy done something to hurt you?"

"No." My voice resembles the croak of a frog.

"Hogwash. Now tell me what happened. If that cowboy hurt you, I'll kick his ass into next week."

"Hogwash?" I croak. My laugh makes me sound like I'm underwater. "Kick his ass into next week? You sound like you're from Hootertown except for that uppity accent that would be really annoying if you didn't have that deep sexy voice."

"Did he hurt you, Jamie Lee?"

I sigh. "Not physically. Griff would rather cut off his arm than ever raise a hand to a woman."

"But he hurt you, somehow."

"Not on purpose. It's a long story."

"I've got all night."

"What about Jessica?"

"Jet lag and appletinis caught up with her. I took her back to the Inn but I wanted to check up on you."

"Thanks, but I'm okay."

"Hogwash."

I have to giggle. He has me feeling better already. "You're learnin' redneck-ese, but your accent needs some work."

Parker folds his long frame into my easy chair and rests his arms on his knees. "I spent so much time in foreign countries with my mother that I always tried to pick up the local lingo in an effort to fit in. I don't think it ever really worked for me." He crooks one eyebrow. "So you think my voice is sexy?"

"Incredibly. Everything about you is sexy. Surely you must know that."

He shrugs those wide shoulders of his and then runs his fingers through his hair. "I was always such a fish out of water everywhere I lived and a bit on the geeky side to make matters worse. Tall and gangly, always with a camera in my hand."

I grin. "Well, you've filled out quite nicely."

"You're shifting the focus away from yourself, Jamie Lee. Enough about me. Now tell me . . . what happened to make you cry?"

I give Parker an abbreviated version of how my concho belt got hooked behind Griff's belt buckle, but enough information for him to get the gist of the situation. After a long sigh, I say, "You'd think the whole thing would have helped my cause, but Griff will never think of me as anything other than Luke's little sister. See, we have sort of a history that he can't quite get past."

Angling his head, Parker says, "Go on."

I rearrange the frozen peas on my ankle and then begin, "Well, when I was a junior in high school, there was this field party that I shouldn't have been at, but that never seemed to stop me. My brother Luke always made it his duty to keep an eye on me, but he was off at college, so the burden fell onto Griff's shoulders."

"What's a field party?"

I grin. "A whole bunch of pickup trucks out in a big grass field parked in a circle with iced-up coolers full of beer. There's usually a bonfire or two and kids makin' out on blankets. This particular night was a Payton College frat party, and when Griff got wind of me bein' there, he showed up to drag me home. I was pretty tipsy and I made this move on Griff . . . who was twenty at the time and I was seventeen. I had crushed on him all my life, and since I finally had boobs, I figured I'd give it a shot."

"What happened?"

I shrugged. "Griff had been at a party that night, too, and was a little lit up as well. I flirted, managed to get him to kiss me and suddenly we were sheddin' our clothes. If Griff hadn't come to his senses at the last minute and pulled back . . . well, we would have gone all the way. He was appalled and disgusted with himself. No one knows of this except Macy so keep it on the down low." When he nods, I continue, "Griff's never quite forgiven himself when what happened that night was really all my doin'."

"Have the two of you ever discussed this?"

I give Parker a shake of my head. "It sort of came up recently, but no, we've never discussed that night openly. For a while Griff avoided me, but we became close friends over the years, especially through some hard times. His daddy died of cancer and then my daddy had his heart trouble and we were there for each other. God, and then when Luke's football career ended and that bitch dumped him and Luke went off the deep end, Griff pretty much dragged him back home. Other than Macy, Griff's been my best friend and I guess in some ways I'm scared of losing that too."

"I hear a big 'but' in that last statement."

"But the thought of him with another woman makes me crazy. And God help me, that man's kisses make me go weak in the knees." Putting my hands to my cheeks I say, "Good Lord, I'm givin' you way too much information."

"Jamie Lee, your honesty and your candor are what I like most about you. Don't ever change that," he says, leaning forward in the chair. "But you never did tell me exactly why you were crying."

I nibble on my lip for a moment.

"You can tell me," he assures me. "Nothing you say to me will go further than this room."

"I feel like you're my therapist."

"You're beating around the bush. Spill."

"Well, Macy is of the opinion that I need to get Griff's boots under my bed so I can find out once and for all if he will rock my world. She thinks I need to find out if this is just an infatuation."

"His boots under your bed?" He chuckles and says, "I've never heard it put that way before."

"I just don't know if I can make that happen and if I do and it doesn't work out then will we ever be able to go back to bein' friends? And what if he rocks my world but I don't rock his? Wouldn't *that* just suck? And what if—"

"Whoa, hold the phone," Parker says with his hands up in the air. "I think that you'll have to agree that there's nothing in life worth having that doesn't involve a bit of a risk. Yeah, you might risk your friendship, but, Jamie Lee, is that what you want from Griff? To be his buddy?"

"Well . . ."

"Yes or no."

"No."

"Well then, if you're asking my opinion, I think you need to stop messing around and just go for it."

"But what if—"

"Jamie Lee, believe me, there's no way you're not going to rock that cowboy's world."

"Ya think?"

"I'd be willing to bet the farm."

I find myself frowning. "Yeah, well, after what happened tonight Griff will be avoiding me. I just don't see any way to make it happen."

Parker runs his fingers through his hair. "Hmmm, well, you were telling me that you wanted to add tanning beds to your shop, right?"

"Yeah . . . oh, I get it. I need to hire Griff. Yeah, but he's busy puttin' on a deck for Irma Baker."

"Perfect. Tell him you've ordered the beds so you have to have the stalls built right away. Offer to let him work after hours and then you need to find reasons to be in the shop while he works and basically drive him crazy. Wear those little cutoff shorts, tiny tank tops, and do a lot of bending over."

I laugh so hard that the frozen peas fall off of my foot. "You are so bad. Do you think I can pull this off?"

Parker gives me a slow smile. "I have no doubt." He stands up and comes over to kiss me on top of the head. "I've got to go back and work on my presentation to your city council. Jessica loves Hootertown as much as I do and we really want to film the movie here. Do you think we'll have much opposition? I know that there are those in this town who think I'm a Hollywood hotshot up to no good, especially where you're concerned."

I have to chuckle. "There's no doubt that you've created quite a stir in this sleepy little town. Nothin's been quite the same since you arrived with your flashy silver

Jag, but I think it was about time we had a bit of a wake-up call."

"I'm not usually one to get things stirred up."

"Well, it's too late for that. Hey, would you like to come over to my mama and daddy's farm for lunch tomorrow? She always cooks up her famous fried chicken and buttermilk biscuits after church. You can bring Jessica. I hate to admit this, but even though she shamelessly flirted with Griff, I kind of like her."

"Thanks for the offer, but we really do have piles of paperwork to do."

"I understand. If you change your mind, call me for directions. Mama always has an abundance of food."

"Thanks. I will. Good night, Jamie Lee."

"'Night, Parker."

After Parker leaves I get ready for bed thinking that I might as well get a good night's sleep, but of course Macy calls to see how my ankle is feeling just when I've snuggled underneath the covers. She happens to find the belt incident with Griff amusing even though I try to explain to her that the whole thing was quite an emotional event, not to mention that my belt is ruined.

"I'm sorry, Jamie Lee," she says in between guffaws. I'm just picturin' the whole thing. What I wouldn't have given to have been a fly on the wall."

When I get to the part where I accidentally cop a feel Macy laughs so hard that she drops the phone. It occurs to me that she might have been drinking but I politely refrain from asking.

"Macy," I shout, "get a grip on your person and listen. Griff called me desperate."

"What!?"

"You heard me. He thought that my faster-than-the-speed-of-light bull ride was a desperate attempt to make myself look impressive to Parker."

"You didn't divulge the real plan, did you?"

"Of course not. That really was desperate, not to mention mean."

"It seemed like a good idea at the time," Macy says as if this is a good defense.

"Macy, girl, if I had a dollar for every time you've said that we could buy us a Harley or something just as sweet."

"Oh, shut up."

"You damned well know it's true."

"I didn't mean that skinny Jessica chick any real harm and you know it."

I sigh and say, "Yeah, I know."

"So Griff called you desperate, did he?"

"Yessiree."

"Well, then I guess he's just gonna get a taste of what a couple of desperate rednecks can throw at him, and let's just say that he'd better duck and run. You got any ideas?"

I think about Parker's suggestion, and chuckle. "Yeah, but it'll have to wait until tomorrow. My wild bull ride has left me too tired to go into it now."

"You gotta be kiddin'. You're actually gonna make me wait?"

"I'll tell you after church services."

"You're killin' me here."

I yawn so wide my jaw pops. "Talk to ya tomorrow."

"Jamie Lee! Have a heart!"

"'Night, Macy."

14

Desperate Rednecks

Sunday chicken after church is a weekly event that I rarely miss and usually start thinking about halfway through Reverend Jacobs's sermon when my mind begins to wander. It's not that he isn't a good preacher; it's just that I tend to be a bit of a daydreamer. On this particular Sunday my stomach is already grumbling with hunger pangs a couple of booming sentences into the sermon. Mama gives me a disapproving narrowing of her eyes beneath the brim of her lavender hat, as if I can control the growling of my poor empty tummy. Unfortunately, I had to skip breakfast when the tender state of my ankle made me move at a much slower pace than usual. Mama, of course, looks all prim and proper, while I on the other hand am a bit rough around the edges. I'm sure Mama thinks this is from excessive partying at Dixie's, but in reality my sorry state is from tossing and turning most of the night thinking about Griff. I suppose his comments about my desperation weren't too far off of the mark; he just had who I'm desperate for way wrong. Why can't the man realize that's it's always been about him?

I groan just thinking about it, drawing a glare from Mama and a poke in the ribs from Daddy, who is seated on the left of me, and I have the ridiculous urge to stick my tongue out at them. You'd think I was ten years old instead of twenty-six. Reverend Jacobs drones on and on about forgiveness or whatever and I swear my eyes feel like they're gonna roll back in my head. At one point I suppose I doze off because I'm rudely startled awake when the good reverend bangs his fist on the lectern. I sort of jump and let out a noise that draws another elbow from my daddy and a thinning of my mother's lips that years ago would have meant that I'm grounded without my Barbies.

Luke, looking all slicked back and churchlike, damn him, leans forward from his spot on the other side of Mama, a tradition started back when we were kids and had to be separated. He gives me a disapproving shake of his dark head. This ticks me off so I act like I'm innocently scratching my nose with my middle finger but of course I'm really flipping him the bird. I'm rewarded when he has to disguise his laughter with a fit of coughing. By now we're sort of disrupting things to the point where Reverend Jacobs gives me a look (why me?) and Mama's white-knuckled grip on her hymnal tells me that I'm getting myself in deep doo-doo. Deciding that I'd better shape up, I fold my hands in my lap and force a look of rapt concentration onto my face.

My gaze, however, drifts over to the left side of the church two pews up where Griff is sitting between his younger brother Brandon and his mother. Petite and pretty in an understated way, Annie Sheldon has always been one of my favorite people. She's quiet like Griff and has handled the hardships of running a family farm with dignity and grace. Earthier than my mama, she likes to sink her fingers in the soil and still tends her personal garden even though she's leased out the farm acreage the past couple of years after Griff's construction company started to take off and he couldn't help her run things on a daily basis.

Half the girls in the congregation are checking out Brandon who is looking sexily scruffy like he's just rolled out of bed. He's on the five-maybe-six-year college program at the University of Kentucky since he tends to party more than study. This kind of sucks because I know that Griff wanted to go to college but at the time his family needed him and couldn't really afford the tuition. Home for the summer, Brandon is supposed to work for Griff but he's more interested in his music than school or work . . . not that he doesn't have the talent and charisma to be a country star but the odds say that he should get a college diploma first. Griff loves Brandon to death, but they tend to butt heads over the whole thing, and judging by the sulky expression on Brandon's face, there's been some recent head-butting going on.

My gaze shifts to Griff and, like it or not, my heart kicks it up a notch. Unlike Brandon, who's in a red polo and jeans, Griff is dressed up in neatly pressed khaki pants and a short-sleeved blue dress shirt. His shoes are buffed to a nice shine and his dark brown hair is gelled back from his forehead. He looks a bit tired and I wonder if he, too, had trouble sleepin'. A slight frown furrows his brow and I think that he must actually be listening, but all of the sudden the angle of his head turns in my direction. I do a quick I-wasn't-looking-at-you shift of my gaze but my heart hammers in my chest.

Maybe he was thinking about me the way I was thinking about him?

I *so* want to sneak a peek over to his pew but if he catches me that would be a dead giveaway so I force myself to stare at Reverend Jacobs who is now waving his arms wildly, causing his robe to billow like the wings of a bat in flight.

"So may *today* be filled with love and laughter, faith and forgiveness," Reverend Jacobs booms in the deep powerful voice that used to scare the hell out of me as a kid, "*Today*, not tomorrow or next week, next year, or Heaven forbid before it's too late. *Today*, as the saying goes, is the first day of the rest of your life. Use it wisely."

I'm thinkin' that this is pretty good advice and I should have been listening more closely but at least when Mama wants to rehash the sermon (which has been a tactical move since Luke and I were kids to see if we were listening) I will have something solid to contribute. My usual mode of operation has always been to let Luke answer and then nod my head or maybe argue the point just to look good.

I have always, though, scored big in the singing department, a gift inherited from my daddy. Luke and Mama are pretty much tone-deaf and mouth the hymns as a courtesy to those around them, thank the Lord. I've always enjoyed singing, humming, or even whistling at inappropriate times, much to the irritation to those around me, so to be able to belt out a hymn is an invigorating feeling that brings me feeling closer to God than anything.

When church concludes most everyone tends to hang around outside on the front lawn and chat but I tell Mama and Daddy that I'll see them over at the house in a bit. I wave and smile at everyone but I hobble over to my old blue Bronco as fast as my sore ankle will allow. I don't feel the need to talk about my unfortunate bull-riding incident over and over so I quickly hop up and slide behind the wheel. Let them gossip about me all they want and I'm fully aware that they are doing just that . . . glancing in my direction and talking out of the side of their mouths, which *hello* is a dead giveaway. Right now the only thing on my mind is Mama's fried chicken, creamy mashed potatoes, and melt-in-your-mouth buttermilk biscuits. I do believe she said something about apple crisp. God, my mouth is watering just thinking about it.

Throwing the truck in gear, I remind myself to take it slow out of the parking lot but once I'm on the open road I roll down the windows and let the old Bronco rumble down the two-lane pathway leading to the family farm. Since I live above the Cut & Curl, Sunday is about the only time I hit the open road, so I crank up the radio and enjoy the twenty-minute drive. I'm singing along with Gretchen Wilson when I reach the dirt road leading home. Cassie, the old collie, runs up to the truck barking and wagging her tail, making me think about how much I miss my dog, but then again how confining my apartment would be.

"Down, girl," I say out the window of the truck and

then ease out the door, not wantin' her to mess up my yellow sundress. Of course she pays me no heed and jumps up anyway, putting dusty paw prints on my skirt. "Aw, now just look what you've done," I shout but scratch her behind the ears anyway just for showing me so much love. Like the dog, the house itself seems to be shouting a warm greeting. White, trimmed in hunter green, the rambling farmhouse isn't fancy but it's my mama's pride and joy. A huge flower bed jam-packed full of petunias, geraniums, marigolds, impatiens, and Lord knows what else looks like a patchwork quilt full of color. Bushy Boston ferns suspended in hanging baskets from the roof of the porch are twirling in the breeze.

Limping a bit, I cross the lawn and hobble up the front steps to the wraparound porch with Cassie at my heels. Several oversized white rocking chairs flank either side of the front door, just begging a person to sit down for a spell. An antique wooden barrel has a checkerboard top where I challenged my daddy to many a game. A wooden swing padded with floral cushions hangs from the ceiling, inviting late-night cuddling, but my favorite spot is a white wicker chaise longue where I read Nancy Drew novels until I graduated to Harlequin romances, Stephen King novels, and sweeping historical romances with covers I thought I had to hide from my mama until I caught her reading one.

Lifting up the welcome mat I locate the key, tug the screen door open and enter the house. Cassie, who knows she isn't supposed to come in but is a rule breaker like me, trots in right behind me bold as you please. Mama will fuss but she loves Cassie more than

she lets on and will let her come in from the heat to
sleep on the cool tile in the kitchen. I love the way the
house smells of cinnamon and spice, old wood and
lemon polish.

Other than the size, there's nothing impressive or
pretentious about the interior, which really hasn't
changed much over the years. A fresh coat of paint or
varnish, maybe a new throw rug or knickknack is about
the only variation I've come to expect and I have to say
that I like it that way. Coming home should be *coming
home*, you know? To the left of the hallway is what
Mama calls the parlor. Furnished with cherry antiques
collected by Mama and refinished by my daddy, it's the
only room that could be considered fancy, but even so,
we were allowed to sit on the furniture as long as we
were respectful.

"Come on, girl," I call to Cassie as I start up the staircase leading to my old bedroom where I keep a closet
full of casual clothing for Sundays. "I need to get into
something comfortable." Cassie zips right past me,
pausing on the landing with her tail wagging. She cocks
her head as if wondering why I'm not bounding up the
steps as usual. By habit I'm counting the steps . . . skip-
ping the eighth because it squeaks and gets you busted
if you're trying to sneak in. "Don't ever ride a mechanical bull," I warn Cassie with a shake of my head. "Or a
real one either, for that matter. Just save a bull and ride
a cowboy," I say and laugh at my own joke. But of
course this makes me think of Griff, and I wonder if he
and his mama and brother are coming over for lunch.
They usually do, but Griff was looking tired and Brandon was looking grumpy so maybe they won't. Just in

case, though, I put on my best jeans instead of my favorite ones with the holes in the knees. Yeah, I laugh at
the eighty-dollar jeans in the mall stores that are all
ripped up. . . . Jeez, I guess I've always been ahead of
the trend.

I push through the hangers in my closet and find a
blue button-down floral blouse that I haven't worn in
years and put it on when the worn, soft T-shirts look so
comfy. I hope that the blue will bring out my eyes and
make me appear sweet and feminine. Looking in my
mirror over my dresser I pucker in an effort to make my
lips look plumper. Turning to Cassie, I ask, "Do you
think I'm sexy?"

Cassie angles her furry head at me as if saying, "No,
I think you're crazy."

Looking back in the mirror, I contemplate leaving my
hair down even though I usually pull it back into a
ponytail. I don't want to appear obvious so I pull my
hair up but fashion one of those sloppy buns that look
sexier than a traditional ponytail. Mama will probably
tell me that my hair is a mess and that I should tidy up.
With this thought in mind I stop obsessing about my appearance and head downstairs. Mama and Daddy and
Luke should be arriving soon and I decide that I had better start peeling potatoes to get on her good side because
I'm quite certain that in the retelling of my bull-riding
escapade the whole thing is going to get blown way out
of proportion.

I hobble back to the stairs thinking that sliding down
the banister might be easier but with my recent luck I
would probably crash-land. But then again crash land-
ings have never deterred me so I swing my leg over the

smooth wood and prepare to let go. "Should I do it, Cassie?"

"Don't even think about it." The deep voice, obviously not Cassie's, keeps me from letting go. I look over my shoulder at Griff, who is standing at the bottom of the stairs with his arms crossed over his chest looking all stern and disapproving. "Are you tryin' to break your neck?"

"Did I ask your opinion?"

"No, you asked the *dog,* which is another scary observation, if you ask me."

"Well, I'm not askin' you."

"Jamie Lee . . ." Griff begins in a tone full of unspoken words. With a pounding heart I wait for him to continue but he falls silent. *Damn him.*

"Where is everyone else?"

"Still back at church listening to the embellished story of your bull ride. Rumor has it that you did a back-flip followed by a cartwheel. I came back to warn you that your mama might not be too happy." He pauses for a second and then says, "There's also buzz about your relationship with that Parker fellow. Most people are referrin' to him as Mr. Hollywood."

My grip on the banister tightens. "Well, *everyone* needs stay out of my business." I look over my shoulder and give him a thinning of my lips that says that I'm including him in this category.

"Like that's gonna happen in Hootertown," he says dryly. "Now, come on, Jamie Lee. Don't go slidin' down the banister. You don't need to go hurtin' yourself any more."

"Maybe you don't know what I need," I say under my breath.

"What?"

"I said stand clear, Griff. I've done this a thousand times." Of course it's been about ten years . . .

"Jamie Lee . . ."

Oh, screw it. I let go and zoom down the slick wood much faster then I remember and when I should have landed gracefully with both feet on the floor, my butt collides with something solid . . . something solid that grunts and grabs me around the waist.

Griff staggers backward three or four steps, taking me with him, and then falls to his ass so hard that he bounces and skids across the hardwood floor, and I bounce on top of him. He drops the f-bomb, (a very un-Griff-like thing to do in front of me) because my ass smacks him hard where a guy hates the most to be hit. After a stunned moment I roll off him, totally ticked off that he felt compelled to catch me, until I come to my knees and see that the color has drained from his face.

"Griff?" I venture softly.

Griff's eyes are closed and he's sort of gasping for air while making little wheezing noises. I just know that he wants to grab himself *there* and I'm wondering if I should tell him that it would be okay with me if he did. His fists are clenched at his sides and in my most sympathetic voice I say, "Griff, you can grab your . . . your, uh, *sore spot* if it will make you feel better."

Of course Luke chooses this moment to come through the front door and hears me say this plain as day.

"What the hell have you done to Griff?"

"Why do I always catch the blame?"

With his hands on his hips, Luke says, "Maybe because you usually *are* to blame."

He has a point, but I ignore it. "I accidentally hit into his . . ."

"Balls?"

"Yeah. Do you think he needs ice or somethin'?"

Before Luke answers, Macy comes through the front door, tossin' her keys and hummin' "Amazing Grace" until she sees Griff on the floor and stops in her tracks. "Jamie Lee, what happened to Griff?"

"She hit him in the ba . . . *groin*," Luke answers for me.

Macy's eyebrows shoot up and she looks at me. "With what?"

"Well, my, uh, *ass*." I wince.

"Your . . . *ass*?" Luke says with a frown.

Macy and Luke look at me in anticipation of an answer. Heat creeps into my cheeks. I swallow and say, "I was slidin' down the banister. . . ."

"What?" Macy glances at the banister and then back at me.

"Why the hell did you do that?" Luke demands in an annoying big-brother tone.

By this time I'm sort of blinking back tears. "My ankle hurt and I thought it might be easier," I say in a small and yet somewhat defensive tone. "I told Griff to stand clear. I slid down the damned thing like I was shot out of a cannon."

"Well, you're heavier now than when you were younger," Macy says.

"Gee, thanks for *that* explanation."

Everyone looks down at Griff, who takes a shaky breath and says in a sort of strangled voice, "I didn't . . . want her . . . to hurt . . . her ankle further."

"Awww," Macy says, smiling down at Griff. She turns and gives me a disapproving frown, which makes me feel even more like a heel.

"You think you can get up?" Luke asks.

"Maybe never again," Griff gruffly tries to joke.

Macy flashes me a God-that-would-be-awful look and I wince, giving her a yeah-that-would-suck look in return.

"Um, I think we need to get him up . . . I mean standing before your mama and daddy get home. I don't think they were too far behind me." Macy turns to me and says, "Jamie Lee, I don't remember you turnin' a cartwheel last night."

I roll my eyes.

"Griff?" Luke questions and offers his hand.

"I'm okay," Griff responds and I think that for a guy who always wants to help others he sure has a hard time accepting help in return. He pushes up to his feet but when he wobbles a bit I slide my arm around his waist, only to have him growl, "I'm fine, Jamie Lee."

"I know, but *I'm* not. My ankle still hurts a bit. Will you help me into the kitchen? I'm sure Mama has a mountain of potatoes for me to peel."

"I'll help," Macy offers. "My daddy said to send your mama his regrets. He's fishin' this afternoon."

"How about Brandon and your mama, Griff?" I ask as we hobble together into the kitchen.

Griff sighs as we help each other into the kitchen.

"Well Brandon is busy bein' a shit and Mama's busy babyin' him so you can count them out too."

I nod up to him. "Oh, that bad, huh?"

"The usual," Griff replies. "Maybe someday Brandon will grow up. They're both pissed at me because I fired him for showin' up late three days in a row."

"Oh." I feel his muscles contract with tension and I so want to hug him . . . *hold him* . . . tell him what a wonderful man he is. He eases me down into a chair at the big oak table in the kitchen where, just as I predicted, there is a pile of potatoes and a couple of ancient peelers. "You guys grab a soft drink and watch some baseball or somethin' in the family room. Macy and I have this handled."

"You don't have to ask me twice," Luke says with a wink that makes Macy blush. "Come on, Griff, before they put us to work."

Griff nods.

With heat in my cheeks, I have to ask, "Uh, Griff, has your . . . um, pain subsided?"

"Mostly." He nods and even gives me a bit of a smile.

"I'm sorry. It wasn't my intention to hurt you."

A soft expression crosses his face. "I know."

"You should have gotten out of the way. You knew I was gonna slide down that banister come hell or high water."

"Yeah, just like you knew I'd be there to catch you."

Before I can find my voice he turns and leaves the room. "Why do I let that man get to me?"

"Because you're crazy about him and for the love of God why can't he see that he's in love with you?"

"Macy, every time I'm around him I feel like either smackin' him or kissin' him."

"Mostly kissin' him, though, right?" Macy says softy and my throat goes closed so I can only nod.

Wanting to take the focus off of myself I ask, "So how are things proceeding with you and Luke?"

She shrugs her shoulders. "I'm gonna try this new diet. You eat soup twice a day and you're supposed to lose five pounds the very first week."

"Macy, this isn't about how much you weigh. You worry way too much about that."

"Easy for you to say, Miss Size Eight." She gets so agitated that she whittles her potato down to the size of a grape. "You don't have to do the soup diet with me."

"Yeah, but you know that I will. I'm sorry, Macy. I don't mean to be insensitive." I angle my head and say, "You're avoiding my question."

She picks up another potato. "Not really. I want to whip myself into shape before making a play for your brother."

I'm about to argue when Mama and Daddy come into the kitchen. I can tell by the look on Mama's face that she isn't a happy camper.

With her hands on her hips Mama says, "Jamie Lee Carter, just what were you thinkin' ridin' on that big ol' bull? The whole town is buzzin' about your antics. You could've broken your neck instead of just twistin' your ankle. Explain yourself."

"Mama, I didn't know that crazy ol' Bubba Baker was gonna whip me around like that. Your beef should be with him."

Daddy narrows his eyes. "Is that so? Maybe I'll have

a heart-to-heart with Bubba." Hooking his thumbs in his belt loops, Daddy hitches up his pants and puffs out his chest. Of course he's always been more bark than bite, but I'd hate to see him and Bubba get into a tussle.

Macy's eyes widen as she whittles away at another potato.

"Daddy, please don't get somethin' started. It was a misunderstanding. Hey, Griff and Luke are watchin' some baseball on ESPN. Why don't you join them?"

"Well, all right," he says with a shrug. "Wouldn't be much of a fight anyways."

Mama rolls her eyes.

"What?" Daddy says. "You don't think I could take Bubba?"

"With one hand tied behind your back," Mama purrs and does a shooing motion with her hands.

"Damned straight."

Mama gives him her prim-and-proper look. "Now you watch your language around these here girls. Go on with you now."

After he leaves the kitchen Mama mumbles, "Old fool." I notice though that the color is a bit high in Mama's cheeks and I do think that she's a little turned on by Daddy's blustering. Then, clearing her throat, she says, "You girls get to work on those potatoes. I've got the chicken soakin' in buttermilk. I'm goin' to change out of my church clothes and then we'll get the chicken fryin'."

Macy sighs. "Oh, Jamie Lee, your parents are so cute. Your mama looked like she wanted to gobble your daddy right up."

"Ew." I wrinkle my nose at Macy, but down deep I think it's pretty cute, too.

Mama is back down in the kitchen in short order, dressed in crisp white slacks and a sleeveless green top, but to her this is dressing casual. She dons her apron and before long potatoes are boiling in a big pot, chicken is hissing and popping in a cast-iron skillet, and cornbread is browning in the oven. The apple crisp she promised me is sitting on the counter, tempting me to go over and take a pinch of the brown-sugar topping.

"Jamie Lee, would you and Macy slice up a vegetable medley for me? We'll steam the veggies at the last minute."

"Sure thing, Mama." While her cooking is still traditional Southern fare, she uses low-fat milk and goes easy with butter and salt in order to keep everything heart-healthy. Much to Daddy's sorrow she makes him remove the crispy skin from his chicken, but for the most part she manages to sneak in low-fat versions of his favorite foods without him even knowing.

Daddy might get on Mama's nerves in his retirement and she might nag just a bit too much, but there is such a foundation of love and respect that I believe will hold up no matter what life throws at them. Some people might say that they're lucky but I know that they've worked and fought for everything they have.

It occurs to me then that I take these Sundays for granted. When I get up to get the veggies from the crisper I surprise my mama with a hug. "I just love Sundays, don't you?"

Mama gives me a surprised smile that trembles a little at the corners. "Yes, child, I surely do." All businesslike once again she says, "Now hurry up with those vegetables."

When lunch is ready to put on the table Mama tells me to go and round up the menfolk. Baseball has them glued to the television with a full count on Ken Griffey, Jr. I hesitate, not wanting them to miss the play, and my gaze drifts over to Griff. He's leaning forward with his elbows resting on his thighs. Oh how I long to be able to go over there and wrap my arms around him from behind, and kiss his neck as I tell him that the food is on the table.

He must have felt the heat of my gaze because he shifts in his chair and catches me looking at him like he's Mama's apple crisp. Something hot seems to pass between us but just when I'm thinking that Griff is reading my mind, he frowns and looks away.

"Lunch is on the table," I announce and turn away before Griff can see the disappointment on my face. I never was much good at hiding my emotions but I square my shoulders and head back to the kitchen. Macy, who is putting ice in a pitcher of sweet tea, takes one look at me and asks, "What's wrong?"

"Same old thing. I'm moonin' over Griff and he dismisses me easy as pie."

Macy comes close and whispers, "So what are you gonna do? You're not givin' up, are you?"

"Hell no. Just the opposite. I'm pullin' out all the stops. Mark my words, Griffin Sheldon's boots are goin' to be parked under my bed . . . *tonight!*"

Macy's eyes widen. "Tonight?"

"You heard me."

"How you gonna do that?"

"I have my ways," I boldly proclaim, when of course I have no idea.

"You sure you want to go that route?"

"Of course I'm not sure. I'm not sure of anything anymore but I'm damned tired of waitin' around. Desperate rednecks call for desperate measures."

15

It's Too Late to Turn Back Now

I am admittedly the queen of second-guessing. This is a really sucky thing to be queen of but no matter how hard I try, I can't break this habit. So, of course, I'm second-guessing my plan to land Griff in my bed this very evening. The problem is, I've already put the whole thing into motion and it is rapidly gathering speed like a car going downhill without any brakes.

Griff has agreed to come over to my shop and measure for tanning-bed stalls and I'm dressed to seduce him in tiny denim cutoffs that barely cover my ass and a white tank top that would fit on a toddler. To make matters worse, I put on a push-up bra that has my boobies just about spilling out of my shirt.

Subtle, huh?

I take one look at my sex-kitten self in the mirror and decide I'm way over the top in more ways than the obvious. This idea has disaster written all over it. I've just decided to go upstairs and change into something less slutty when Griff comes walking in. When he lays eyes

on me his Adam's apple bobs up and down like he's trying not to swallow his tongue.

"Hey, Griff," I say while trying not to blush.

"J-Jamie Lee," he says in greeting and although I can
tell he's trying to stay focused on my face, he *is* a guy
and his gaze keeps dipping to my pushed-up boobies.

"I'm thinkin' of puttin' the tannin' beds over there," I
tell him and walk to the back corner of the shop. "Do
you think I can squeeze two in?" The sweeping gesture
of my arm causes my breasts to jiggle, and Griff's
Adam's apple bobs again. Clenching my fists, I force
myself to quit talking with my hands as I wait for Griff
to answer. "Griff?"

"What?"

"Don't you need to take some measurements or
somethin'?" Sheesh, just what is it about breasts that
makes men come undone? My plan included some
bending over and come-hither smiles, but I've already
decided *not* to put the seduction of Griff Sheldon into
action. It's not that I'm chicken; it's just that this isn't
the way I want it to happen. So even though I'm dressed
like a little tart, I decided to be as businesslike as I can
under the circumstances. The problem is that Griff can't
seem to concentrate.

"Maybe we should do this another time."

"Why?"

I'm trying to come up with an excuse when there is a
knock at the door. I look over to see none other than
Parker Carrington waving at me. "I'll be right back."

Griff narrows his eyes and is about to comment but I
hurry to the door and step outside. Parker's eyes open
wide when he sees me too and I'm thinking that guys

are guys no matter where they're from. "Hi, Parker. What brings you here?"

"I'm leaving in the morning."

"For good?" I feel a bit sad at the thought.

"We're going back to L.A. to try and get the movie studio to sign off on the project now that we have our location. If all goes well, we'll be back in a week or so. I just wanted to say good-bye for now." He leans in and gives me a brief kiss on the mouth, and we hug.

"I hope it all works out."

Parker nods. "Me too. Jessica was excited to get some interest from Sarah Michelle Gellar and Freddie Prinze Jr., to play the leads."

"That would be awesome."

Parker leans in again and kisses me on the cheek. He whispers, "Good luck with your cowboy in there. You look sexy as hell."

"I feel ridiculous."

"Well, he's watching us and not looking too happy." Pulling back, Parker gives me wink. "See you soon."

I head back inside, but I'm not prepared for just how unhappy Griff really is. With a glare he says to me, "So now I see why you wanted me to do this another time. You have a date with Hollywood."

Before I can correct him, he goes on, "You know for a minute . . ."

"For a minute, what?"

"Nothin'," He starts messing with his tape measure but a muscle is jumping in his jaw.

"No, tell me, Griff. Go ahead and speak your mind."

He swings around and says, "For a second there I thought you were dressed like that for me."

His comment, so unexpected, just hangs between us for a moment. I have the feeling that he didn't really want to say that either because there's color high in his cheeks. With jerky motions Griff tries to clip his measuring tape back onto his belt, but it drops to the floor with a loud clunk.

"I *was* dressed like this for you." I'm thinking that this will make him smile but I get the patented Griff scowl.

"Why, Jamie Lee? So you can finally finish what you started nine years ago? Are you still that pissed that I turned you down?"

I feel like he's slapped me.

"Why don't we just *do it* and get it out of our systems once and for all?"

So he thinks he can fuck me out of his system? Not even. "Okay, big boy. You're on."

He blinks at me.

"You heard me. You're on." I walk away and stomp up the stairs, swinging my barely covered ass just in case he's lookin'. My heart is pounding and tears are burning behind my eyelids. My sore ankle hurts but I ignore the pain. I keep waiting to hear him leave but instead he starts up the stairs behind me.

Uh-oh.

He's calling my bluff. And God help me, I was bluffing. But I'm also spitting mad so I swing around and taunt him, figuring that I might as well give him something to be sorry about. "Come on, big boy, let's go." I tug my tiny tank over my head and toss it at him.

"Jamie Lee . . ." His eyes are stormy and he swallows. "I shouldn't have said that."

"Oh but you *did*." When he follows me to my bedroom I shimmy out of my shorts and stand before him in my pink push-up bra and lacy thong. "Come on. What are you waitin' for? Finish this thing." I reach around to unhook my bra.

"Stop!"

"Go to hell!" I shout and shove his chest. With a quick snap of my wrists my bra is on the floor and I shimmy out of my thong. "Come on, *do me*, Griff. What, do you need a handwritten invitation?"

"Jamie Lee . . . *stop*," he growls.

"Come on, you know you want to."

Once again he surprises me by pushing me up against the wall. With his hands splayed on either side of my head and he leans in and kisses me . . . *hard* and I kiss him back . . . *harder*. Pent-up anger, frustration and pure need bubble to the surface. I shove my hands beneath his shirt and encounter warm smooth skin. With clumsy fingers I fumble with his belt buckle, unsnap his jeans, and tug on the zipper. He groans into my mouth, kissing me deeper until my knees threaten to give. Needing to feel his skin rubbing against mine I yank upward on his shirt until he gets the message, pulls it over his head, and tosses it behind him.

His bare chest caresses my breasts, teasing my pebbled nipples while his hot mouth makes love to me. I press my palms to his back, enjoying the ripple and play of muscle, while slowly sliding downward, easing his jeans and boxers over his hips. I gasp at the feel of his hot, hard penis against my bare belly while I run my hands over his ass, kneading, caressing, pressing him closer.

His long tapered fingers, big calloused hands, are deliciously abrasive against my sensitive skin. Cupping my breasts he takes a step back and breathes, "Beautiful." He watches me while he thumbs the areolas in slow circles lightly and then with more pressure until I feel like my body is turning to liquid. With a groan he dips his head to lick, nibble, lave, and nip at my breasts until I'm shameless with needing him. With a soft cry I shove my fingers into his hair and arch my back, offering him more.

"God, Jamie Lee . . ." Griff lifts his head and threads his fingers with mine, pinning me against the wall while kissing me like he can't get enough. Heat pools in my belly and sinks lower. I kiss him like a wild thing, moving, arching, squirming . . . pressing my back against the smooth, cool wall.

"Griff, *please* . . . I need—"

"*This?*" He dips his middle finger inside me. "God, you're so hot, so wet."

I gasp when he slides his finger out and caresses my clitoris with slow circular strokes. I shudder. "Yes . . . *no* . . . I want—"

"The same thing I want." He swiftly moves his hands to my waist, lifts me up and enters me with one sure stroke.

"Yes, God yes . . ." My fingers curl around his shoulders and I wrap my legs around his waist. He pauses for a moment and seems to savor the feeling of being so deep inside me. With a sharp intake of breath he slides slowly out and then *in* until I arch my back, letting him know that I need more.

"Jamie Lee . . ."

"Faster," I plead breathlessly.

"Like this?"

"Y-yes!" I hold on tight while he rides me wild and hard against the wall but it's just the way I want him . . . need him. When my orgasm starts to build I wrap my arms around his neck, wanting to kiss him while I come. When his lips touch mine I shatter with a climax that robs me of breath and coherent thought.

Griff thrusts deep and climaxes right along with me while kissing me deeply . . . and it's a good thing because my scream would have awoken the dead or at the very least Rose Jenkins next door.

When the kiss ends Griff pulls back and rests his forehead to mine. I can feel his heart beating a million miles a minute and it makes me smile. His breathing is ragged and his eyes are closed. The blood feels like it's humming through my veins. I love the feeling of him still buried deep and I so want to tip his head back for another delicious kiss . . . "Griff?" I wait in anticipation of what he'll say to me. I know what I want to say to *him* but I want him to say it first.

He looks at me with eyes full of confusion and regret and my words die on my lips. "I'm sorry, Jamie Lee."

Sorry? My happiness melts like a sugar cube in hot tea.

"I lost my head," he continues and then eases himself from me. Reaching down, he pulls his boxers and jeans up.

Sorry? The word rings like a gong in my head and seems to echo. My legs are shaky so I lock my knees, refusing to reach out for him to steady me. Feeling the need to cover myself, I reach down and pick up his shirt and somehow manage to tug it over my head. Clearing my throat and praying not to cry, I say, "Don't beat yourself up, Griff. This was my fault *again*." With a shrug I say, "Look at the bright side. Maybe now I'm out of your system."

"I didn't mean that."

"Didn't mean it or didn't mean to say it? There's a world of difference." Without letting him answer I continue, "You can go now."

"See, this is why I didn't want to . . . to let things go this far." He runs his fingers through his hair. "You're hurt and angry and things will never be the same between us."

"Yeah, well, there's the fundamental difference between us, Griff. I never wanted things to stay the same." After taking a deep breath I decide to put it all on the line. "Even at seventeen I knew I loved you. For years I pretended otherwise, but every guy I dated I compared to you." Poking him in the chest I say, "And guess what, Griff? They all came up short."

"Jamie Lee—"

"And yes I dressed like Jessica Simpson in a misguided effort to land you in my bed—not to get you *out* of my system but to start something *lasting*." I poke him again. "But I'm done. You hear me? Done. Game over."

"Jamie Lee, I—"

"No, Griff, don't." I swallow the hot moisture clogging my throat. "I was wrong to taunt you into this just as I was wrong to try and seduce you at seventeen. I'm trying to force something that you obviously don't want, and for that I am truly sorry. But this whole unrequited thing is gettin' way old. You have my word that it won't happen again. Now go, because I do believe I'm goin' to have a bit of a meltdown." I give him a trembling smile. "You've seen me in meltdown mode and it isn't one bit pretty."

He shoves his hands in his pockets and I wonder if he does this so he won't reach out and hug me but man oh man, I could sure use a hug about now. "I can stay for a while."

"That would be kinda weird, don't ya think?" I swipe at a tear. "Y'all better hightail it outta here before the dam breaks."

"I can't leave you like this." He hangs his head and manages to look as miserable as I feel.

"I'll live, Griff. I'll get me some bourbon on ice and ride it out."

"I have to ask you one thing," he says and slowly raises his head to look me in the eye. "We didn't use, um . . . protection. If anything, that is, if you end up . . . you know, pregnant, you'll tell me, right?"

"You don't have anything to worry about on that score," I tell him. I know he wants to know if I'm on the pill but I'm not and I want to give him the impression that I *am* so he doesn't worry because the fact of the matter is that I could very well be pregnant. I had condoms all stacked up and ready for my ill-fated seduction but they're in the drawer on the nightstand right where I put them. The funny thing is that the thought of carrying his child doesn't even faze me. "I'm okay. You can go."

Griff just stands there for a minute and I get my hopes up thinking that he's gonna say something wonderful like *Jamie Lee, I love you.*

He clears his throat, swallows, and finally says, "You know I'd do the right thing by you, right?"

My heart shatters into a billion pieces. *Do the right thing as in forced to marry me.* Knowing that my voice would crack, I just nod. Of course he would do the honorable thing; it's his way. Griff is upstanding, trustworthy, hardworking, and kind. It's why I love him.

Too bad he doesn't love me in return, at least not in the way that I want him to.

Griff looks like he wants to say something but that it's stuck in his throat. Knowing that whatever he wants to say would just make me more miserable, I shoo him with my fingers.

"You want me to send Macy over or something?"

"No! Don't you breathe a word of this to anybody. I'm tired of this whole damned town talkin' about me."

"But—"

"But *nothin'*!" I'm gettin' a little pissed. "Griff, if you don't leave this minute I'm gonna kick your ass into next *week*." Of course like that could really happen. He's standing there all bare-chested and muscled and I'm just a little shit smothered by his big shirt. But I come up on my tiptoes and clench my fists and give him my best kick-ass glare, which is pretty damned difficult since I'm ready to burst into tears.

Still, Griff stands there, clearly wanting to comfort me in a situation in which that is impossible. Finally, he nods slowly and then leaves.

I stand there for a long tortured moment blinking back tears and breathing ragged. I really want to throw something or punch a hole in a wall but instead I walk on stiff legs over to my bed and lie down. Curling my sorry self into a tight ball, I let the tears come. Usually, my crying jags are noisy . . . full of wailing, sniffing, stomping, and nose-blowing.

But not this time.

This time I cry silently into my pillow. Streams of hot tears leak from beneath my eyelids. It doesn't help that I'm wearing Griff's shirt, which smells of his aftershave and the outdoors, a heady scent that is uniquely his. If I had the energy I'd tug it over my head but I don't.

The phone rings and I know it's probably Griff. I ignore it the next three times it rings and then finally reach over to the nightstand and turn the ringer off. When there isn't a drop of liquid left in me I finally stop crying. My throat feels parched, my eyes burn, and I kind of have to pee, but I defiantly wallow in my misery, ignoring my bodily needs, until I finally fall into an exhausted sleep.

16

Better Late Than Never

"Spray me a little more, Jamie Lee," Miss Irma tells me. "I want ta look good for the Fourth of July picnic."

"All right, then, close your eyes." I give her curly do another liberal shot of hair spray.

"Now that's better," she says, reaching up and touching her stiff hair. "I'll wrap my head in toilet paper tonight when I go to sleep to keep these here curls stiff and perky. It's a little tip your mama taught me years ago. Works like a charm even though it makes you look like a danged Q-Tip."

"Okay, you're all done." I tug on the Velcro strip holding her cape around her neck and then shake it free.

"Good. I need to get back to make sure Griffin and Brandon are still alive. Yesterday I had to pull them two apart."

"I thought your deck was done," Macy says from where she's folding up towels.

"Just about. The recent rain held things up a bit."

I refuse to ask questions concerning Griff but Macy

does it for me. "Brandon and Griff got into it?" I act un-
interested but my ears perk up.

Miss Irma stands up and waves her hands in the air.
"Woowee, they sure 'nuff did. Second time in less than
a week. Now most times I'd have to say that wild card
Brandon is at fault . . . shows up late and whatnot, but I
have ta say that Griffin has been outta sorts lately and
has been a bit hard on the boy."

"Really?" Macy draws the word out and gives me a
look. I scowl at her and start tidying up my station like
I don't give a fig.

Miss Irma nods vigorously but of course her hair
stays put. "Yep, and that Brandon's a looker, too. My
niece Katie Lynn has been comin' over with the pre-
tense of havin' lunch with me, but I know it's to see
Brandon. Not that I blame her. I reminded them boys
that shirts are optional."

"So Griff has been grumpy lately?" Macy prods, but
Miss Irma doesn't need much proddin'.

"Shoowee yeah! Not that he's not polite to me and
all, but he's been a-scowlin' and a-gripin' at Brandon at
every turn. And he looks a little rough around the edges
like he hasn't been sleepin' right."

"Is that so?" Macy says slowly. I feel her eyes on me
but I refuse to look at her.

"Danged straight," Miss Irma says gruffly. "Brandon
nailed in a board crooked or somethin' and Griffin
growled at him and all the sudden they was goin' at it."

"What did you do?" Macy asks.

"Turned the hose on 'em." She grins and wags her
eyebrows. "Now that was a sight seein' them two drip-

pin' wet and all fired up. I thought me and Katie Lynn was gonna swallow our tongues."

Macy chuckles and normally I would too, but nothin' has been normal since that night with Griff. It's been goin' on two weeks and the hurt hasn't gone away.

"I'd better get home," Miss Irma says and I shuffle over to the cash register to ring her up. "You okay, sugar? You seem a bit down in the mouth."

"I'm fine, Miss Irma," I lie and muster up a pathetic smile.

She nods her head but doesn't seem convinced. "Well, I'll be seein' y'all at the picnic tomorrow, right?"

"Sure thing," I reply but I'm not planning on going. Mama will have a hissy fit. The Fourth of July picnic is the biggest event in Hootertown and as Mama will remind me dates back to the Civil War days. She'll expect me to have a picnic basket prepared for the auction where the menfolk bid on said baskets. Whatever. I'm not going. I'm not up to smiling and for God's sake I'm still fending off questions about the danged bull ride. Parker is supposed to come into town for the event but I'm still not going.

"Jamie Lee you've got to snap out of it," Macy says after locking the front door and flipping the CLOSED sign over. She puts her hands on her hips and tries to look all big and bad. "You been mopin' and sulkin' and . . . and you need to do your roots!"

"Who cares?"

Macy frowns. "You should. It's a reflection on our shop."

I roll my eyes and toss the soiled towels in the hamper with more force than necessary. "You sound like Mama."

"Geez, you're in a bad mood. You PMSing?"

I feel heat creep up my neck.

"You want to go out for a beer or two and loosen up? Maybe shoot some pool?" she asks, trying another tactic.

"No."

"You haven't had a drop to drink in goin' on two weeks. Now I'm not one to promote drinkin' but come on, you've got to have a little fun. Hey, you wanna go to Nashville this weekend?"

I shake my head.

"Look, Jamie Lee, I know this thing with Griff, that you by the way *refuse* to discuss, is getting outta hand. You're moody as hell; refuse to even go out for a couple of drinks. What is up with . . . *holy shit!* Are you . . . are you . . . are you . . . *pregnant*?" The p-word comes out a high-pitched squeak that will bring dogs running.

"Three days late."

Her hand goes to her chest, her eyes bug out and she blinks rapidly. "Who . . . w-who . . . did you have *sex* with?" She whispers the word *sex* like someone might hear.

"Bubba Baker," I tell her, going for sarcasm. Any other kind of humor is totally beyond me.

She gasps and by the stunned look on her face she must be picturing it in her head. Ew. That could never happen no matter how jacked up I was. I consider letting her dwell on this a moment longer because that's the kind of mood I'm in but she looks ready to pass out so I correct her even though it's hard for me to get his name past my lips. "It was Griff, Macy, you dolt."

Her shoulders slump in relief. "Don't you ever fuck like that with me again!" Her eyes narrow but then go wide when it hits her. "Ohmigod! You had sex with Griff?"

"No, I stole his sperm and injected myself with it. Of course I did."

"Don't be so bitchy . . . you sound like you're PMS-ing. Maybe you're gonna start."

I shrug my shoulders.

"You want to start, right?"

"Of course. I mean I wouldn't want to be carryin' Griff's baby."

Macy angles her head at me. "You sure 'bout that?"

I flop down into my station chair. "I would never want to trap him like that, but . . . there is a part of me that"—I swallow the emotion that's been choking me for days—"would be happy. Am I crazy or what?"

Macy comes over and pats my hand. "No, you're not crazy, just in love."

I shrug. "Well it's not like I have any say-so in the matter anyway. If I am, I am."

"You gonna tell him?"

"Not 'til I know for sure."

Macy nods. "Should we go and get one of those test thingies?"

I chuckle without humor. "We'd have to go out of town to get it. Lordy, word of me purchasin' a pregnancy test kit would spread like a brush fire in California."

"Good point."

"Well then, let's go. We'll even cross over into Tennessee." I stand up and give Macy a hug. "Thanks for puttin' up with me."

"That's what friends are for." She gives me an extra squeeze and says, "I'll be over in an hour or so okay? I'll drive."

"Yeah." Normally I would protest Macy driving since she tends to do things like look at you instead of watching the road when she's talking and she's pretty much always talking. She also tends to tailgate, speed, and miss turns. But considering my state of mind I find it best that she drive, which says a lot about how screwed up I am.

After changing into my favorite jeans and a worn Toby Keith T-shirt I head into the kitchen in search of something to eat. I grab a slice of leftover pizza and almost snag a beer when I remember that I shouldn't be drinking. After grabbing a bottle of water instead, I warm the pizza in the microwave and then take a bite even though I haven't been hungry all day.

I've always been such an upbeat person that being depressed feels foreign and weird, like I'm not myself, which I suppose I'm not. I feel like I need to shake myself like a wet dog and *just snap out of it,* like Macy said, but I can't. Unable to force another bite of pizza, I toss the rest in the trash and then decide to watch some TV until Macy honks her horn.

It's not surprising that nothing catches my interest but just why is it that every commercial seems to be for a baby product? With a moan I turn the TV off and just sit there and stare at the blank screen. When my cell phone rings I let out a little yelp and scowl at the damned thing. Picking it up I see that the call is from Griff and I do what I've done for almost two weeks and simply refuse to answer. Just to torture myself, though, I listen to the voice mail.

"Jamie Lee, it's Griff. Call me."

My heart thumps, first at the mere sound of his voice—it really ticks me off that he has that power and probably always will—and then that he sounds upset. Did Macy call him? My heart beats even harder at the thought. Surely she didn't. I listen to the message again with the absurd thought that I might be able to figure it out by the inflection of his voice. Okay, this time he sounds angry rather than upset.

Angry? Would he be angry that I'm pregnant?

God, this whole thing has the nasty pizza doing cartwheels in my stomach, making me need to go use the bathroom. Macy's horn blows but I really have the urge to go so I ignore her second blast on the horn. Patience is not one of Macy's strong points especially when there's some sort of drama going on.

I rush to the bathroom, tug down my jeans, and there it is . . .

My period.

I sit there for a moment feeling an odd mixture of relief and regret. Deep down I know it's for the best for so many reasons, but still . . . I feel this sense of loss for something I never had in the first place.

Now, what in the hell is up with that?

A loud banging on the bathroom door brings me out of my musings. "Jamie Lee, you okay?"

"Yeah, I'll be out in a minute."

When I emerge from the bathroom Macy is standing there in the hallway leaning against the wall. She gives me an anxious look and says, "Ready?"

"We don't need to go. My bitchiness was PMS after all." I smile but it feels forced.

"Let's celebrate," Macy says, a little too brightly.

"I don't want to celebrate."

"Let's bitch, then. About everything we can think of to bitch about."

"Now you're talkin'." My ankle is feeling better so I stomp down the hallway. I hated not being able to stomp. Macy follows and stomps right along with me even though she's not much of a stomper. I snag a couple of longnecks out of the fridge and hand one to Macy. "Let's go out on the deck."

She nods and follows me outside. We sit down in our chairs, unscrew our beers, tip them back for a long pull, and then rest the wet bottles on our thighs, totally in sync like we've choreographed the whole thing. Although it's still warm and muggy, the sun is sinkin' lower in the sky and a bit of a breeze ruffles our hair. Insects are hummin' and a gray squirrel chases another squirrel round and round up a tree, making me chuckle.

"That's a good sign," Macy says with a smile.

"What?"

"Hearin' you laugh."

I twirl the beer bottle on my leg. "Well, I'm damned tired of cryin'. This whole bein'-pathetic thing really blows."

Macy sits up straighter in her chair. "Well then fuck bein' pathetic. Let's be . . ."

"Assertive!"

"Yes, let's assert ourselves." She blinks at me. "Just how are we gonna do this?"

"Damned if I know. As you might recall we had this

same conversation not long ago. Let's face it, Macy. We're full of bullshit."

She almost chokes on a swallow of beer. "That's not true. We had promised to go after what we want."

I give her a look.

Macy shrugs. "Yeah, we're big talkers aren't we?"

"Well, that didn't work for me, anyway. I *went* after Griff and look where it got me. I blow off the attention of the amazingly hot Parker Carrington and actually convince him to pursue Jessica. And then once again throw myself at Griffin Sheldon with disastrous results."

Macy gasps. "No you didn't."

"Yes to all of the above." I take a long swallow of beer and then sigh.

"Jamie Lee, I know this is bold of me but I just have to know. How was he? Did he rock your world or was he just, you know, *okay*?"

"Rocked my damned world."

"Oh. I suppose it would have been easier if things didn't work out because he had been, like, a pencil-dick or something."

I sputter my beer. "Oh, lord-a-mercy."

"I'm guessin' that wasn't the case."

"I'm not gonna discuss Griff's . . . thingie with you but no, that was not the case."

Macy slaps at a mosquito so I lean over and light a citronella candle on the small table between us. "Without goin' into the details I'll tell you the series of unfortunate events that occurred that night." I wet my whistle and then go on. "Well, I was dressed for the seduction of Griffin Sheldon wearin' Daisy Duke shorts and a tiny tank with a bra that pushed my boobies just about up to my chin. But then I decided that this wasn't the way I want things to go down. See, I was thinkin' that I wanted a more subtle approach instead of in-your-face-*do*-me, but Griff showed up before I could change my clothes and blew that all to hell."

"Lordy, lordy."

"It gets better or worse dependin' on how you look at it. Parker showed up on his way out of town and kissed me good-bye. Griff saw the whole thing and thought I was dressed like a hoochie mama for Parker. We exchanged words."

"Oh no."

"Oh, yes. *Why* I don't know, I told Griff that I dressed like that for him, not Parker. Instead of bein' pleased, Griff accused me of wantin' to finish what I started when I was seventeen." Even though I was determined not to cry, I feel tears well up and spill down my cheeks. "Macy, he said that we should just *do it* and get it out our systems."

"Oh, Jamie Lee . . ." She pats my leg. "I can't believe that Griff would be so harsh. That's not like him."

I shrug. "Our tempers were flairin'."

"So you had, like, angry sex?"

I nod, thinking that there was no one else on earth that I would divulge this kind of personal information to. "At first, but it turned into something else. Well, at least for me."

"So, now what?"

I swipe at the tears. "I'm done."

"What do you mean, *done*?"

"I'm done wishin' and done hopin' for somethin' that

will never be. And I'm absolutely done chasin' after the man."

"Will you ever be done hopin', Jamie Lee?"

"That's just it, Macy. I don't know. I've managed to suppress my feelings for a long time but now that they've bubbled to the surface like a damned volcano, I just don't know." I drain the last of my beer and than blurt out, "Maybe I'll just have to move away and start fresh."

Macy gasps. "You wouldn't! Jamie Lee, tell me that you wouldn't."

"No, course not," I reassure her, but for the first time in my life, I wonder . . . "You ready for another beer?"

Macy nods. "Sure."

I come back out with a couple of cold bottles. We sip and talk until the moon comes out and the bullfrogs start singing.

"Just stay here tonight. I don't want you drivin' home," I tell Macy when we both start yawning. She agrees and we drag ourselves inside.

"You really not goin' to the Fourth of July festivities tomorrow, Jamie Lee?"

"You got that right."

"Well then, me neither. We'll boycott the whole damned thing. Just to prove a point."

"What point might that be?"

"Don't know."

I laugh as I head for my bedroom and Macy turns toward the spare bedroom where she's slept more times than I can count. "'Night, Macy."

"'Night, Jamie Lee."

17

A Hootertown Holiday

"Jamie Lee, it's your mama." I pull the covers up over my head but Macy pulls the quilt down and thrusts the phone in my face. I shake my head and mouth, "Tell her I'm in the shower."

Macy mouths, "I won't lie to your mother."

I narrow my eyes and pinch my lips shut.

Macy sighs and says sweetly, "Mrs. Carter, Jamie Lee is in the shower. Oh, have we made our baskets yet?" Macy's eyebrows shoot up and she gives me a what-should-I-say look. I shake my head.

"We're workin' on them."

I shake my head harder, *not* a good thing to do with bit of a hangover.

"Um, what's Jamie Lee makin' for her basket . . . ? Um, she said to tell you that um, you'd be surprised."

I groan after Macy hangs up. "Why'd you go and tell her that? We're boycottin' the damned thing, remember?"

"I suck at lying, Jamie Lee! I said that she'd be surprised."

I roll my eyes instead of shaking my head.

"She's gonna be pissed."

I push the covers back and sit up. "Well, that's too damned bad. I don't have anything in my kitchen to make for a picnic basket so it's a moot point, anyway."

Macy chews on her bottom lip, meaning that she's having second thoughts about our boycott. "Surely there's something in your pantry?"

I groan louder.

"Well, is there?"

"Aw, Macy. Look, I'll watch the parade, but I'm not gonna do the basket auction. You got that?"

"You must have somethin' in your pantry." Macy does this little pout that always works with me and she knows it.

"I'll go look in a minute if you make a pot of strong coffee."

Macy smiles. The coffee machine is one of the few kitchen appliances that she's mastered. "Deal."

I flop back down onto the soft pillow with a long sigh but soon the delicious aroma of coffee brewing entices me to get up and get going. After tugging on yesterday's jeans and the Toby T-shirt that's conveniently lying on the floor, I pad on my bare feet into the kitchen.

"We need to go to the grocery store," Macy says while poking around in my pantry.

"It's closed because of the holiday and I'm sure we don't have time to go all the way to the Super Wal-Mart."

"Oh. So now what do we do?"

"Boycott like we planned."

"That was the Bud Light talkin', Jamie Lee. We can't boycott the auction. It's a tradition—"

"That dates back to the Civil War days. I know! Geez, Macy I swear, I don't have to worry none about turnin' into my mama 'cause you're doin' it for me." I grab a big mug and pour myself some coffee. After stirring in some cream and sugar I take a sip. "You find a Mountain Dew?"

"Yeah," she says glumly.

"Okay, let me see what I can round up." After rummaging around I have a meager bounty of odds and ends on the kitchen counter. Turning to Macy I ask, "Do you have anything at your place?"

"You know I don't cook. You're always in charge of the baskets."

"Well then, this is it." I do a sweeping gesture with my arm. I'll do ham and cheese and you can do peanut butter and jelly sandwiches. That's as good as it's gonna get."

"Your mama is gonna have a fit. What about dessert? You usually do chocolate chip cookies or brownies. Don't you even have a brownie mix?"

"I consumed everything remotely chocolate this past week. I don't think we have time . . . wait a minute." I pull a box of Rice Krispies cereal from the pantry and locate a bag of marshmallows.

"Rice Krispies treats? Your mama's not gonna—"

"Mama will just have to get over it. Do you want to do this or not?"

She nods.

"It goes quick in the microwave."

"You can do it in the microwave?"

I grin. "Don't let Mama know. She thinks food prepared in a microwave oven will kill you."

"Wow," Macy says. We look through the little window as the marshmallows swell and expand over the top of the spinning bowl. "It's alive!"

I chuckle and feel my Debbie Downer mood ease up just a bit. "Okay, now you have to add six cups of Rice Krispies and stir it up while it's hot and gooey."

"Me?"

"You can do this, Macy. I'll butter the pan."

"Okay," she says, but doesn't sound confident. "Ew, it's all stickin' to the spoon and bowl."

"When it's mixed up scrape it into the pan and pat it down, but make sure to butter your hands."

"Ew."

"Hey, cookin' is messy. I'm gonna make the sandwiches. We've got to hurry if we want to watch the parade." I'm in the middle of smearing peanut butter on Wonder bread when my cell phone rings. I glance at the caller ID and let it ring.

"Aren't you gonna answer it?"

"No, it's Griff." I calmly add the strawberry jam to a slice of bread even though my heart is thumping.

"Yeah but don't you want to know what he has to say?"

"I've got to get over him once and for all, and talkin' to him isn't gonna do that. Besides I'm still a little shook about the whole thinkin'-I-was-pregnant thing."

"I understand," she says softly and then frowns at the mess she's making.

I'm about to take over but my doorbell rings. I hurry

over to the door and open it not thinking that it could be Griff until it's too late. "Well hello there!" I'm surprised to see Parker standing in my doorway.

"Aren't you going to ask me in?" he asks with that sexy grin of his.

"Oh, I'm sorry. Come on in! Don't tell Mama about my lapse in manners. Macy and I are making picnic baskets for the auction."

"Auction?"

"Yeah, you bid on them and the proceeds go to various charities."

"Hey there, Parker. Jamie Lee, this stuff is stickin' to my hands!"

"Did you smear butter on them?"

"Crap, I forgot."

"Smear some on now."

"Ew, gross!"

Parker observes Macy's lumpy buttery hands and looks skeptical.

"Macy, let me finish or we'll never get to the parade." I bump her out of the way with my hip and grease up my hands. "Parker, do you want somethin' to drink?"

"A beer would be nice."

I glance at Macy, who opens the fridge. "Um, Jamie Lee, I do believe we depleted your stash. How about a bottle of water or a Coke? So, is Jessica with you?"

"Water would be fine." After taking a swig, he says, "Jessica is back in L.A. taking care of business." His smile fades a bit and I wonder if he had wanted her to come with him. "It looks as if the movie project is moving forward, though. I came back to scout out a few more locations and to get all of the legal work and permits done so we can return in the fall to hopefully begin filming. The autumn season will be what we need for the story line, and the college students will be in town and can be extras."

"Cool," Macy says. She claps her hands together but they stick. "Can Jamie Lee and I be extras? I wanna scream really loud and get killed."

Parker chuckles. "Sure. Count on it."

"You don't have to do that, Parker," I tell him, but I'm thinkin' that it would be really fun.

"I insist," he says. "By the way, how's it going with your cowboy?"

"It's over," I tell him while I wash the stickiness off my hands.

"I never thought you were a quitter," Parker comments.

"Good try, Parker. I'm not quitin', just movin' on." When he looks like he wants to say more, I change the subject. "I hear the sirens from the fire trucks. Let's go on down and watch the parade."

I grab a bottle of water out of the fridge and hand one to Macy. We head out to Main Street in front of the Cut & Curl and sit on the curb. The street is lined with families waiting for the biggest annual event in Hootertown to begin. The sirens are getting louder. We can hear the drums of the marching band. A cheer goes up when the band comes marchin' down the street and strikes up a lively rendition of "America the Beautiful." There are so many people in the parade it's a wonder how there's anyone left to watch, but then again Hootertown is full of tourists visiting Lake Logan, so much of the crowd lining the street is out-of-towners. I find myself scanning the crowd for Griff and then curse beneath my breath.

Forcing a smile I wave to the float full of Girl Scouts who are throwing Tootsie Rolls to the crowd. Parker catches one and hands it to me. Leaning closer he says in my ear, "You okay?"

"Not really. How about you?"

"Hanging in there. So you're really throwing in the towel?"

"It's hopeless, Parker."

"Oh yeah? Well, don't look now, but your cowboy is across the street looking like he wants to come our way."

"That's only because he thinks you're playin' me and he needs to be my friggin' knight in shinin' armor."

"Really?" He says this like he's coming up with another plan.

"No more schemin', Parker. This isn't a scene in a movie where you can change the ending."

Macy leans over and asks, "What are you two cookin' up?"

"Nothin'." I give Parker a pointed I-mean-it look.

"I hear you," he says with a smile that's supposed to look innocent, but I get the feeling that he's up to something.

"I mean it, Parker. Griff just isn't that into me and I've got to get over him and move on with my life."

"You know what I say to that?"

"What?"

"Hogwash."

I shake my head at him. "You should be makin' romantic movies instead of horror flicks." I turn my attention back to the parade, hating myself for trying to catch another glimpse of Griff. I'm not nearly over the man and I don't know if I ever will be. Maybe moving away is the only answer. With that sad thought in my head, I turn to Macy and say, "We'd better go on up and finish our baskets and then shower. If I show up lookin' like this Mama will have a cow right here on Main Street.

"We'll see you in a bit, Parker. Macy and I have to get cleaned up for the festivities."

"Okay. I'll see you over at the auction."

Macy follows me back upstairs. We pack our picnic baskets and label them using little note cards. I cringe as I write my items on the card. I usually spend days plannin' my menu and I have to chuckle when I remember last year's basket.

"What are you laughing at?"

After taping the note card to the wicker basket I say, "I was rememberin' my basket from last year when I got the idea to do somethin' a bit different. I had seen this segment on "Good Morning America" for a French picnic . . . you know, pâté, wine, cheese, salami, and chocolate mousse for dessert."

"Yeah, didn't go over too well," Macy says. "Didn't Griff finally start the bidding?"

I nod. "Yeah, and he won. You should have seen him tryin' to choke down a cracker full of chicken-liver pâté." I chuckle but then bury my face in my hands.

Macy comes over and gives me a much-needed hug. "Chicken-liver pâté. Come to think of it I remember that now. What were you thinking?"

"Damned if I know," I tell her, half laughing, half crying.

"We don't have to do this, Jamie Lee. We can take our baskets and go out to the lake or somethin' if you want to."

I step back and wipe my eyes. "No, I'm not gonna run and I'm not gonna hide."

"There's the spirit," Macy says, and we do our little handshake. "I'll drop the baskets off on my way home to shower and change. I'll meet you at town square in about forty-five minutes, okay? Everything's gonna turn out all right. You just wait and see."

I nod, wishing I could believe her.

18

Hollywood Versus Hootertown

As luck would have it, bad luck that is, my basket is raffled off first. My mama is beaming as my big wicker basket with the traditional red-and-white-checkered cloth is held high for all to see. A hush falls over the crowd but then Bubba Baker, who seems to be the bane of my existence lately, reads off the contents.

"Miss Jamie Lee Carter has provided for your eatin' pleasure . . . ah, ham and cheese on white with mustard or mayonnaise on the side?" He says this like it's a question and he can't believe it. "Oh, and p-potato chips? One green onion and one barbecue?" This time he looks over at me like this is all a practical joke. Two cans of Coke and Rice Krispies treats for dessert?" He looks ready to chuckle and I swear if he does I'm gonna slide tackle him. Macy must have felt the anger oozing from my pores because she puts a restraining hand on my arm. I just know that Mama is glaring at me even though I refuse to look in her direction.

There is really awkward silence when no one bids.

My daddy looks ready to raise his hand, which would be humiliating to the extreme. See, everyone knows that the other baskets will contain luscious items like fried chicken, chocolate cake, apple pie, and potato salad, whereas my basket sounds like a brown-bag lunch.

"We should have stuck to our boycott," I hiss at Macy.

"You think I could sneak over there and retrieve my peanut butter and jelly sandwiches while no one is lookin'?"

"Macy, everyone is lookin'."

"Well, then create a distraction."

"Oh, you mean like smackin' you silly for talkin' me into this?"

"Twenty dollars!" Parker says, raising his hand. I smile over to where he's standing in the crowd of men who are bidding.

"Goin' once, goin' twice . . ." Bubba says, obviously thinking that no one other than Parker will want my basket.

"Thirty!" Griff counters and of course my heart starts to thump.

"Goin' once—"

"Forty!" Parker shouts, drawing a collective "ooooh" from the crowd.

"Fifty!" Griff shouts back.

Bubba looks at Parker who smiles calmly and says, "Seventy-five."

"Eighty!" shouts Griff.

The crowd gasps, my mama included. We're headin' for a Hootertown record.

"Ninety!" counters Parker.

"One *hundred* dollars!" Griff says loud and firm.

Everyone, including me, looks over at Parker. I know that his pockets are a helluva lot deeper than Griff's, but Griff has this look on his face that says, "I ain't losin'."

Everyone hushes, even the babies in the crowd. All eyes shift to Parker.

"Goin' once?" Bubba says and hesitates. "Goin' twice?" He looks at Parker and then slams his gavel on the makeshift lectern with a thump. "Miss Jamie Lee Carter's basket is sold for a new Hootertown record of one hundred dollars!"

The crowd roars and some of my self-esteem returns. People are clapping Griff on the back like there's beef tenderloin and champagne in the basket instead of ham and cheese and Coke. Of course, it's a hometown-pride thing that Hootertown Griff beats Hollywood Parker.

"Aren't you gonna go over there with Griff?" Macy asks me. "You're supposed to go eat with him, you know."

"There's no written contract, Macy."

"The man just forked over one hundred dollars!"

Everyone is looking at me so I put a smile on my face and head over to where Griff is payin' for my basket. Macy's basket is up next and I hope that the crowd doesn't ridicule her peanut butter and jelly. I give Parker a wink when the peanut butter and jelly sandwiches are mentioned. He raises his hand and starts the bid off at twenty bucks. I'm hoping that Luke will outbid him but I can see that Parker is determined to get his first taste of the classic sandwich.

But the rest of the world seems to fade into the background when I reach Griff. He's standing there holding my basket with a slight smile on his face.

"Thanks for bailin' me out, Griff. It seems to be your mission in life for savin' me. I know that my basket is sorely lacking this year. My pride, thanks to you, has been somewhat salvaged. "

He gives me a funny look that I wish I could read. "I happen to like ham and cheese." Holding out his hand, he says, "Come and share it with me?"

See, this is where I need to be strong. It's so easy to stay in love with him. "I . . . *can't*."

"What? I won your basket. You *have* to." He looks so disappointed that I almost cave.

"No, I don't." I start walking away but he follows.

"It's a Hootertown rule."

"You know that I don't have any problem breakin' the rules."

"What if Hollywood had won?"

This stops me in my tracks right in front of the Cut & Curl. "Ah, so this is what this is all about. *Winning*. I had forgotten how competitive you are."

"No, you've got it all wrong."

"Right, you just had a craving for ham and cheese . . . or was it the Rice Krispies treats?"

"Dammit, Jamie Lee . . . *no*, I just wanted . . ." He threads his fingers through his hair in a gesture that I know so well.

"You just wanted to save me," I finish for him. "I *get* that." Facing him squarely I say, "Griff, get over the guilt still hangin' over your head from nine years ago and from two weeks ago. Just let it go . . . let *me* go." I turn away because I'm feeling the damned urge to cry.

But of course he feels the need to keep following me. I keep walking but when I get to the bottom of my steps Griff puts his hand on my shoulder.

"Jamie Lee?"

I reluctantly turn around. I look up into his face and for the first time I see how tired he looks. "Yes?"

He swallows and then says, "I have to know . . . if . . ."

I feel my eyes widen when it hits me. "You want to know if I'm pregnant, don't you?"

He swallows again and then slowly nods. "Well, yeah, it's been on my mind and I realized that—"

"You don't have to save me this time, Griff. I'm not carryin' your baby, so you can stop losin' sleep over it."

"I wasn't losin' sleep over that—"

"Stop! Just . . . *stop*." God, I hate that my voice goes all shaky. "Griff, I don't want you to come to my rescue ever again." I poke him in the chest. "You hear me? Never! Not . . . not . . . ever! If I need help, I'll call nine-one-one!"

"Jamie Lee, wait!"

But I don't wait. I run up the stairs and into my apartment, twisting the lock to keep Griff from coming in. Too bad I can't lock him out of my damned heart.

I stay in my apartment for the rest of the day, telling everyone who calls that I'm not feeling well. Macy probes me for details and wants to come over, but I refuse on both counts. Later, I watch the fireworks from my back deck while nursing a glass of bourbon on ice. Music and laughter in the distance make me feel lonely, lost, and more than a little confused.

19

Never Say Never

When I come down to work four grumpy days later, my mama is standing at my station, which causes me to yelp and almost drop my mug of coffee.

"Mornin', Jamie Lee."

"Mama, just what are you doin' here?" I ask while thinking that I should have the locks changed.

"Sendin' you on a much-needed vacation."

"What?"

"You heard me. You've been chasin' away customers with your bad attitude."

"I have *not*."

"Jamie Lee, you have been downright, well, I'll just say it, *bitchy*."

"But—" Before I can finish my thought, Macy rushes in and says, "She's not puttin' up any resistance, is she?"

"Resistin' what?" I ask.

Macy smiles. "You're goin' for a week of R & R up at my grandpappy's cabin on Lake Logan. Your mama and I stocked up a big cooler full of supplies. It's already loaded in your Bronco. We even packed up some romance novels and DVDs so all you have to do is run upstairs and throw some clothes in a suitcase."

"But—"

"But nothin'," Mama says. She shoos me with her hands. "Go, child! Don't go lookin' a gift horse in the mouth."

I blink at them both for a minute but then smile and get all choked up. "Thank you. I really need this."

Macy rolls her eyes and does her little head-bopping finger-pointing thing at me. "Don't I know it. You've been grumpy as an ol' grizzly bear." She says this with a shaky smile.

"Thank you, too, Mama."

"Oh, go on with you. This gives *me* a much-needed vacation from your daddy. Men should not be permitted to retire."

"Well, first I had better get a few things in order. I need to order some supplies and make a few calls and I can maybe get out of here by this afternoon."

Mama says, "I swear your daddy must be poppin' those little blue pills. Why, just this mornin' he—"

Putting my fingers in my ears I say, "Okay, you convinced me, I'm outta here!" I laugh at my mama's tactics as I hurry up the stairs to pack. It doesn't take me long to throw the basics into a duffle bag and head out the door. As promised, my old Bronco is loaded up with grocery bags overflowing with snacks and a big cooler already iced down with beer, Cokes, and more food than I could possibly eat.

I crank up the radio, roll down the windows, and

head out of town. The drive is a pleasant one on a windy road through lush farmland. I had forgotten how beautiful the countryside was through here. The breeze smells of fresh air and damp earth. I breathe deep and blow it out, clearing my head of perm fumes and sad thoughts. Feeling my mood lift I slide in a Keith Urban CD and sing along.

When Lake Logan comes into view on the left, I smile. The water looks blue and inviting and suddenly I can't wait to go for a swim. There are fishing boats and party barges dotting the water but I pass by the touristy side of the lake and head to the far end where the cabin is located. Kicking up dust, my Bronco bumps over the lumpy dirt road leading to the log cabin nestled back in the woods. When it comes into view I smile. I've created plenty of memories here over the years, first as a kid and then as a teenager sneaking up here to party.

This is the only time, though, that I've come up here by myself, and I realize that I need some solitude, some downtime, and to just kick back and chill. After killing the engine I grab my purse from the passenger seat and hop from the Bronco, thinking that I want to open the windows and get the place aired out before lugging in my stuff.

Unlike the luxury accommodations on the main part of the lake, this handcrafted log cabin is on the rustic side but that's part of its charm as far as I'm concerned. A fieldstone sidewalk cuts through tender green grass begging for the sunlight that's filtered through the tall trees. Two stone steps lead up to a wide front porch meant for sittin' and sippin' something cold in the summertime and hot in the crisp fall weather. Handmade rocking chairs flank the front door and before the cool morning breeze is gone I mean to be rocking in one of them.

The screen door opens with a squeak and I insert the ancient key in the lock, jiggling it a bit to get the door to open. Because Macy's daddy comes up here frequently to fish and is pretty free with lending the cabin out to us there's only a slight musty smell in the air that will be gone after I throw open the windows. The cabin is cozy with only a living room that opens to a dining area and a small kitchen to the right. One bath and a bedroom are at the back of the cabin. A narrow staircase leads to a semifinished loft where we slept as kids on air mattresses or snuggled in sleeping bags.

Irish linen curtains are a frilly touch that breaks up the rustic feel and a hunter-green-and-white braided rug adds a bit of color to the gleaming hardwood floor. The couch is a dark green weave and a bit on the lumpy side but big enough to fall asleep on in front of the fieldstone fireplace. The only modern addition is the sliding glass doors Griff put in when he built a deck off the back of the cabin to take advantage of the magnificent view of the lake, no easy task since the backyard is basically a straight drop to the edge of the lake. I walk over there and flick the lock up, and then slide the door open with a whoosh to let in the fresh air.

Unable to resist, I push open the screen door and step out onto the deck. With a deep intake of breath I admire the sight of the sun sparkling off the water and then close my eyes and turn my face up to the sun. I can hear the buzz of a motorboat, the hum of insects, and the gentle rustle of leaves blowing in the summer breeze.

"Ahh." I let out my breath with a smile thinking that as soon as I unload the Bronco, I'm gonna slip into my bathing suit and work on my tan . . . oh, or should I read in the front-porch shade? Or then again maybe I'll head down the steep steps leading to the private dock where I can take a dip in the cool water . . .

"Jamie Lee?"

"Eeeeek!" I scream and jump about a foot into the air. Spinning around, I come face to face with Griff. With my heart just about jumping out of my chest, I say, "You scared the crap outta me. What are you doin' here?"

"I came here to repair some rotten boards on the deck."

"Well, come back another time."

"It won't take me long."

I narrow my eyes at him. "Do Macy and Mama know you're here?"

He shakes his head. "No, but I stopped by the shop to get my hair trimmed, and when they told me that you were here, I decided to come out and repair the deck so you didn't fall through the rotten boards. Macy was unaware of the problem but Luke and I were here fishing just last week and I even commented on how dangerous it was."

"Didn't we just have a recent conversation where I specified that you were not to come to my aid or rescue *ever* again?"

"I don't see how this falls into that category. I'm making a repair."

I blink at him for a minute while trying to come up with an argument, but I'm distracted by the fact that he's shirtless and wearing cutoff jeans that are more ripped than intact. A tool belt is making the mere shreds of denim ride low on his hips.

"I'll be out of your hair in no time. Just go on about your business. Except for a little poundin' you'll never know I was here."

I'm wondering if he's meaning that as some sort of sexual innuendo but he gives me this deadpan look so I'm not sure. God, I suddenly need a beer. "Just show me the rotten boards and I'll avoid them."

"What if you forget?"

"I have a very good memory, which apparently you don't. Just show me and go."

"I'm already here and I'm not leavin' until I fix the damned deck." He sort of growls this and I'm thinking he's really sexy when he goes all alpha male on me. That, combined with seeing way too much of his skin, has me breaking into a sweat.

Damn him.

With a lift of my chin and one eyebrow, I nod. "Fine. Fix it and let me get on with my vacation." I flip my hair over my shoulder and walk away like I'm all cool and collected instead of turning to warm jelly. To my dismay, he walks out with me but then turns to his truck. I lift my hatch and lower the tailgate on the Bronco and start grabbing grocery bags while trying really hard not to watch Griff heft two boards over his shoulder.

Squeezing the bags way too hard, I avert my gaze and head back inside the cabin. It takes another trip to gather all of the snacks and my gear. I head back out for the

last but heaviest item, the big blue cooler. Knowing that
Mama and Macy hefted it up into the Bronco together, I
can only pray that I can handle it on my own. I scoot it
to the edge of the hatch and then, looking around to see
if Griff is out of sight, I grab the handles on either side
and attempt to lift it.

"Crap." I take a deep breath, bend my knees and
manage to lift the damned thing up maybe an inch before having to plunk it back down.

"Need some help?"

Of course I yelp and place a hand to my racing heart.
"You need to quit sneakin' up on a person. And no, I
don't need any help." I stand there waiting for him to
leave so he can't witness me struggling with the mother
of all coolers. I make a mental note to purchase Mama
one of those kind on wheels. If it only had wheels I
could maybe wrestle it to the ground and the rest would
be a piece of cake. If only . . .

When Griff just stands there all brawny and everything, I say, "Don't you have some repairin' to do?"

"Let me carry the cooler inside for you."

"I can do it," I tell him through gritted teeth. Determined to prove this, I take a deep breath, grab hold of
the handles and hope for adrenaline to bridge the gap
between my lack of physical strength and my determi-
nation. I heft the cooler up a good three inches and for
a shining moment I think I've accomplished my task . . .

Oh shit. I stagger backwards and of course the smart
thing would be to set the damned thing down but I'm
gripping the handles so hard that my brain can't quite
convince my fingers to let go and so I continue to stagger while gathering up a surprising amount of speed.

What's that law about a thing in motion staying in motion? Well, I'm a perfect scientific example about now. "Whoa!"

Griff, who finally had the decency to let me struggle in private, comes running up behind me and puts his hands beneath mine, savin' me from landing on my ass and havin' the cooler land on top of me, crushing me to death. God, what a way to go.

"Got it," he says with the ease of one much stronger than me.

Of course I can't let go because his hands are covering mine. The fact that his bare chest is plastered to my back and my ass is nestled very near to his groin is not at all lost on me.

We stand there for a moment but then Griff, bein' the voice of reason, says, "We're gonna have to set this thing down together. Lean forward slowly and ease it to the ground, okay?"

I nod and begin leaning. This makes my ass burrow deeper into his groin . . . yes I'm *sure* now that it's his groin . . . When the cooler is safely on the ground, Griff releases his hold but takes his sweet time straightening up and backing away from me.

"You sure you don't want me carryin' that inside for you?" His voice carries a thread of humor and something else that sends heat all the way to my toes.

Without turning around I say, "Suit yourself." With my head held high I march inside the cabin, making a mental note to join Gold's Gym . . . well, make that Jerry's Gym, the Hootertown answer to fitness.

I busy myself putting away snacks but make the mistake of looking up when Griff enters the kitchen carrying the cooler with apparent ease. If possible, his jeans or lack thereof have ridden lower on his hips, practically defying gravity. His muscles are straining with the weight of the cooler and I notice that his skin is gleaming with a fine sheen of sweat.

"Where do you want it?"

Right here, right now, every which way you can.

My mouth has gone all dry, making it difficult to speak. "Right now . . . uh . . . here." I point randomly.

He sets the cooler down and wipes perspiration from his brow with his forearm. While he isn't looking, I watch a trickle of sweat roll down his chest and disappear beneath his jeans.

"Jamie Lee, could I trouble you for a cold beer?"

"Oh, uh, sure. Help yourself to anything in the cooler. There should be some beer in there."

"You mean you don't know?"

I shrug. "Mama and Macy packed it up for me. They sort of kicked me out of the shop for a week."

"Why's that?"

I shrug. "I needed some time off." Still a bit shaken by his presence I say a bit too sharply, "Don't you have some work to do?"

"Huh?"

"The rotten wood."

He frowns for a minute. "Oh yeah. Sorry. I'll finish my task as quickly as possible." He holds up the can. "Thanks for the beer." Tipping it back he takes a long pull and I watch the long column of his throat, his Adam's apple bobbing, and feel my own sweat pop out on my forehead. I turn away before I do something stupid like kiss him.

When Griff leaves, I unload the cooler and crack open a Coke instead of a beer, thinking that I need a jolt of caffeine and to keep my wits about me until he leaves. I take a drink while heading to the bedroom to change into my bathing suit. A nice dip in the lake will cool me off and with any luck Griff will be finished with his repairs by the time I get back.

After tossing a bottle of sunscreen and a towel into a big tote, I head out the back door. The back deck leads to a steep path leading down to the private dock. Primitive steps have been carved into the hillside and paved with stones to make the descent easier. I pause on the deck and look for Griff. I can hear a hammer pounding but I don't immediately see him until I start down the steps. His head is bent and he's removing the bottom step, which must be some of the rotten wood he was talking about. I'm a little disappointed because I had it in my head that he was making the whole needed-repair story up just to come out here to be with me. Ha. When will I ever learn?

When I get halfway down the deck steps he looks up from his task. Pushing up from his crouched position he moves out of the way so that I can pass. "Careful," he says when I reach the bottom mangled step. He offers his assistance, and I don't want to be rude, so I grasp his hand and step over the mess. "Where you goin'?"

"Down to the lake for a swim."

He frowns. "You shouldn't swim by yourself."

I barely refrain from rolling my eyes. "I'm just goin' down to the dock for a dip to get cooled off. I'm not really swimmin' out far, not that it's any concern of yours." I move to brush past him but he puts a hand on my arm.

"The water's up from the recent rain so it's deep even by the dock."

"Thanks for the heads-up," I say with a polite tilt of my head. "I'm a strong swimmer, so I'll be fine. I've swam in this lake quite a bit, Griff."

"But never alone."

Okay, now I am getting pissed, but I refuse to let him bait me. "I'll be fine." I start down the hill.

"Okay, well, keep an eye out for snakes."

This stops me in my tracks. Being a farm girl I'm not afraid of much. I can stare a bull down, bait a hook, gig a frog, pluck a chicken . . . ew, maybe not *that,* but you get the picture. There isn't much that makes me scream. But slithery snakes and creepy spiders and the sight of blood make me go weak in the knees. Of course Griff is well aware of this but I know he's just trying to scare me. If I didn't know better I'd say that he's wanting me to ask him to go swimming with me. "I'll keep my eyes peeled."

"Yell if you need me, okay?"

I whip around so fast that my ponytail hits me in the cheek. "No I will *not* yell because I will *not* need you. Griffin Sheldon, you are not responsible for my well-being, do you hear me?" He doesn't nod or say anything but since I'm shouting I'm guessing he heard me, so I continue on down the hill while muttering beneath my breath. It's difficult to stomp in flip-flops while making my way down the steep path, but I give it my best shot. "Snakes, my sweet ass," I mumble as I reach the dock. "Tryin' to scare me," I grumble and kick off my flip-flops. "I wouldn't yell for that man if the damned Loch Ness monster had me in its clutches."

I flick a glance up the hill to see if Griff's watching me but he's pounding away on the new board. He was right, though, the water is up quite a bit, spilling out of its banks. The rocky bottom keeps the water clear instead of muddy, making it possible to see your toes in the water. I eye the surface a bit warily but the only creatures I see are little fish schooling around. Still, the whole snake thing has me a bit spooked so I unfold my towel and sit down, just letting my toes dangle in the water. I remember to slather on some sunscreen, getting my back the best that I can. After a while, though, I'm starting to roast, so I'm either gonna have to jump in or head back up the hill.

I make the brave decision to take the plunge . . . well, actually, I sort of ease myself using the metal ladder attached to the wooden dock. The water is deliciously silky and cool against my heated skin. Lifting my arms above my head I let my body sink beneath the surface with a smile. Kicking back I float for a bit, letting the water soothe me. I can hear Griff pounding away in the background but I try not to think about him and let my mind wander for a bit while I float.

"Oh crap." I've managed to drift a bit too far away from the dock so I start swimming back. I'm a pretty good swimmer so I slice through the lake rather quickly. I'm almost to the dock when I pause to catch my breath. I'm treading water when suddenly I see it.

A snake.

Of course before I can stop myself I let out a blood-curdling scream that probably travels for miles and then echoes. The snake slithers away but I'm coughing from swallowing a gulp of water so I can't immediately swim back. Plus I want to make sure that the snake is really gone. So I'm coughing and treading so I don't see Griff until he's almost down the hill. I'm wondering how he can manage to run so fast on the rocky path when he slips. Flailing his arms, he lands on his ass and then does this rolling thing a couple of times before sort of jumping right back up in a rather impressive fluid motion. I'm so busy watching that I forget to swim and out of the corner of my eye think I might have seen the snake.

Shit.

Something slithers against my thigh and it's probably a bluegill but then again it might be the snake so I feel the need to scream and splash around in an effort to scare it away. In the midst of my splashing, I see Griff dive into the water and swim out to me. I grab a hold of him and wrap myself around his body.

Trying to keep us afloat, Griff says, "Jamie Lee, what's wrong? You hurt?"

"A s-snake . . ." is all that I can manage.

"Did it bite you?"

I imagine a knife, Griff sucking out the poison and I shudder before remembering that I haven't been bitten.

"Jamie Lee?"

"N-no. I don't think so . . . but it might have t-touched me." I cling harder to him just thinking about it and we almost dip beneath the surface.

"Hold on and I'll get us back to the dock." He somehow manages to swim with one arm while I remain wrapped around him. We're barely clearing the surface but he has us back to the dock quickly, all things considered.

"Can you climb the ladder?"

I nod.

"Well, then, you have to let go of me."

"Oh." I pull my face back from the crook of his neck and by accident my lips brush against the rough stubble on his chin. Desire flares so hot and potent that I look at him in surprise. His eyelashes are spiky and wet and there's such heat in his gaze that well, I just *have* to kiss him.

It's not just a little peck either. I mean why bother. Oh no, I slant my mouth over his mouth, squish my boobs to his chest, and kiss him with all I've got. I channel all of my pent-up emotion into the kiss . . . anger, frustration, fear, but all of that quickly melts into something softer, sweeter . . . *deeper*.

The slippery sensation of his warm wet skin rubbing against mine is pure bliss and so sensual but I need more. Reaching up I unhook my bikini top from around my neck, sighing deep in my throat when my bare breasts slide up against Griff's hard chest.

He sucks in a breath, tugs his lips from mine, and gazes down at me for a heated moment. "Jamie Lee . . ."

I'm thinking that he's gonna ask to make love to me and I'm thinking that I'm gonna say yes when he suddenly tenses. The soft look on his face turns to a slight frown and he says, "Let's head on up the ladder."

I blink at him, dazed and more than a little confused. "But—"

"For once, Jamie Lee," he says softly, "just do what I say."

Of course this pisses me off and I defiantly stay put.

His eyes widen just a fraction and he seems to be watching something behind me in the water. It hits me all of the sudden that it's probably Mr. Snake and I swallow. The look on my face must have said it all because Griff nods. "Slowly," he says softly in my ear.

I nod and I really want to move but fear has paralyzed my limbs.

"Jamie Lee, you really need to climb up the ladder. The damn thing is swimmin' this way."

Adrenaline pumps through my veins but moving slowly isn't an option that my brain obeys. Letting go of Griff I put my feet on the ladder, splashing, slipping, and not making any progress. Griff gives my ass a big shove and I'm propelled upward onto the dock with him close behind me but he must slip on the wet metal because I hear a splash. I scramble to my knees and scream when I see a big ol' snake bearing down on Griff. The snake dips beneath the surface and I pray that it doesn't latch onto Griff.

"Hurry up!" I shout as he's climbing up the ladder too slowly for my liking and I wonder with panic if he has been bitten.

"I'm comin'." Finally Griff successfully climbs out of the water, dripping wet and breathing hard, and flops onto the dock. He swipes his dark hair out of his eyes and says, "Now just what was that all about, Jamie Lee?"

Of course this could mean any number of things but first things first. "Are you bitten?"

"No."

"Thank God." I rock back on my heels, feeling almost dizzy with relief. "Was it a cottonmouth?"

He's on his back still breathing hard. "No, those are rare around here, but the way you were screamin' for me I thought perhaps it was. It was only a harmless water snake more afraid of you than you were of it."

"And you know this how?"

"It didn't have the triangle head of the venomous cottonmouth, and because of the inner white surface of its mouth that this snake *didn't* have."

"Well *somebody's* been watchin' the Discovery Channel." Some of my good humor fades with his being unbitten and all smug with his snake knowledge. "I wasn't screamin' for your help. I was . . . trying to scare the snake away and I do believe that it worked, both times. Did I yell your name? Huh?"

"I believe you did."

"Did not." Did I? Maybe, but I'm not gonna admit it.

"So what about the kiss, Jamie Lee?"

"It—it was an emotional reaction to my near-death experience with the snake."

"It was harmless."

Does he mean the snake or the kiss? "I didn't know that."

"So just what are you doin' now?"

"What?" Oh crap. I had forgotten all about my bathing-suit top being undone. I gasp and cover my boobies with my hands and he has the nerve to chuckle.

"Too late."

"You—you took advantage of my distraught condition. I was scared to death! And—and all of my senses were, like, heightened . . . making me vulnerable to your *unwanted* advances." Standing up I tell him, "I want you to finish up fixin' the damned step and leave." I march up the hill with my head held high and with as much dignity as I can muster while holding my hands over my boobies and knowing full well that his gaze is on my bikini-clad ass.

20

As Luck Would Have It

I stomp into the house and would have slammed the door but I don't want to give him the satisfaction. I'm tying my bathing-suit top back in place, cursing my sorry self for losing control with Griff once again, wondering if this pattern will ever end. God, when I thought he was in danger I thought my heart was gonna stop.

I love the man. Desperately. I could travel an hour away or halfway around the world and it wouldn't matter. I'm gonna love him 'til the day I die and there is just no stopping it. I can hear him hammering and hopefully he'll be finished soon and leave me in peace. At least then he won't be under my nose half naked and . . . *holy crap*. As luck would have it, right there on the white kitchen sink is the biggest, hairiest spider I have ever seen in my entire born days. I take a step back so as not to disturb it while looking for a weapon with which to end its life. Of course I've never been very good at killing anything, even something as horrible as a big hairy spider. But knowing I won't be able to stand not killing it, I quietly pick up a nearby *Field and Stream* magazine and roll it up. Barely breathing, I creep up next to the sink, raise the magazine, and stand there for God knows how long gathering up the courage to strike.

My heart thumping against my ribs, I'm thinking that this is stupid, being scared of such a small creature. I'm just ready to smash it when it starts crawling toward me all nasty and hairy and I try so hard to swallow the scream bubbling up in my throat but it just comes out sort of involuntarily and *oh crap* was it a generic scream or did I just scream for Griff?

A moment later he comes bursting through the back door so my guess is *yes*.

"What's wrong?" Still clutching his hammer, he's out of breath and his eyes are wide.

I point to the spider. "Would you mind killin' it for me?"

With a shake of his head Griff pries the magazine from my fingers, whacks the spider and then washes it down the drain, the whole process taking perhaps fifteen seconds.

"Thank you," I say primly. "By the way, screamin' your name was an involuntary reaction so you'll have to—"

"Shut you up?" He pulls me to him in one quick-as-lightin' movement, lowers his head, and kisses me senseless. My hands go up to his bare shoulders and I have it in my head for a fleetin' second that I'm gonna prove some sort of stupid point by pushin' him away. But where Griff is concerned I have no willpower and I find myself clingin' and kissin' him back.

When the kiss finally ends Griff puts his forehead

against mine and for a moment all we can do is catch our breaths.

"For the record, you kissed me this time," I tell him in a voice that's supposed to be firm but comes out all husky.

He chuckles low and sexy but then tips my head up so I have to look at him. "I have a confession to make . . . well make that several confessions."

"These are good and not creepy weird, right?"

He chuckles again. "Ahh, Jamie Lee, what am I gonna do with you?"

I have a few suggestions but I really want to hear the confessions first. "Okay, spill."

He takes a deep breath and says, "Well, for starters . . . *damn,* this is more embarrassing to admit than I thought." He blushes a bit and then says, "There wasn't any rotten wood to fix. I made that up."

"So you could keep an eye on me?"

"No, Jamie Lee. I was tryin' to . . ." He shrugs. "God . . . I feel like such a girl."

"Oh, *I* get it." I push a fingertip through a tear in the jeans. "You were tryin' to get me goin'." I can't help but smile. "Hey you stole that idea from me."

"Yeah, well it worked like a charm on *me* so I thought I'd give it a shot on *you.*" Griff sucks in a breath when I rub my finger back and forth. "I talked to Hollywood."

My finger stills. "About what?"

"You."

I school my features into what I hope is a fairly calm expression. "And?"

"There's always been something special about you,

Jamie Lee. You're more than just beautiful. You're smart and talented. Even those college girls come over to your shop to get their hair done. I knew that you had offers from fancy salons and I guess I always had it in the back of my head that you'd up and leave Hootertown." He takes a deep breath and then continues. "When Hollywood came to town, you started talkin' about needin' some excitement and I felt like I wasn't good enough for you." He shrugs. "Maybe I've always thought that."

"You've got to be kiddin'," I tell him but I can see by his expression that he's not.

"Even by Hootertown standards, I've come from pretty humble beginnings. Couldn't even afford to go to college."

"Look at you, Griff. You have a thrivin' business and—"

He puts a gentle finger to my lips. "Let me finish."

I nod but it's really hard not to reach up and hug him. Is it possible to love a person even more by the minute?

"When Hollywood took a likin' to you I thought to myself that you'd ride off into the sunset with him and end up in diamonds and pearls."

I really want to interrupt him but I don't.

"Well, like I said, Hollywood and I had a heart-to-heart over a few beers and he told me somethin' that you said to him." Griff gives me a serious look. "He said that he asked you what you wanted out of life and you said that you wanted a hardworkin' man with a good heart who would treat you right. A few grandkids for your mama and a little bit of land." He smiles and my heart goes crazy. "Now, *that* I can do."

"It's all I ever wanted."

Griff angles his head. "Yeah, well, Hollywood said somethin' else that got to me in a big way."

"Wow, the two of you bonded."

Griff grins. "I hate to admit that I like the guy."

"God, what else did he say? Someone really needs to tell me to quit runnin' my mouth off."

"That's part of your charm, Jamie Lee."

"Really?"

"*Most* of the time."

I hook my thumbs in his belt loops and tug. "Tell me what else Parker said."

"He said that you weren't into wine and roses . . . didn't need all of that stuff. But I disagree."

I wait but he just stops. "Go on . . ."

Griff shakes his head. "No, you're gonna have to make yourself scarce and just wait."

"Come on, you know that I really suck at waitin'."

He taps me on the nose. "When we'd go fishin', my grandpappy used to tell me that patience is a virtue."

"One which I do not possess."

"Then how about this one: good things come to those who wait."

I wrinkle my nose.

"Then humor me. Go in the bedroom and stay put for the afternoon. Watch a movie, read a book, take a nap . . . whatever. Just do this one thing for me, okay?"

"Okay. Just this *one* thing," I try to joke but my voice cracks and suddenly he's kissing me. I reluctantly pull my lips from his and head toward the bedroom.

"Don't come out until I say so, and no peekin'."

I nod, but think *Right, like I'm not gonna peek*. I head

back to the bedroom and sort through the DVDs that
Mama and Macy packed. I slide in one of my favorites,
The Princess Bride, and settle on the big bed to watch
it. . . .

Something that smells wonderful wakes me up. My
stomach rumbles, reminding me that I must have
skipped lunch. And then I remember that Griff is here,
and holy cow he must be cooking dinner for me. I really
want to peek but, steeling myself against the urge, I
head into the bathroom and take a hot shower. I dress in
my best outfit, which is not all that fancy, just a simple
yellow sundress that I threw in my bag thinking I might
be heading straight to church as I leave the cabin on
Sunday. After blow-drying my hair and putting on my
makeup I sit on the bed and wait.

"Jamie Lee?"

Ahh, finally! "Yes?"

"You can come out now."

"Okay." I stand up but suddenly I'm really nervous.
Checking my appearance, I add a bit more lip gloss,
take a steadying breath and open the door. The aroma of
grilled steak is stronger as I pass through the kitchen
and enter the dining area.

I stop in my tracks and cover my heart with my hand.
The table is covered with a linen tablecloth and is set for
two. Tall white candles are lit, flanking a bouquet of
long stemmed red roses. Soft music is suddenly playing
and I turn to see Griff entering the room.

"You look lovely," he says and hands me a glass of
red wine.

"So do you . . . look handsome, I mean." Does he

ever. He's wearing black dress pants and a blue button-down shirt open at the throat. His usual work boots are gone, replaced by shiny leather loafers. I wave a hand toward the table. "You went to a lot of trouble. The table is beautiful."

"You're worth it."

He takes a step closer and my heart kicks it up a notch.

"You deserve something special."

I take a sip of my wine and it's surprisingly good. "I like this wine."

Griff takes the goblet from me, takes a swallow and then sets it down on the table. "I wanted to wait until after dinner for this but I just can't wait any longer."

I'm about to make a comment about having dessert first, but his expression is so serious that I refrain. He reaches in his pocket and pulls out a velvet ring box and I swear I think my legs might give out. He bends down on one knee . . . and my hand goes to my chest.

He clears his throat and says, "Jamie Lee, would you do me the honor of marrying me?"

Of course this is the one time when my voice fails me. I feel a tear slide down my cheek and I can only nod. I throw myself into his arms but because he's kneeling and all, he loses his balance and we both go tumbling to the floor. "Yes," I finally manage, laughing and crying and kissing him until I remember the ring!

I come up to my knees and tug him up with me. Knowing what I want he opens the box and there is a simple yet oh-so-elegant solitaire sparkling at me. He takes it out of the box and slips it onto my shaking finger.

"Do you like it?" He looks so hopeful that my heart just melts.

"It's perfect. Just perfect."

"I love you, Jamie Lee."

"I love you, Griff," I say and throw myself into his arms once again but this time he's ready for it. We're in the middle of a really hot kiss when my damned cell phone rings. I ignore it but then a minute later it rings again.

"You had better get it," Griff says.

I walk over to the coffee table where I left it lying and answer it.

"Hey, Jamie Lee," Macy says all innocent-like, but I look over at Griff and he nods sheepishly, letting me know that she knows. "What's shakin'?"

"Nothin'," I say and Griff rolls his eyes at me. "I'm just about to have a simple little dinner." I crook my finger at Griff and than have to pause and admire my ring. Griff grins and comes over to wrap his arms around me from behind.

"Well I just thought I'd give you a shout, you know, just to see what's goin' on."

Normally I would torture her a bit more but I really want to get back to kissin' Griff so I attempt to say this calmly but I end up shouting, "I said *yes* and the ring is amazing and I love him so damned much and of course you're gonna have to be my maid of honor and I'm hanging up now because I just have to kiss him again."

The phone slides from my fingers and hits the floor with a thump. I lean into him while he kisses my neck. "I have another confession to make," he says in my ear.

"Oh great, now comes the weird and creepy part after

I've already said yes. So do you like to get spanked or want to wear my underwear or somethin'?"

He chuckles and then says, "I planted the spider in the sink."

I gasp and twist around in his arms. "You didn't."

He nods, backs up and starts running. Of course I chase him and he heads right for the bedroom . . . imagine that? I'm about to tackle him but I stop in the doorway and can only stare. There are rose petals strewn all over the bed and ohmigod a bottle of champagne on ice. Fat candles are everywhere ready to be lit. My eyes meet his and I don't want to ruin the moment by bursting into noisy tears so I swallow hard and whisper, "Wow. I thought I knew just about everything about you, Griff, but this romantic side is such a *bonus*."

With a grin he reaches in his pocket and pulls out a list. "I had a little help."

"Macy?"

He nods. "And Hollywood. You weren't supposed to see this until after dinner. Let's go eat."

I go over and sit down on the bed. "Dinner can wait."

"Hey," he says with a mock frown. "Who is gonna wear the pants in this family?"

I make quick work of his belt and zipper and tug hard.

He chuckles as he steps out of his pants. "I guess that answers *that*."

Oh, but Griff pulls me to my feet and quickly takes over. He kisses me slow and easy while the sweet scent of roses fills my head. I unbutton his shirt and let my hands glide over smooth, warm skin and a delicious ripple of ab muscle. Griff is so big and so strong but his reassuring words of love whispered in my ear make me ache with wanting him.

Taking a step back, I unzip my dress and shimmy out of it, letting it puddle to the floor. Griff sucks in a breath when he sees that I'm not wearing any underwear. "I was feeling lucky." I try to joke but the heat of his gaze is making me tremble.

Griff smiles and says, "God, I love you."

With a little hiccup I push him back onto the bed against the pillows and then straddle him. "Keep your eyes open, Griff, and watch me make love to you." Holding his shoulders I sink down and let him fill me. At this angle it's almost too much and then again not enough. Easing up to my knees I begin a slow sensual rhythm, savoring each stroke.

Griff watches through half-lidded eyes. The heat of his gaze is like a warm caress on my body, making me feel flushed, hot. I want to go faster but instead I let the passion build slowly. I can feel him growing thicker, harder, while his chest rises and falls with deep breaths. A trickle of sweat runs from his temple to his chin and I think that he looks so masculine, so beautiful.

"Jamie Lee . . ." he says in a low throaty voice and thrusts upward taking me along with him. Intense pleasure, absolute happiness washes over me in a long moment that seems suspended in time and place. Finally, I collapse against his big, warm body and let out a long sigh that makes him chuckle.

With my cheek resting on his chest I ask him, "I can't remember ever *not* lovin' you, Griff. What took you so long to figure out that you felt the same way?"

He strokes my hair for a long moment. "When I

thought you could be pregnant. The thought of you car- ryin' my baby just turned me inside out. I want that, you know."

"God, Griff . . ." I push up to my elbows, lean in and cover his face with wet kisses until he's laughing and I'm laughing and then we're wrestling on the bed. Rose petals are flying and in the midst of my laughter I think to myself that Griff's grandpappy was right. . . . Good things come to those who wait.

If you liked *Dark Roots and Cowboy Boots*,
then you'll love LuAnn McLane's next fun
and sexy Southern romance

The Real McCoy

On sale May 2007

Read on for a sneak peek. . . .

"The hell you say, Jamie Lee! You *can't* get married in two months!" I stop sweeping up snips of hair from around my station and give my best friend an I-can't-believe-it look. Of course it is *her* wedding, *her* life, but that's beside the point. "Just how can I lose twenty-five pounds in eight weeks?"

Jamie Lee fists her hands on her hips. "Macy McCoy, you don't need to lose twenty-five pounds!"

"Okay, twenty, then. Whatever! It can't be done unless I resort to liposuction or a tummy tuck. But the last time I checked, a plastic surgeon hadn't hung his shingle here in Hootertown, Kentucky."

"You wouldn't really do that, would you?" Jamie Lee looks at me with a bit of concern.

"Of course not," I admit, but then sigh. "Can't you give me at least six months?"

"I want to get married while it's still nice weather, and Griff doesn't want a long engagement." Jamie Lee gives me an apologetic shrug. "Besides, you look fine. So what if you have a few curves?"

"That's a politically correct way of sayin' that I have a fat ass."

"It is not!"

I turn around and slap my left cheek. "This butt is as big as the broad side of a barn! I should have 'See Rock City' tattooed right here," I proclaim, and smack myself again for emphasis. It sorta stings since my white capri pants are rather thin, but I'm trying to make a point here.

"Well, *that* would be interesting," says a deep voice laced with humor. Without turning around I know who that voice belongs to. *Well, hellfire.* I suddenly wish the floor would just open wide and swallow me right up. I shoot Jamie Lee a why-didn't-you-tell-me-Luke-walked-in-the-shop look.

Jamie Lee gives me an innocent I-didn't-know shrug and then turns to her brother. "Macy was just saying that she'd like to lose a couple of pounds before my wedding."

"Is that right, Macy?" Luke asks, which means that I have to turn around and face him.

"Um, well, yes, I suppose." I just know that my cheeks—the ones on my face this time—are flaming. I can't believe that Jamie Lee just said that to him, knowing what she knows about me, which is basically everything, and I shoot her a look that says as much. She blinks at me, all innocence again, which clearly means that she has an agenda here of some sort, and I have the sneaking suspicion that I'm not going to like it.

"Maybe Luke can help you out—you know, be like your personal trainer. He's got all that expensive equipment at the Payton College workout center."

"What?" I choke out, and my fingers curl around the broom I'm holding. I knew I wasn't going to like her agenda. And I don't. Not one bit. In fact, I hate it.

"Sure, I could do that," Luke offers with a warm smile that gets me even more flustered.

"Luke, I know you're busy with the football team and all. Plus, I was thinking of joining Jerry's Gym right here in town."

"Jerry's Gym sucks," Jamie Lee interrupts, and ignores my glare. "The equipment is falling apart, and Jerry constantly hits on all the women who go there. Ew, the guy is smarmy, Macy."

Luke frowns as if this bothers him, but I'm sure it's just in a brotherly-concern kind of way. "Well, it's settled then, Macy. You can exercise at the college. I'll show you the machines and give you a workout schedule."

"But what about all of those football players? I'll feel a little out of place."

Luke waves a hand at me. "You can come in after work, or early, if you prefer, when the team isn't there. You would be quite a distraction," he says with a wink.

Of course I have to blush, even though I know he's just teasing. See, I've been in love with Jamie Lee's brother pretty much forever, but he's always been the hometown hero, the high school star quarterback and all that, so I never really thought I'd have even a remote chance of shagging . . . um, I mean, *snagging* him. He was a big college star too, on the fast track to the pros until a shoulder injury ruined his career. Not that he didn't try to battle back with two operations and then months of therapy, but his arm was never the same. Luke's bitch of a girlfriend (sorry, I call 'em like I see 'em) dumped him after his injury—when, of course, I would have showered him with tender loving care, but that's a moot point since I'm not and will never be Luke Carter's girlfriend.

I do have aspirations in that direction, but though Luke may have gone through a couple of rough years before returning to Hootertown to coach the Payton College football team, he is still *Luke Carter* standing there all tall, buff and out of my league. His blue Payton Panthers golf shirt is stretched across wide shoulders and bulging biceps, and of course here I am stretching and bulging in all the wrong places, namely my butt. Okay, maybe I'm being a little hard on myself, and I am prone to exaggeration (my ass isn't *that* big), but I just can't see a hottie like Luke going for an ordinary girl like me.

"So, when do you want to start, Macy?" Luke asks, and I realize that both he and Jamie Lee are waiting for my answer.

"Luke, really, I don't want to impose. I know how busy you are gearing up for the football season."

"No way. You'll be a breath of fresh air after working with all of those big sweaty bodies. Not that I won't make you sweat," he says with a crook of one dark eyebrow. "You just might hate me after eight weeks."

"Impossible," I say before I can stop myself (a frequent problem of mine) and then of course blush all over again. My damned face must be the color of a tomato hanging heavy on the vine, but Luke just laughs, thinking I'm kidding.

"Don't be too sure of that," he warns, making me think, *Holy cow, maybe he's serious,* but then he chuckles. "It'll be fun," he promises with the enthusiasm of one used to strenuous exercise. I have my doubts, but nod my head and conjure up a smile.

"And you won't have to worry about me hitting on you like smarmy Jerry," he adds.

"Oh sure." Of course I keep my smile frozen on my face, but my heart plummets. With little jerky movements, I begin sweeping up the already-swept floor.

"So, what brings you here, Luke?" Jamie Lee asks,

and I'm grateful to have his attention diverted. "Doesn't look like you need a haircut. Maybe you want some highlights?"

"Yeah, right," Luke scoffs. "And a bikini wax, too. I just stopped in to pick up some hair spray for Mama. She said you would know the right kind."

"This must mean she's down to her last three cans," Jamie Lee says with a chuckle. She gets the hair spray for Luke and then walks him to the front door. I continue to sweep the clean floor like it is my main mission in life.

"I'll call you, Macy," Luke says with a wave.

"Okay." I give him a little smile. God, how long have I hoped to hear those three little words from Luke Carter? Of course, in my fantasy, he was asking for a date, not setting up a workout schedule. "I don't know how I'll repay you," I add. *A little sex, maybe?*

Luke shrugs. "Oh, a home-cooked meal once in a while would do the trick."

"Sure thing," I answer in a very tiny voice, thinking that it wasn't the trick I was hoping for. My cooking skills are . . . well, I don't *have* any cooking skills.

After Luke leaves, I pounce on Jamie Lee, but of course she knows I'm going to do this, so she's all fired up and ready. "Just what the hell was that all about, Jamie Lee?" My voice is high-pitched with suppressed panic. "Explain your sorry self! Do you think I want to present myself to your brother in spandex and a sports bra? And a home-cooked meal? My specialty is Dinty Moore stew and macaroni and cheese from a box! Ohmigod, what did you just get me into?"

Jamie Lee juts her chin out. "I simply saw an opportunity and took it. That's what friends are for, you know. May I remind you of our recent pact of going after what we wanted, namely Griff and Luke? I have lived up to my end of the deal."

"Smugness is very unbecoming," I inform her.

To her credit, Jamie Lee lowers her chin a notch and her expression softens. "Macy, I might not be getting married to Griff if you and Mama hadn't sent him up to the cabin with me. I needed some intervention and you came through. I'm only tryin' to return the favor."

"I will thank you to mind your own doggone business."

"You know that's impossible."

I have to chuckle because it's so true. "I'm still mad at you for doing this."

"Why? Now you have eight weeks to entice Luke."

I roll my eyes. "Yeah, grunting and sweating in a gym . . . that's gonna entice Luke for sure. Maybe my Dinty Moore stew will get the job done."

"Quit selling yourself short, Macy. Things are gonna work out between you and my brother. I can just feel it."

"Well, if nothing else, I'll end up with a buff butt, right?" I say brightly, but my smile trembles.

"Girl, you're gonna get the butt and the boy, you mark my words."

Signet

LuAnn McLane

HOT SUMMER NIGHTS
0-451-21907-4

You'll find America's favorite pastimes in Sander's City. The town's love affair with baseball sparks some scorching affairs off the field, and the men are fair game. Here are three stories that will remind you there are other ways to score—and that hitting a home run has always meant something a little different when the playing field moves from the stadium to the bedroom.

When the sun sets, temperatures rise. So turn up the air-conditioning, pour a cool drink, and let LuAnn McLane make your summer nights hotter than you've ever imagined.

Available wherever books are sold or at
penguin.com

S394

Signet

LuAnn McLane

Wild Ride
0-451-21762-4

A SCORCHING COLLECTION OF HOT STORIES:

In "Whip Lash," the owner of the Wild Ride Resort—a sexy, edgy adult amusement park—and a travel writer uncover an excitement that's more exhilarating than any roller coaster.

Jenna and her childhood crush have scored a vacation at the Wild Ride Resort. They agree to keep things platonic, but sharing a room makes the temperatures rise—and makes Jenna wonder if some things really are "Worth the Wait."

An ex-rodeo star turned country music singer discovers that when love comes knocking, you had better "Hold on Tight."

Available wherever books are sold or at
penguin.com

S394

All your favorite romance writers are
coming together.

SIGNET ECLIPSE